RESOLUTIONS

BY

TERI RIGGS

Decadent Publishing Company
www.decadentpublishing.com

This book is a work of fiction. Names, characters, places, and incidents are the products of the author's imagination or used fictitiously. Any resemblance to actual events, locales or persons, living or dead, is entirely coincidental.

Resolutions

ISBN: 978-1-61333-606-9
Cover design by Tibbs Designs

Published by Decadent Publishing Company
www.decadentpublishing.com

Printed in the United States of America

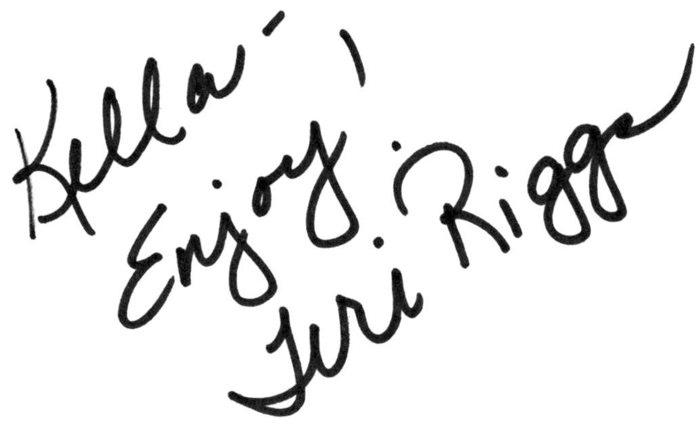

~Dedication~

Thanks to Michael, my soul mate, and to my girls for always believing in me.

~Praise for Resolutions~

"Ms. Riggs is a new voice in romantic suspense."

"...Finally A Real GI Jane...It is so rare that you can find a strong heroine that can hold her own with men, especially a trained operative." ***~D. Johnson, Amazon reviewer***

"The action and suspense were nonstop. Eve was believable as a tough and persistent female protagonist. And I liked how she and Mac's characters developed throughout the story." **~Marie, Amazon reviewer**

"...When a Touch Feels Like A Million Butterfly Kisses... Author Teri Riggs' romance novel, Resolutions, has done an amazing job writing a love story demanding your heart and soul..." **~Just Booked**

"...Not your average love story...This has tons of action, steamy sex, and twists and turns the whole way through." **~Dirty Hoe's Book Blog Reviews**

"Resolutions is a fast-paced action novel that includes a steamy romance and plenty of wit. A big thank you to Teri Riggs for creating a strong female protagonist who can also show a soft side without coming across as needy or reliant upon the opposite sex." ***~Sage Adderley, Amazon reviewer***

"...Perfect Romantic Suspense...This is an action packed book from beginning to end." ***~Kaylyn Davis, Amazon reviewer***

Chapter One

San Carlos Lucas, Colombia
Mendoza Compound

An ear-piercing cry interrupted the computer's steady hum, twisting Eve Taylor's gut into a tight knot. She grabbed her gun, crouched low, and surveyed the dark room. The excited chatter of a howler monkey had pushed her sixth sense into overdrive. Laughing it off, she willed her heart to slow to a semi-normal rate.

"Damn," Eve whispered into her mic. "Curious George just scared the bee-jeesus out of me."

"Hey, the monkey's telling you to speed things up in there," Rex, the partner she'd left hidden deep in a shelter of tropical foliage, answered. "What's taking so long? It's fucking hot out here."

"Relax, Rex, I've almost got it. Keep your eyes open, but loosen the tight-ass grip you've got on your weapon. Don't want you taking out any of our chattering friends by mistake." *Not to mention letting Mendoza's men know we're here. Too much tension puts the team at risk.*

"What makes you think—"

"You always go overkill on the trigger when you're pumped."

She needed to ease him down a notch. "I'll lay odds that loud-ass monkey scream got a few of your pistons knocking."

"Miss Know-It-All," Rex said wryly.

"That I am. Now don't be so impatient."

"I'm not impatient. I'm pissed. I can't believe Mendoza somehow managed to block the satellite signal. Beaming up the intel would've been much faster—not to mention easier. And why didn't we know about this before arriving on site?"

"What can I say? Mendoza can afford all the latest geek toys. We should be grateful Blackburn got the password to us before his cover was blown and Mendoza took him out." Blackburn was one of many good IDEA agents killed during the war to stop Mendoza's reign of terror.

She glanced at her watch and finished copying the drug lord's computer files onto a flash drive. She popped the drive out, sealed it in a plastic bag, and tucked the package safely into one of the zippered pockets of her camouflage pants. The blocked signal may have slowed her down, but it hadn't stopped her from getting what she needed. Plus a bonus. One big fucking bonus.

Eve turned the laptop off and the screen flickered to black. She picked up her 9mm Glock from the desk, the solid grip both comforting and commanding. Soundlessly, she slipped through the double French doors into the fading cover of the night.

Avoiding the landscaping and security lights, she crept across the compound's large backyard. Eve reached the perimeter of the pool house, stopped, put on a pair of night vision goggles—NVG's—and surveyed the grounds. Two guards passed far to her left. She spotted her team, alert and waiting for her. Randi Ford, the farthest away, hid beneath the cover of a large, dense breadnut tree near the wall her team had scaled to gain entrance to the compound. Danny Carlyle knelt to one side of a closer tree and Rex Brewer, her partner and best friend, crouched near a large storage shed.

Her tiny earpiece crackled. "Eve, got you in my sights. Any other problems with the files?"

Other than the damned blocked sat signal? I'd say so...if I could. Fucking Mendoza was a lot more dangerous than the IDEA first assumed. Eve couldn't share the details until she showed her boss what else she'd found in the bastard's files.

A flutter of guilt hit her belly dead center. Withholding the unexpected info she'd found from her team made Eve uncomfortable. This mission had just grown more important than anyone could've imagined. She shook the self-reproach off, moved into the deeper shadow of a tree, and watched the guard's silhouettes fade in the infinite darkness. Eve cleared her throat. "The password intel was right on the money. If these files don't nail Mendoza's ass, it isn't gonna happen."

"Exactly what I wanted to hear, partner," Rex whispered, sounding more in control.

"Jesus, Rex, what a fuckin' miracle," Danny chimed in. "You finally stopped whining."

"Bite me, dude. I don't whine."

Eve smothered a smile. Her team's focus and black op skills were unsurpassed. The fun-and-games attitude eased their tension. She couldn't knock what always seemed to work. She wondered what they'd think if they had any inkling how intense this op had just gone.

"Eve," Rex said. "You've got about a hundred yards until you'll reach Carlyle."

"Yeah, I see him. Be hard to miss those Dumbo-size ears."

Rex and Randi's muffled laughter rumbled over her ear bud. Eve looked through her NVGs. Danny grabbed his crotch, a smirk plastered on his lips. "Hey, doll face, if you think my ears are big, you should see my—"

Gunfire erupted.

Danny clutched his chest and dropped to the ground. Eve, a tingle coiling up her neck and settling in her scalp, stood in horror, her chest constricted in a tight knot. A bullet whined past her right ear and she dove for cover, returning fire while rolling onto her side.

"Danny's down," Randi yelled.

No shit. Eve crawled to a better position behind a low bush and searched for the source of the gunfire. Mud and leaves stuck to her, thorns scratched across her clothing. *Crap.* "This area is supposed to be secure."

"I don't know where the hell these guys came from," Rex growled.

"Sounds like two shooters." Eve took off her NVGs, improving her depth perception. "I spotted muzzle flashes about twenty-five yards back on my right, near the flowering bushes. You see them?"

"Negative on that." Rex's voice held frustration. "How about you, Randi? Got 'em in your sights?"

"I can't see anyone."

Eve's heart pounded hard and loud in her ears.

"Carlyle's not moving," Rex said. "Cover me while I check on him."

"Copy that." Eve emptied her Glock into the bushes and reloaded without missing a beat. The acrid smell of fired weapons filled the air.

The barrage of bullets ceased and Eve replaced her NVGs.

Rex checked his fallen teammate's pulse. He looked up, shook his head, grabbed Danny's mic and ear bud, and shoved them in his pocket. "No pulse. Carlyle's dead."

Aw, Danny. Eve had seen men die before, but Danny wasn't just a member of her team. He was a friend. Losing him hurt. She shuddered then sucked in another deep breath to clear the onslaught of sorrow. She fought back tears she didn't have time for and concentrated on getting the rest of her crew and the flash drive out safely.

She shook the heaviness from her arms. Reluctance trickled into her voice despite her best efforts. "Time to pull back. The extraction chopper will be at the rendezvous point in ten."

"Dammit," Rex said. "Eve, he—"

"I know. Danny was a good man. But we've got to go. ASAP!"

Gunfire sliced the predawn air again, forcing her into action. "Grab Danny. No way are we gonna leave him here for

Mendoza's bastards to mutilate."

"I'm on it."

Eve closed her eyes, willed herself to stay calm. "You need help?"

"I've got him," Rex yelled, barely audible over a volley of gunfire. "You worry about getting your own sweet ass out of here in one piece. Randi's already at the wall."

Eve said, "Randi, the wall still clear?"

"For now, but we need to hurry." Randi's voice wavered. "All this gunfire's gonna bring out Mendoza's men in hordes."

"Too late," Rex shouted. "Reinforcements are already here."

"Let's get a move on." Ready to sprint to the wall, Eve patted the pocket holding the flash drive, wishing she'd taken the time in Mendoza's study to put it in her boot heel hidey hole. "Where the hell are these guys coming from?"

Rex, still firing his M-16 at the enemy, slipped an arm around Danny's body and heaved him over his shoulder.

Eve covered him with her weapon, stayed low, and began a zigzagging run toward the wall. As she neared the cover of the trees, a bullet slammed into her left shoulder, dropping her on impact. Pain sliced through her and she fought to stay conscious. She rolled onto her hands and knees struggling to get up. Her left knee screamed from the blunt force of her fall.

Rex put Danny down and moved toward her. "Eve, stay down! I'm on my way."

"Negative on that. I repeat, negative on that. I'm okay. You get Danny to the extraction site. I've got your back."

Eve forced herself to stand, hadn't had time to straighten to full upright when another burst of gunfire echoed in the air.

Rex took a hit and tumbled to the ground.

Holy crap. "Rex!" Bullets flew around her as she tried to get him to answer. Her fingernails bit into her palms, and she fought to keep her voice steady. Sweat trickled down her forehead, and she wiped it.

"Rex, can you hear me? How bad are you hit?"

No response.

"Rex, answer me!"

Still nothing.

"Shit, shit, shit." Eve stared at the blood pulsing from her shoulder. "Randi, get over the wall and haul ass to the rendezvous point."

"I can't leave you and Rex."

"Randi, I'm ordering you to retreat. Now move!" Eve gritted her teeth, fighting pain and frustration.

"What about the flash drive?"

It would take Randi longer to backtrack than for Eve to reach the wall, even stopping to check on Rex.

"The intel is secure. I've got it and I'm still in the game. I'll be right behind you. Go, go, go!" Fragments of Randi's breathless agreement—or argument—she couldn't tell for sure, crackled through Eve's earpiece, followed by the rustling of the agent's hurried retreat.

Eve reloaded and fired off several more rounds, inching her way toward the line of breadnut and mango trees near Rex and Danny. She fought the veil of blackness threatening to take her down. *Dizziness. Shit, where's that coming from?* Covered with sweat, she began to shake. By the time she reached the trees, Eve knew she'd underestimated the severity of her injury. A horrible judgment call, rendered even worse knowing what else Mendoza was involved with.

She wouldn't get to Danny and Rex. She couldn't reach the wall. Even if she did, she didn't have the strength to climb it. She'd lost too much blood. With her injured shoulder growing numb, she was one handed. Her knee popped with blinding pain every time she tried to bend it. It'd be impossible to tuck the flash drive into the hiding place in her boot. And she damned sure wasn't willing to risk another team member's life by calling Randi back. There was no time. Danny and Rex were already dead.

No longer able to stand, she went down on her good knee, pulled the knife from its ankle sheath, and struggled to dig a hole. The smell of wet dirt encircled her like a veil. She buried the flash drive, covered it with mud and rocks then topped the mound with a scattering of wilted leaves. She peeled a piece of bark and carved a small V into the inner layer of the mango tree nearest her buried treasure.

Nausea and pain hammered her. Still she managed to cover her tracks and crawled on one knee back to the area behind the pool house. Eve glanced at her fallen teammates one more time and cringed, a sharp pang of guilt smacking her insides. She prayed Randi had reached the extraction point in one piece. Randi would regroup and bring another team back for Eve.

She dug out an iodine gauze pack from a pocket, tore the wrapper open with her teeth, and pushed the gauze into her wound. It stung like a son of a bitch, but it had to be done.

The flash drive was safe, at least for now, and a surge of satisfaction rose in her throat. The wet ground grew colder by the second. Or was Eve going into shock? Was she dying? That'd be one hell of a note. Who'd retrieve the flash drive if she were dead? Who'd get the vital new intel to the IDEA? So many lives were at stake. She snorted. Apparently, anyone could've done a better job than she did.

Occasional bursts of gunfire echoed in the distance as the distorted voices of Mendoza's men moved closer. The damned monkey started chattering again. She flipped onto her back and forced her breathing and heart rate to slow. The night's stars faded into the orange-red sky of morning sunrise and a welcomed calm washed over her. For the first time in her life, Eve wished she was still back home in Duncan Falls, Iowa with her four overprotective brothers. The Alpha Four, she called them. They'd be royally pissed if she didn't somehow get out of this mess.

Her mind turned to thoughts of Mac, the only man she'd ever loved. Maybe he'd been right after all. Maybe she wasn't cut out for this line of work. Maybe she did need him. So many maybes.

Eve closed her eyes and the maybes and darkness took her.

Chapter Two

San Carlos Lucas, Colombia
One week later

"Don't give up," Eve squeaked. Her throat burned like hell, but she forced herself to say the words out loud, needed to prove she was still alive. She had no intention of dying in the small, dark prison cell hidden deep in the musty underground chambers of Miguel Mendoza's huge compound.

"Please, God, let me survive the next round of interrogation." It was going to happen. The relentless bastards had already covered her body with cuts and bruises inflicted with unrivaled skill and enthusiasm.

Fever from the bullet wound to her left shoulder made pain and exhaustion her constant companions, kept her weak. Sheer determination kept her fighting to stay alive. She had to get the information back to the IDEA before it was too late.

In spite of the heat and humidity, Eve shivered, curled into a ball on the stained, pitted floor of her prison. Dried, splattered blood of past prisoners marked her cage. The lingering stench of stale urine, feces, and vomit had her continuously pushing back waves of panic and nausea.

Trickling through a six-inch hole near the ceiling, light

splintered the bleak darkness. Eve cringed at the scratching sound of tiny feet and the occasional flash of cat-size rats skittering by.

"Go away. Find somebody else's bones to pick today." She rubbed her throat, tried to soothe the burn. "And take your friends with you." She refused to think about what other types of creepy-crawlies shared her space. Instead, she fine-tuned her third escape plan.

Will it be third time's the charm, or three strikes you're out? If her newest attempt at freedom proved successful, she'd grab the hidden flash drive and be out of San Carlos Lucas by morning. *Mission complete.*

Eve wasn't about to let Mendoza win his little game. He'd kill her if he did. She'd be of no further use to him. No matter how many times he beat her, she wouldn't talk. He wanted to know what information she'd obtained and demanded she hand over the flash drive she'd downloaded with the names of associates, buyers, warehouse locations, dates of upcoming drug deals, and more. Much more than the IDEA ever imagined.

Turned out the arrogant bastard conspired with an Afghani terrorist group plotting a major strike against the Pentagon. They'd failed in their 9/11 attempt to annihilate the building and the people inside. To get the job done this time, they planned to use a bio-chemical toxin developed by Mendoza's chemists and delivered by a prototype U.S. military aircraft. The weapons could kill millions of people in the surrounding area, reaching as far as the White House. How he'd get hold of the aircraft was anyone's guess. The bastard would do anything for money. So hell yes, he wanted the flash drive back and Eve dead.

"Sorry to disappoint, buddy."

Eve relished the frustration escalating on Mendoza's face. Did he know she'd gotten past his encrypted codes and found the hidden file on the terrorist group? Eve was a computer expert and for the most part, was up to date on the latest cyber gadgets, but she'd never seen anything similar to the way his files had been concealed. If she hadn't been looking for a way around the blocked satellite signals, she wouldn't have found the file. Yeah, she'd let Mendoza speculate and second-guess how well he'd buried the data.

Let him worry if someone on her team had carried the intel from the compound and passed it to the International Drug Enforcement Agency's joint task force or Homeland Security. If Mendoza believed the flash drive was in their hands, he had to ask himself when and where they'd come for him. And were they already in hot pursuit of the terrorists he'd been dealing with?

In one of her more creative moments, Eve hinted she was on the take and planned to auction the flash drive to rival drug cartels. Enemies could be plotting his demise already, she'd told him. His files had been breached, but she'd only admitted to finding information on his drug and money laundering business.

Still, he had to question whether she'd uncovered the Afghani plans. He wouldn't want a bunch of pissed off terrorists after him. And pissed they'd be if U.S. forces foiled their planned attack on the Pentagon and D.C. area. Mendoza would be a hundred times better off in the custody of IDEA than with the Afghani fanatics on his ass.

Mendoza had no clue what she'd found. If he did, she'd already be dead.

If her split lip didn't hurt so much, she would've smiled. "The man is beyond frustrated." The longer Eve kept him guessing, the longer he'd keep her alive. And the longer she stayed alive, the better her odds were for escape.

She was drifting toward sleep when heavy boots pounding in the hall signaled the guards' return. Garbled voices grew clearer, the footsteps closer. The guards fumbled with a key ring before a lock clicked as they unbolted her door. The heavy metal frame crashed against the wall, a bang echoing through the darkened chamber. Eve was too exhausted to be afraid of the minion guards anymore. She'd save her fear for a bigger fish. Like a piranha named Miguel Mendoza.

A pair of calloused hands jerked her to her feet.

Eve drove the elbow of her good arm into her nearest

assailant's stomach. Satisfaction reigned as her elbow sank into his large belly.

He rewarded her with a solid cuff to the right side of her face.

She staggered, ears ringing and spots flashing in her vision.

It took a few seconds to regain her balance. Before she could high five herself, a flashlight blinded her. She swatted it away. Several blinks later, her eyes adjusted only to find Mendoza standing before her, arms crossed, and a smug look on his face.

Damn. Looks like the bigger fish has arrived. Inklings of fear threatened to ruin her tough woman act.

Ignoring Mendoza, she spoke directly to the guard with the rough hands and rock solid slap. "Hey, Paco, do you mind? You're interrupting my nap time here."

"Do you have any idea who you are toying with?" Mendoza's deceptively smooth, silky tone caused Eve's insides to knock and rattle.

She shoved aside exhaustion and covered with a cloudburst of sarcasm. "Sure, I know. I can quote the memo. You're an evil drug kingpin responsible for smuggling well over sixty billion dollars' worth of cocaine into the United States during the last four years alone. You also run the largest money laundering operation in Colombia. You're ruthless and brutal, murdering anyone who stands in your way including, but not limited to, several agents of the IDEA task force team. Basically, you're an all-around prick. Oops!" She covered her mouth. "The last bit about you being a prick...well, that was my own little add-on."

Eve kept her focus steady on him, refusing to show weakness or fear. And she did fear him, a fear that could paralyze if not kept in check.

Mendoza walked with a limp, courtesy of a gunshot wound to his right thigh three months ago, and used a cane to help keep his balance. His long, straight black hair, pulled back in a low ponytail bound with a thin strip of leather, drew attention to his high chiseled cheekbones. Clean-shaven, his angular face and pretty-boy look disguised the monster inside. His six-foot tall lean, muscular body gave him an air of intimidation, one he used to his advantage.

"Well, well, Miss Taylor," he said in a soft, controlled voice. "I see you are still a feisty little one."

"That's Agent Taylor to you." Eve jutted her chin out, stood with her legs apart.

His head shook. "Spending quality time in our fine accommodations has not improved your attitude at all, has it, *Miss* Taylor?"

Stepping closer to Mendoza, Eve pushed her dirty, matted hair out of her face, and looked him straight in the eyes. "No, Miguel, I'm afraid it hasn't. But, to be honest, I've been trying to squeeze in a few days of R&R." She shrugged her good shoulder, put on her best nonchalant act. "Although this place wasn't exactly first on my list of top destinations, I'm at least finally getting a much needed vacation. All this five-star resort lacks is a swimming pool, hot tub, and decent room service."

Mendoza smacked her across the face, causing her to momentarily sag against the hands holding her.

She regained her balance, shook loose from the men, and rubbed her burning cheek. "What's the deal with you and your crew of flunkies slapping me around? Is it just something men with small penises like to do or what?"

An enraged look covered Mendoza's face. *Bingo*. She'd scored big time.

Mendoza's dark eyes narrowed into menacing slits. "Ah, my *querida*. Ever the comedienne, no? Tell me, how funny is this?"

He yanked her closer and pulled off the dirty makeshift bandage from her shoulder.

She flinched at the instant sting and got a whiff of the sour, decayed flesh of her infected wound. If there'd been anything in her stomach, she would've hurled all over the shitheads.

Mendoza dug the tip of his polished ebony cane into the red-rimmed hole.

Eve saw stars and doubled over, wrapping her arms tight around her waist. The cell floor seemed to move in waves beneath her. When the ground settled and the throbbing began to fade, she sucked in a deep breath and stood straight again.

"Are we finished with this game?" Mendoza asked.

Never. She pointed to his cane and panted past the pain. "I see you're ready to enter the company picnic's three-legged race. I hear the competition is tough this year."

Fury filled his eyes, making them impossibly darker. Jerkily, he pulled his gun and shoved the muzzle against her head. A red flush inched up his neck as his finger twitched against the trigger.

The metal chilled her skin. Eve certainly pushed all the right buttons today. The man was pissed. *Maybe it's time to back off a bit.*

"You really do try my patience, *querida*," Mendoza growled through clenched teeth.

A lifetime seemed to pass before he let out a long, frustrated sigh. Eve froze, waiting for him to regain control and put his gun away. *He doesn't want to kill me. At least not yet.*

He rubbed his leg with a fisted hand. "Mark my words, the man who betrayed me will pay dearly for this when I find him."

Eve was well aware of who shot Mendoza, crippling him. Dillon McKenna. She'd loved Mac once. The pain he'd caused was greater than anything Mendoza's idiots had inflicted. He'd left her and hadn't bothered to look back. Didn't fight for her, or for what they'd had together.

A familiar twinge tugged her heart. How could the mere idea of that man still bring on such raw anguish and hurt? Even now, while fighting to survive another day, her disloyal body ached for Mac's touch. Eve hated he still made her feel so much. Needing to shake the emotions, she focused on mocking Mendoza. "Trusted the wrong man, did you, Miguel?" *Ditto. I trusted him, too.*

"We will not discuss the *cabron*!" Mendoza's voice cut like a razor through rice paper. He circled her nonchalantly. "Let's talk about your unfortunate situation. Your pitiful attempts to escape have failed miserably. Only one rescue attempt has been made by your fellow IDEA agents."

Eve tried to hide a flicker of hope. IDEA must think there's still a chance she's alive. Or maybe they tried to retrieve another copy of Mendoza's files. Either way, the possibility of finding her increased. They had to rescue her. Had to know about Mendoza's new side business.

He wore a smug smile. "Also...unsuccessful. I'm afraid we were forced to dispose of your poor, unlucky amigos. They screamed like pigs while they died."

"You bastard." Eve pushed away images of the doomed IDEA team. It was painful enough to remember what happened to her own crew. Danny, the constant comedian of the team, the man brave enough to call her doll face—and get away with it—was dead. Rex, her partner, was dead, too. He'd been her mentor and friend. Hopefully, Randi had gotten back in one piece. She'd at least cleared the wall, so her chances were good. Eve ran a hand down her face and refused to dwell on the fates of her team. She needed to focus on staying alive.

"I think it would be in your best interest to tell me what you've done with my files."

"It'd make life easier, wouldn't it? You're not sure if you should make a shitload of changes to protect your interests. Interruptions are bound to cost you millions."

"There will be no changes."

"What will your new customers think when they find out how easily I breached your security?" *Wait till they see how big a screw up they're dealing with.*

"New customers? Keep talking."

"New? Old? Whatever." *Still worried about how much information was downloaded, Miguel? Plant the seed and live a little longer.*

Eve offered him an innocent look, topped it off with a shrug.

"I grow tired of your games. Tell me who has the flash drive. Now!" Mendoza boomed and she jerked her head back.

Eve looked away, ignoring him.

"Did you pass the flash drive to one of the agents who got

away?" Mendoza dug the cane into her shoulder.

Her knees went weak, her mind spinning. Eve cried between grinding teeth, "Go to hell!"

"*Querida, por favor*. Please, we must end this."

He let the cane drop to the floor and motioned to another man in the cell. A fireplug with legs moved next to her.

"You remember Carlos. He loves to play with pretty little things like you."

It wasn't likely she'd ever forget him. He'd taken his turn beating her several times. Carlos hadn't been around for a couple of days, and Eve had hoped he'd dropped dead from a bad case of painful penis rot. No such luck.

Eve concentrated on his uni-brow as he leered, his gaze taking in every inch of her body. Her stomach roiled at the way he mentally undressed her. Taking a step back, she tugged her barely-there tank top.

"Carlos, would you like to spend some special time with Miss Taylor, maybe get to know her a little bit better?"

"I would like this very much, Miguel." Carlos looked to Mendoza eagerly and licked his lips.

"Of course you would. But I am afraid you'll not have Miss Taylor until I've had a chance to enjoy her many charms myself. I like her spirit." Mendoza arched a brow. "I may even keep her around awhile."

"*Sí*, Miguel, I will gladly wait my turn."

Mendoza grazed a knuckle down her bruised cheek. "Remember, Carlos, no one is to have her until I've had my fill."

The notion of Mendoza or any of his men raping her was repulsive. Still, Eve managed to stand defiantly. To keep from shaking, she let her mind drift, thinking of the many ways she would like to kill the revolting men standing before her when—not if—she got the chance.

Mendoza took Eve's left hand in one of his. Raw pain shot up her arm, settling in her injured shoulder. He pulled her closer. "I will give you one more chance to tell me where the flash drive is."

Eve didn't answer. *Back to the quiet game.*

"Did one of your friends take it with them?"

Still no answer.

Mendoza squeezed her hand harder, and Eve bit back a moan.

"Is my property hidden here on the grounds? Do you plan to sell it? Maybe make a little money on the side?"

Eve forced a smile and tried to tug her throbbing hand away from Mendoza's tight grip. "Same old questions. You're starting to sound like a broken record. Give it a rest, Miguel."

He shook his head, making an animated tsk, tsk, tsk sound. "It is not wise to be so uncooperative, my lovely *querida*."

Mendoza dropped the hold he had on her and took her hand in both of his. His dark eyes narrowed, and he gave her wrist a quick, hard twist. Her bone snapped, sending a loud, clear popping noise echoing off the concrete and dirt walls. Eve screamed and dropped to her knees, skinning off a thin layer of flesh. Her injured knee roared at the new assault.

He pulled her to her feet, and studied her face. "I will give you until tomorrow morning to tell me where my property is. If you still are not talking, Carlos and his men will take turns breaking your bones—one every hour—until you give me what I want." He ran a manicured finger casually over her cheek, wiping away a traitorous tear.

Cradling her wrist, she squeezed her eyes shut, refusing to let another drop escape.

"Why must you make this so difficult?" The forced concern made her stomach roil.

Eve tried to swallow the thick lump stuck in her throat. Mendoza didn't expect an answer. And he wouldn't be getting one.

He faced Carlos. "She is to have no more food or water until further notice."

Eve wasn't sure what drove her to set herself up for more punishment. PMS? Bad hair day? Temporary insanity? Whatever the reason, the sarcastic words tumbled out before she could pull them back.

"Now there's a real loss, Miguel. No more bug-infested fried mush, or bacteria-polluted piss water."

Mendoza wrapped a large hand around her neck, fisted his other and drove it into her face three times, each blow accentuating a word. "You...*Puta*...Bitch!"

With one more solid, cast-iron punch, he knocked Eve to the floor. "When I'm finished with you, I will kill you myself. Very slowly and very painfully."

Mendoza gathered his cane, used it to push Carlos out of his way, and limped from the cell, leaving a mile long string of Spanish profanities hanging in the air.

Eve promptly passed out.

Chapter Three

The offices of Resolutions, Inc.
Washington, D.C.

Dillon "Mac" McKenna's fist hit the solid, mahogany desk with a loud thundering whack. "Dammit, Hutch. What do you mean you're not sure if Eve is still alive? What kind of bullshit is that?" *She has to be alive.*

Mac's boss and Resolutions' owner, Robert Hutchinson, leaned forward in his chair. "I'm telling you what's in the report. Her team was ambushed leaving the Mendoza compound a little over a week ago. One agent was killed. Two other operatives, Ford and Brewer, were able to get out. Eve went down with a hit to her shoulder, but the surviving team members saw her get back up.

"Brewer said she ordered them to move out, she'd cover their six. He took a bullet and blacked out. When he came to, he started his retreat and soon realized Eve never made it to the wall. By the time Brewer zeroed in on her, Mendoza's men had Eve surrounded, and he had to rabbit."

Mac balled his hands into fists, the veins along his neck bulged painfully with anger. He fought to reduce the boiling rage inside him to a simmer. A former Army Ranger and Delta Force soldier, he believed in the Ranger Creed, No man left behind. "You mean to tell me the bastard just left her there with Mendoza and his men? They're bloody animals!"

"Brewer had no choice."

"There's always a choice." Mac clenched his teeth around the words.

"Brewer wouldn't have escaped himself if Ford hadn't backtracked and helped him to the extraction site." Hutch's argument lacked enthusiasm. He didn't buy into bullshit excuses either.

"That's a load of crap. Did they get the intel out? Eve risked her life for it." He lowered his voice a notch, almost choked on his next words. "May have died for it."

"Brewer says it's still with Eve, probably tucked into the heel of her boot, or stashed on the grounds somewhere. IDEA sent in a recovery team. The move turned into one royal clusterfuck. Mendoza's men took out the whole rescue team. The IDEA task force head, John Sanders, has contracted us to go in and extract the intel and Eve. The strong emphasis being on the flash drive's recovery."

Mac bristled. "I'll get the fucking flash drive, but Eve comes first."

"You've got to remember Sanders and the task force has been after the bastard more than two years. They've been under fire from Senator Long and his Appropriations Committee. Sanders had a lot riding on Eve and her team making a successful retrieval." Hutch steepled his fingers. "We won't leave her. That's why I'm sending you in. You know Mendoza, his compound, and the surrounding area better than anyone. You're Eve's best shot."

"Damn straight. I should've killed Mendoza while I worked undercover."

"Your mission was to locate and extract the chemist, not take out Mendoza. Without jeopardizing your job, you still managed to pass on information the task force used to shut down two major drug deals."

"If I'd been able to get the intel Eve was after, she wouldn't be in this mess."

"The password wasn't available to you at the time."

"Dammit. This is beyond fucked up!"

"Can you handle this op, Mac? You have to be prepared to set aside personal feelings," Hutch said.

"I'll deal." Mac sucked in a deep breath and exhaled evenly. "Eve is part of my past. I no longer have personal feelings about her. Doesn't mean I want to see her hurt. No one should be left behind with Miguel Mendoza. I know what he's capable of."

Hutch nodded again, a look of satisfaction on his face. "I'm not sure what you'll find—or won't find. Like I said, Eve could be dead."

Mac settled back in his chair, the leather creaking, and crossed his arms. "Eve's not dead. I refuse to consider the possibility. She might be going through pure hell, but she's alive."

Mac, no longer able to sit still, stood, and paced. Unease knotted his gut and fear stole the air from his lungs. Mendoza was known to enjoy both the torture and killing of his victims. The idea of her suffering had beads of sweat dotting his forehead. His heart pounded erratically, every beat echoing loud and clear in his ears. He swiped a sleeve across his brow.

Even though Eve wasn't his anymore, he couldn't shake the overwhelming urge to shield her. He was well aware of what could happen to an unprotected woman...and to the people left behind who loved her.

Mac sucked in a long, calming breath, and stopped in front of Hutch's desk. He planted both hands on its smooth surface. His fingertips went white from pressing hard against the dark wood. He leaned forward calmly and spoke with a composed and clear voice.

"Mendoza will pay for ever having touched Eve."

☙

San Carlos Lucas
The Mendoza Compound

Beefy hands wrenched Eve awake from a fevered sleep, pulled her from the cell, and shoved her into a musty-smelling hallway. *I'm being moved?* A guard pushed her with one hand, keeping a tight grip on an AK-47 rifle with his other.

Her shoulder throbbed in perfect cadence with the pains shooting through her broken wrist, and she had one badass headache from being punched in the face a few too many times. Using her good hand, she walked fingers across one cheek, then the other. The right side was totally numb. Her eye had swollen shut, and she couldn't see a damn thing out of it. She ran her tongue across her teeth and tasted the tart, copper flavor of blood. Three teeth loose. *Well, at least they're still in place.*

In spite of the relentless pain, she stayed determined to survive whatever Mendoza dished out. She wasn't a quitter. No, sir. Duncan Falls, Iowa didn't grow quitters. Eve ignored the constant ache in her ribs, courtesy of a guard's overzealous kick, and took in a deep breath. She willed herself to stay alert, to keep pushing. *Escape. Third times the charm.*

Eve slapped the guard's dirty hand. "Hey, Pedro, stop being so damned pushy. Where we going anyway? We got a hot date I've forgotten about?"

He looked puzzled then shoved her again.

"Don't understand English, do you, Diego? Bet you understand this." Eve drove her elbow into the guard's face. Thick rubbery cartilage gave, and she whooped triumphantly.

Blood squirted from his nose and he screamed.

Eve stepped back. "Yep, I'm pretty sure you understand that."

Unable to grab the guard's assault rifle, she clutched her injured shoulder, and took off in a slow jog, no longer able to push any harder.

Her escape was short lived. When she reached the stairs, Carlos, the fireplug with legs, was waiting. He pointed a mini Uzi at her, and she froze.

Eve glanced at his weapon then cut loose with a crooked, all-knowing smile. "You know what they say about men with small guns...."

The bloodied guard she'd left behind, winded and holding a dirty hankie to his nose, caught up with them. His expression screamed pure outrage. He pointed his rifle at Eve.

"Carlos, *lo seinto, por favor—*"

Fireplug's disgusted look and sharp wave stopped any further explanation the guard might offer.

"You are no happy here, *señorita*?" Carlos spoke to Eve with a heavy accent. "Miguel's feelings will be crushed."

"You're right, Gomez, I am no happy here."

Carlos spun Eve around, steered her up the stairs into the large foyer of Mendoza's villa. The sound of the bloody-nosed guard's labored breathing followed.

Eve's good eye needed a moment to adjust to the late afternoon sun. Ignoring the pain in her ribs, she gulped the fresh air drifting through the open windows and doors. She savored the clean, after-the-rain smell from an earlier tropical downpour. Finally focused again, she scanned the room, memorizing its layout.

The coolness of the colorful tile against the cuts and bruises on her bare feet was soothing. She glanced at an ornate iron chandelier hanging from the center of the high ceiling. Bright and airy, the tasteful décor accentuated the sharp contrast to her dingy, dark hole of a prison cell. Eve hadn't expected a low-life scumbag like Mendoza to have such good taste. It both surprised and appalled her. Everything had been paid for with illegal money. No telling how many people Mendoza had killed to get the place. The idea left a sour taste in her mouth.

She pushed the nausea back and looked at Carlos. "Hey, Juan, how many drug sales and dead bodies did Miguel have to make in order to build this little hacienda? Or did he merely kill the owners and move in?"

Ignoring her question, Carlos propelled her through the

doors of the study she'd broken into just days before. He guided her to stand before Mendoza.

"Look at you, *querida*. Your eyes are exhausted and glassy with fever. This *muy bonita*, very beautiful body of yours is filthy and battered." He rested the back of his hand on her forehead. "Your fever seems higher than it was this morning. I am impressed you are even standing."

She slapped his hand away.

"Come now, let me help you. It would seem infection has set in. You really should have immediate medical attention."

"Your concern is touching."

He offered her a glass of water. Water not tainted with flecks of rust and other floaties. She stared at it, would've licked her lips if she'd had a drop of spit left.

Could be poisoned. Could kill me. Oh fuck it. She needed fluids, or she'd die anyway. Eve guzzled the drink, the cool liquid sliding past her cracked lips and down her dry throat. She should've felt guilty, but she didn't.

"See, you are thirsty. Surely, you must be hungry, too."

Mendoza poured another glass. Again, she downed the water.

"Wouldn't a meal and a hot bath be nice? Once you are clean, we could dine together. I think I would like the woman beneath all of this filth." He ran his hands over her breasts and worked them slowly south. "Yes, I think I would like her very much." He rubbed between her legs, thrusting his hips toward her.

Eve attacked Mendoza, legs kicking, good arm swinging. Her mind and body screamed with rage. He punched her damaged shoulder. Mind-numbing pain flooded her body, and blood oozed from the infected wound.

Laughing, Mendoza pushed her against his desk. Strong legs held her in place, and he captured her hand with the broken wrist between his hands the way he'd done the night before. His sturdy fingers stroked hers before settling on her pinky.

Realizing what her tormentor planned to do, Eve tensed, her

breath catching, her chest tightening. She squeezed her eyes shut and gasped.

He snapped her little finger, and a muffled scream escaped her throat.

"I warned you. A broken bone every hour," he said with a smile. "Now tell me where the flash drive is."

Fighting back the urge to scream again, Eve answered, "*No comprende, asshole.*"

Mendoza shook his head. "My poor, poor, foolish *querida*. So brave are you, no? Can't you see this is not going to turn out well for you? Your body is weakening. Even your sharp wit is beginning to dull."

Time was running out. Still, she wouldn't give Mendoza anything. She held her broken hand against her chest and squirmed to break his hold.

He released her and signaled Carlos. "I guess we haven't been persuasive enough with Miss Taylor." He gathered some papers, threw them in the briefcase parked on one side of his desk, and snapped the lid shut.

"Take her back to the cells. I'd love to stay and get better acquainted, but I have an important business obligation to see to in Buenaventura. I'll return tomorrow morning. We will continue this conversation then."

Important business obligation? Like a drug shipment headed north to his U.S. suppliers? Killing some poor bastard? A rendezvous with his new BFFs, the terrorist group?

"So, Miguel, what makes you think the IDEA won't be waiting to surprise you? Or maybe another cartel, ready to move in on your operations?"

Mendoza thrust out his chest, a smirk in place. "I've made some adjustments."

"Gonna cost you a fortune to *adjust* all your plans." She mirrored his smug stance.

A flash of red snaked up his neck, settling in his face. He cracked his knuckles and his nostrils flared. "Take her back now, Carlos."

"*Sí,* Miguel. I will keep a good eye on this one." Carlos pointed his mini Uzi at Eve and motioned her toward the door.

Eve moved, but Mendoza stopped her. He cupped her chin firmly. "Many days have passed and IDEA has not made a move on any of my operations. I'm thinking maybe your incompetent team was not so successful in the mission to steal my files."

"Correction. They haven't made any moves you're *aware* of. They're probably taking out your associates first, saving the big fish from the scummy little pond for last. Exactly how long has it been since you talked to your *tus amigos que son una mierda?*"

Alarm flickered across his face. *He's buying this load of crap? This feels better than breaking the guard's nose.*

"My piece of shit friends? Such un-ladylike words. *Querida,* save us both a lot of grief. *Por favor.* Give up this foolishness, and tell me what I want to know."

Eve retreated into her silent mode. Ignoring Mendoza really seemed to make him livid. *Piss him off. Make me happy. Ahh, it's the little things in life.*

"Too bad you choose to disregard my wishes." He released her chin and said to Carlos, "Break a bone every hour until she is ready to talk. Call me when she's had enough."

Carlos clasped his hands to his chest, the feet that usually rocked, seemed to bounce several times. "*Sí,* Miguel."

Eve shuddered at the sadistic gleam in Carlos' eyes.

ଓ

Mac stared out the Black Hawk's open cargo door. His gut twisted into knots and sent acid bubbling up his throat. He listened to the steady whump-whump-whump of high-powered rotor blades propelling him and his extraction team toward San Carlos Lucas. A million bright stars twinkled across the cloudless night sky. He rotated his shoulders, rolled his head from side to side, and his mind focused on the mission ahead.

Leaning back against a small duffle bag filled with medical supplies, hands fisted tight on his lap, he mentally prepared for every conceivable scenario they might encounter at Mendoza's compound.

Cade Warner, his partner this mission, sat across from him sorting through two larger duffels filled with weapons and ammo. He pulled out a box of grenades and flash-bangs. "Wanna review the extraction plan one more time?"

"Not unless you feel the need." Mac shifted forward and tossed Cade the bag of medical supplies.

"I'm good to go." Cade stuffed a couple of the flash-bangs inside the pockets of his camouflage pants. "Want to talk about her?"

"Nothing to talk about. I haven't seen Eve in two years. She's history. She and her chicken-shit partner are together now."

"Understood." Cade adjusted his radio headset and turned the volume back on.

The time for offset talk was over.

It annoyed Mac—and maybe stung his pride a little—how quickly she'd moved on after they split. Brewer had moved in on Eve so fast her sheets were probably still warm from the last time she and Mac had made love. Make that smokin' from the last time they'd made love.

The times they'd spent between the sheets had been good. Days and nights filled with sex hot and steamy enough to melt Alaskan ice glaciers. Global warming had nothing on them. He grew hard just thinking about it. Eve only had to walk into the same room with him, and he'd grow hard. But there'd been more than just the sex. She made him whole. When he was inside Eve, Mac felt like he was home. No other woman would ever make him feel the same. He grunted with a half-laugh. Obviously, she hadn't shared his feelings.

Now, he didn't even know if Eve was dead or alive.

Mac put on his headset. Breathing in the hot night breeze flowing through the open cargo doors, he listened to the radio chatter. Cade entertained the team with a shitload of his never-let-the-truth-get-in-the-way-of-a-good-story anecdotes. Cade's tall tales would make a two-dollar hooker blush. Occasional bursts of laughter, with frequent rounds of, "You are so full of shit, Warner," washed over Mac. He blocked out the bantering voices.

If only he could block memories of Eve so easily.

Chapter Four

San Carlos Lucas, Colombia
The Mendoza Compound

Eve's battered body finally surrendered to the unrelenting fever, letting delirium sneak past her weakening barriers. Falling in and out of consciousness, her dreams were vividly realistic. Soothing dreams of her family and the gently swaying cornfields of her hometown were history. Images of her team, bodies stilled by death, haunted her sleep. Rivers of red flowed from them like floodwaters from a Texas gully-washer.

She had to escape. The thick, wet blood burned her skin and the sour, coppery smell stung her nose. Struggling to crawl away, she sank into soft, cool soil. The crumbling dirt gave way and she was sucked through a large black hole into the endless darkness below, quiet cries of desperation filling her mind on the downward spiral.

Two guards, each took an arm, yanked Eve to her feet, and held her steady. The pain in Eve's injured shoulder wrenched her from her nightmares. She couldn't stand on her boneless legs right now if she tried, but she was able to see Carlos clearly. He smiled and his ugly, rotted teeth made him look like a junk-yard dog.

"*Señorita*, you must tell me what you've done with Miguel's property. This would make him very happy, and make me look very good if I recovered the files from you."

He'd leaned in close enough she gagged at the stench of decay and alcohol on his breath. Using all the innocence she could muster, Eve said, "What files? I have no idea what you're talking about, Gomez."

"I am Carlos, not Gomez." He smacked her hard, splitting her lip. The burning sting shot all the way down to her toes. "You never learn. We know you stole Miguel's files. It does no good to refute this. Why do you bother?"

Eve licked her lip, tasted blood, and spat at Carlos' feet. "Listen, José, and listen well. I have nothing to say to you or your boss."

Carlos nodded to the guards holding her.

One man grabbed her injured hand and yanked her toward Carlos.

Eve howled, no longer giving a damn if she let the tears fall. For the first time since being captured, Eve wasn't sure she could handle more abuse. A shiver of doubt curled up her spine, through her body, and lodged deep in her soul.

"You make me do this, *señorita*. I have no choice." Carlos selected her ring finger and snapped the bone.

Eve screamed and prayed for unconsciousness, wanting the darkness to take her under again.

He loosened his grip.

Eve snatched her arm back. Pain rocketed from her fingers, through her wrist, and to the bullet wound in her shoulder, causing her to cry out again. The guards let her slip to the floor and she fell gratefully into a well of semi-consciousness.

Eve vaguely heard Carlos leave the cell, one guard following, on a mission, he'd said, to find a bottle of tequila. The other two stayed behind. One of them tore open the filthy, tattered tank top she wore.

She wanted to scream, but her mouth refused to open.

He roughly fondled and pinched her already bruised breasts.

Her breath shuddered, and she began to tremble. The second guard soon joined him. Eve forced her mind to shut down further, their laughter and taunts becoming distant like stars in a night sky.

They poked her with their feet, tried to shake her awake. Pain shot through her, but she couldn't muster a retort until they touched her mutilated hand.

Eve let out a wake-the-dead-level scream.

☙

Mac and Cade inched through one of the abandoned passageways deep in the underground belly of Mendoza's compound. A muffled scream echoed through the tunnels, bringing them to an abrupt stop. Another scream filled the air. Mac instantly recognized the voice, her shriek cutting through his heart like a knife.

"Eve." His heart hammered against his ribs.

They slid the AKs from their shoulders and followed the sound of Eve's cry, dashing to an opening outside an ancient dungeon. Ignoring the smell and occasional hand reaching through barred doors, Mac sped toward Eve's whimpering, his hand tight on his AK, a finger on the trigger. *Son of a bitch! They kept her in this rat-hole for a week?*

Reaching her cell, Mac zeroed in on the two guards kicking mercilessly at Eve and swung the weapon back on his shoulder. He jumped the man about to deliver the next blow, snapping his neck with a single twist.

Cade took out the second guard with equal skill. After collecting the dead men's weapons, he pulled both corpses into the shadowed corners of the cell while Mac hurried to Eve's crumpled body.

Mac got a good look at her and blinked. Almost every inch of her skin was black and blue. Not sure if she was still alive, he fell to his knees, afraid to touch her. "My, God. What have they done, baby?"

Her chest moved with sluggish breaths. Eve was alive, and a veil of relief swept over him.

Checking her injuries closer, he noted fresh bruises layered with faded ones. The ones covering her pale cheekbones were especially colorful. Blood trickled from a fresh cut on her lower lip. Mac ran his hand around her ribs and she flinched. Next, he checked the shoulder wound caked with dried blood.

"Gunshot to the shoulder—" Mac choked, then tried again. "Dammit, it's infected. Broken wrist, two fingers, and possibly a couple of ribs. Multiple cuts and bruises." He pinched the skin on the back of her uninjured hand. "Dehydrated."

Cade scooted next to Mac. "Christ, she looks like death warmed over. Let's get her the fuck out of here."

Mac took off his outer shirt and wrapped it around Eve, covering her naked and bruised chest. He scooped up her feather-light body. The fire burning in his belly escalated to a scorching level. "Someone will fucking pay for this."

Eve took a deep, labored breath and her body jerked.

Mac firmed his hold. "She's regaining consciousness."

Cade nodded.

Anxious to get moving, Mac eyed the empty hallway. Before he'd taken his first step, Eve caught his jaw with a solid cuff, hard enough he stumbled backward. She fought tough, her good arm punching wildly at him. Her following blows missed, hitting only air. Arching her back, she screamed, her voice raspy.

Mac covered her mouth. "Shhh, Eve, its Mac. We're getting you out of here."

Another weak flail died quickly when he touched her cheek. "Stop fighting me."

She looked at him. "Mac?"

"Yeah, baby, it's me. Hang in there, okay?"

Eve's head sagged against toward him. "I...ummm...I'm tryin'."

"I know you are." He smiled down at her. "You're doing fine."

"Danny's dead. And Rex...we've got to check on Rex." Her

eyes blinked several times. "Need to get...I buried...flash dri—" Eve passed out.

"Damn." Cade looked at Mac. "You wanna try to wake her again, see if she can tell us where she buried the flash drive? We can grab it."

"She won't be coming around any time soon." Mac studied her limp, injured body. "Fuck the flash drive. She's out cold. Let's get her out of here."

"Yeah, she's had enough. You take point. I've got your six."

They took off in a controlled jog, made their way out of the cell area, and headed into the dark, musty tunnels. Mac's heart pounded anger-driven adrenaline through his body. Still, he managed to gently and effortlessly carry her. Eve had been in the hands of a cold-blooded bastard for a week. He wasn't sure how she managed, but somehow she'd survived. After he got Eve safely back on American soil, he'd return to Colombia. Miguel Mendoza would be a dead man.

"Cade, alert the team. Time to fire up the Black Hawk. I want Beauchamp ready on the mini guns." Mac kept his tone steady, steadier than he really was.

Running shoulder to shoulder, Cade said, "Eve needs checked ASAP. You wanna shoot for home ground?"

"Negative. I don't think she'd make it. There's a small clinic in Bogota sponsored by Resolutions. The doctor handles this kind of emergency for us all the time. Alert Corelli we're gonna make a medical stopover."

Not wanting to cause her more pain, Mac worked hard to avoid jarring her. He counted on Cade keeping a close watch on their surroundings while he concentrated on the almost lifeless woman in his arms.

In record time, they'd passed through the tunnel. Cade stepped in front of him and jiggled the hidden lock buried behind the gate. The iron door swung open, and they passed through. Metal clicked as Cade secured the lock behind them.

"Looks like Lady Luck is on our side, Mac. Mendoza and his men still haven't figured out the gates in the tunnels can be opened."

Mac, who hadn't bothered with prayers since his mother's death, began a round of praying even John the Baptist would be proud of. He prayed their luck wouldn't run out. Prayed he could get Eve to the chopper safely. And he prayed she wouldn't die. Hell, at this point, he'd pray for world peace if it'd help.

Alongside Cade, Mac plodded through the slippery jungle muck, his leg muscles propelling him forward at an even pace, rivers of sweat running down his back. Thick fronds from the tropical foliage slapped him, leaving a trail of scratches on any uncovered skin. Occasionally, a small, panicked lizard darted for cover from his steps.

Mac sighed with relief when the groundcover became less dense. "Not much farther."

About two hundred meters from the Black Hawk waiting to be boarded, their luck did run out. Bullets slammed the ground all around them. Mac curled Eve closer. "Looks like Mendoza's men have caught up."

"Bastards!" Cade went down on one knee and returned fire, giving Mac a better lead. A burst of enemy rounds fired above their heads.

Mac looked over his shoulder and caught a glimpse of Cade shooting back with his HK416, dropping men with the keen accuracy the specially-made-for-Delta-Forces assault rifle was famous for. Backing up Cade from the chopper, Jackson Beauchamp gripped one of the door-mounted mini guns, laying down a flurry of suppressing fire.

Mac reached the Black Hawk and signaled Cade to make a run for the open cargo door. Under the cover of Beauchamp's fire, Cade snaked his way backwards until he caught up, and climbed on board. Cade reached for Eve. Mac passed her motionless body to his partner's waiting arms, his own suddenly feeling strangely empty. Mac jumped on board, his gaze never leaving Eve. Cade laid her down, then jumped to the door mounted mini gun. Beauchamp moved to the second mini gun mounted on the opposite side.

Mac again used his body to shelter Eve. "Get us airborne, Corelli. Go, go, go!"

The powerful Black Hawk vibrated and lifted off.

Mac turned to Cade at the same time a bullet grazed his friend's cheek.

Cade, one hand still firing the mini gun, slapped his wound with the other, rubbing a streak of blood away. "Fuck me! That stings like a bitch."

Mac bit back a smile. "You okay?"

"I'm fine, but now the fuckers have pissed me off." Cade launched one of the short-range missiles into the remaining group on the ground still firing at them. A small fireball erupted, sending bodies flying and a cloud of smoke spiraling skyward. All movement on the ground stilled. The chopper banked left and flew in a zig-zag pattern away from the flume of smoke covering the now quiet terrain.

Cade and Beauchamp let go of their mounted weapons. Cade took another swipe at his cheek. "Teach them to fuck with me and my pretty face." He knelt next to Mac. "You need help?"

Mac worked furiously to stop the bleeding in Eve's shoulder. "She's burning up. Beauchamp, can you haul out one of the large bottles of water from the cooler? I'll need a couple pieces of cloth, too."

"On it." Beauchamp reached for the water.

Mac tossed Cade the duffle. "Grab an IV kit so I can get some fluids running. Find the tube of antibiotic cream for your cheek, and slap a Band Aid on it."

Mac had just started Eve's IV when Corelli, manning the controls of the Black Hawk, signaled for Cade and Mac to put on their headphones.

Corelli said, "ETA to Bogota, one hour. The doctor will meet us at the landing strip and then it's about a ten-minute drive to his clinic. I filled Doc Peterson in on what injuries we're dealing with. He'll set up for surgery before heading to the air strip."

"I called the Resolutions office and let Hutch know how the extraction went. He said he'd fill in the head of Agent Taylor's task force, SAC, John Sanders," Jake Chapman said. "Hutch wants another update when the doctor gets a look at her."

"Any chance of speeding up the ETA?"

"Sorry, Mac. I'm a damn good pilot, but we're at full speed and the wind is with us. On the ground in one hour is already pushing the envelope."

"Just asking." Mac got the IV in on the first try and set the fluids to run wide open, thankful for the basic combat medic training Delta Force provided.

Mac nodded at the bottle of cold water Beauchamp held. "Soak the towels and cover her forehead, neck, and limbs. We need to get her fever down before she starts convulsing. She's showing signs of shock."

Beauchamp, Cade, and Mac worked to keep Eve covered in cool cloths. Using gauze, Mac staunched the bleeding from her shoulder. He cleaned some of the dirt off her, swearing at each lesion and bruise he uncovered.

Yep, Mendoza's days are numbered.

☙

Bogota, Columbia

The Black Hawk touched down on the tarmac in Bogota one hour later. The sun had begun to rise, casting off layers of glowing pink, purple, and orange.

As promised, the doctor stood waiting, prepared to whisk Eve to his clinic. Cade drove while Mac rode in the back seat with Eve and the doctor. Mac held the IV bag in one hand, her uninjured hand in his other. He found it odd how he couldn't quite let go of her yet, that he needed to feel the warmth of her skin, wanted the assurance Eve was still alive.

Cade cut the ten-minute drive down to five. Mac carried Eve into the clinic and put her on the gurney the doctor had prepared. After a quick exam, a piggyback infusion of antibiotics, and several x-rays, the doctor took Eve to surgery.

Mac put in several miles on the clinic's tile floor, every step filled with unease. "Cade, what the fuck is taking so long in there? Is the doctor doing a brain transplant?"

"Park your ass and catch a breath. You want Eve patched up right, don't you? They've not been back there very long, and he's working alone."

Still Mac couldn't get his constricted muscles to relax. His fists stayed clenched, his jawline tight.

The door to the surgery area opened and Mac's head jerked. "It's about time, Doc."

Cade stepped out and Mac went to Eve. His heart skipped a beat at the sight before him. She was even paler than before. A fierce ache shot through him. Had he really hated this woman for the past two years? He smoothed back the tangled mess of hair from Eve's forehead. A sudden urge to plant a kiss there hit him square in the gut. Taking a deep breath, he cleared his head, and ignored the impulse. Their relationship was over. She'd walked away, and he'd let her. There was no going back.

"How'd the surgery go, Doc?"

"Pretty much as expected. I cleaned the bullet wound and set the breaks. I bathed her the best I could under the circumstances. I applied a wrist to elbow cast and taped the two broken digits together. If you're going to fracture your wrist, a Scaphoid break is the best type to have."

"Speak English, Doc."

"Basically it means the break is closer to the thumb and will heal faster because there's a better supply of blood needed for healing." The doctor added a syringe full of something to Eve's IV fluids. Mac raised a brow.

"Relax, Mr. McKenna, it's just a painkiller." He tossed the used hypodermic in a red trash container. "She did quite well considering the beating she's taken. The fever took its toll, but her excellent physical condition should help speed the healing process. Applying the iodine gauze field dressing was an excellent call on her part. If she hadn't, the infection would've killed her by now. All things considered, she's a lucky young lady."

"She doesn't look too damn lucky to me."

"The bullet to her shoulder hit high enough to miss bone and major veins. Her ribs are bruised, not fractured. Seems like luck to me."

"Was Eve...was she...?" Mac stuttered, finding the words hard to say. He didn't even like thinking them.

"You're asking if Agent Taylor was raped. The answer is no. That's one cruelty she didn't suffer. I didn't find any signs of vaginal tearing or bruising."

"Thank, God." Mac ran his hand through his hair. He caught a strange vibe from the doctor. "There's more? Spit it out, Doc."

"Although there's no sign of rape, I did find severe contusions on her breasts, leading me to believe she was sexually assaulted in that manner."

"Fucking bastards!" Mac punched the wall, wishing it was Mendoza's face. He tapped his fingers against his thighs, searching for a calm he'd never find until Mendoza burned in hell.

"How long until we can fly her back to D.C.? I want Eve out of Colombia and back on home turf before Mendoza finds where we've got her stashed."

"I understand, but she's safe here. This is a Resolutions clinic, and your boss personally hired me. I'm not only your basic MEDEVAC, patch and go doc. I'm ex-Delta Force myself."

"It's not that I don't trust you, Doc. My pilot this mission is a former patient of yours. He's got nothing to say except good things about you. You wouldn't be here if Hutch didn't trust you completely. I just think I'll breathe easier when Eve's out of Colombia altogether."

"Understood." The doctor pulled back Eve's cover and checked the thick dressings covering her shoulder. "The anesthesia should wear off soon. The next twenty-four to forty-eight hours are critical. I'd like her to stay put at least three days, but I'd prefer to give her a full five or six for rest and IV antibiotics before you move her. I've hung the CLOSED sign. No one in the barrio will bother us. Give her a little time to re-coup."

"I'll give you three days, but five or six? Well, that's debatable. I need to get her home. Cade and I will stay here with Eve. Hutch arranged for a guard to keep watch on the front door."

The doctor nodded. "Good. She'll heal faster if you give her time to regain some strength for the trip. I'll leave you with her while I clean my surgery area. Yell if you need anything."

Mac pulled a chair close to Eve's bed. Overwhelmed by the need to touch her, he slid the side rail down quietly. He didn't bother to fight the urge and held her hand with the IV attached. Mac studied her face and neck before releasing his hold to lift one side of the covers. The doctor had dressed her in a tank top and baggy pair of boxers. A kaleidoscope of bruises marked her exposed skin.

Skin he remembered smelling.

Skin he remembered touching.

Skin he remembered tasting.

"Mac?" She spoke in a whisper-low voice.

He let the sheet float down over her. "Yeah, baby, I'm here. Go back to sleep. You need the rest."

Eve's wobbly hand cupped his cheek, startling him. Her touch was cool and shaky, her face shrouded in pain. The small thread holding Mac together snapped. A surge of anger started low in the pit of his belly before rising and becoming caustic in his throat.

"Dammit, Eve. I knew this would happen if you took this job. You needlessly put yourself in danger."

Her hand jerked back as if scorched. "Thanks for pointing out my flaws. You couldn't resist the 'I told you so,' could you?" Her voice splintered, and she sucked in a deep lungful of air.

Mac wished he could take his words back. They'd tumbled out before he could stop them. *Damn. Hadn't she suffered enough without me adding more crap to the pile?*

"I'm sorry, Eve. I shouldn't criticize."

He'd wasted his apology. She'd retreated into

unconsciousness.

ꝏ

Thirty minutes later, the doctor came to check on Eve. Mac welcomed the distraction. "You're retired Delta Force, Doc?"

The doctor straightened his shoulders. "Lt. Colonel James Peterson, former First Battalion, Seventy-fifth Ranger Regimen, and Delta Force retired, at your service." He snapped off a well-honed salute. "Been out damned near twenty years now. I stepped down from active duty not long after the Iran-Iraq War."

A sudden sadness wash over Mac. "My mother was a nurse with the United Nations during the First Persian Gulf War—as she called it. She was killed in 1988 while treating injured Basij teenagers near the Basra-Iran border."

"The Basij. Misguided teenage volunteers used for suicide missions. Human wave attacks setting off land mines and clearing the way for Iranian ground attacks. Such a waste." Peterson looked to Mac. "Any chance your momma was Maggie McKenna?"

Mac's head pounded. The last time he'd seen his mother he'd begged her not to go. She'd kissed him on the cheek, told him not to worry, and left without another word. His dad didn't try to stop her. Didn't try to protect her.

"Yeah, she was my mother." He couldn't keep the anger or the grief out of his voice.

The other man smiled. "Maggie was a fine woman, and a damn good nurse. You can be proud of her. I had the opportunity to meet her on base at Fort Bragg before I shipped out, even got a chance to work with her a couple times."

Mac wasn't sure 'proud of her' was the phrase he'd use to describe his emotions back then. Fucking angry came to mind. Senseless waste definitely topped the list. But he wouldn't go there right now. "Did you know her?"

"Well enough to recognize I liked her style."

"Did she seem happy?" He'd always wondered why she'd chosen a dangerous job instead of her family.

"Yes, she did. Always had a smile on her face. I didn't realize Maggie hadn't made it back." Peterson shook his head, his face a mask of sadness. "What a shame."

"You have no idea."

"You're right, I don't. You must've been a kid when she died."

Mac tried to smile. "According to Mom right before she shipped out, I was thirteen going on thirty."

"I'm finished here, so I'll get out of your way and let Agent Taylor rest. In the meantime, I'll put the coffee on and rustle up some food if you'd like."

"Thanks. I appreciate the offer."

Mac dug out his satellite phone and dialed the Resolutions' office.

Hutch answered on the first ring, as if he'd been waiting on the call for hours. He probably had.

"We've got Eve at the clinic. The doctor cleaned the shoulder wound, wrapped her ribs, and set her broken wrist. He started her on antibiotics, but she's still running a high fever."

"Prognosis?"

Mac looked down at the battered woman in the bed. "We're in the wait and see mode. Doc wants to keep her six days, three minimum. He says the clinic is secure."

"It's one of ours. Of course it's safe," Hutch said. "I assume Doc put up the CLOSED sign. The locals think he's an old drunk who goes on occasional benders. They're used to him disappearing. They won't suspect he's got anyone in the clinic."

"What's the word from Eve's boss? Did you tell Sanders we had to pull out without the complete package?"

"Affirmative." Hutch grunted. "He wasn't real shot in the ass when I told him Eve said she buried the flash drive and couldn't stay in the game long enough to tell you where. Her boss is a smart man, and he agreed with your decision to leave the intel behind and get Eve out. He's bought some time by putting the word out Eve brought the flash drive back with her. He doesn't want Mendoza to know it's still on compound grounds."

"Makes sense if another task force team is going back to retrieve the flash drive. It'll go smoother if Mendoza thinks Eve has his property, and he's not expecting another break in." Mac already had a vision involving IDEA's next trip in. It included him tagging along and Mendoza dying a long, painful death.

"Any chance she's mentioned the exact location the flash drive is buried since you've been at the clinic?"

"Nada. She's only coherent a few seconds at a time."

Hutch said, "Too bad. At least Sander's rumor gives IDEA a little wiggle room until a definite plan is in place. Our mission's complete. I'm meeting with him and the task force heads later today for debriefing."

"Resolutions may be finished with Mendoza, but I'm not. I'm going after the bastard."

Chapter Five

San Carlos Lucas
Mendoza Compound

Miguel Mendoza sat behind his hand carved, mahogany desk, dressed in his three-thousand dollar Armani suit, surrounded by all the things money could buy. The best furniture. The best chandeliers. The best cigars. The best of everything. His illegal businesses had made him wealthy and powerful.

His new venture would quadruple his worth. He'd be unstoppable, a man people feared. Like the two men standing before him now. One stood shaking, sweating, and chewing on his bottom lip like it was a wad of gum. The other shifted from one foot to the other. The guy doing the foot dance was Carlos Salazar, Mendoza's right-hand man and a full-time pain in his ass.

The man with Carlos was the surviving guard on duty when Eve escaped.

Mendoza bared his teeth like a snake ready to strike, eager to spew its venom. A face he'd practiced many times in front of his bathroom mirror. "I don't understand how guarding one woman could be such a hard task. Last time I saw her she could barely stand, much less make a daring escape.

"Look around." Mendoza gestured around the room. "I have

only the very best of everything. Why can I not seem to employ help who are the best? Is this asking too much? Do I not deserve this?"

"Miguel, of course you deserve to have the best of everything." Carlos said sympathetically as his feet shuffled faster. "This escape was just an unfortunate event."

"Unfortunate event?" Mendoza growled. Unfortunate didn't begin to describe what happened.

"*Sí*, Miguel, very unfortunate." Carlos rocked faster. "*Señorita* Taylor did not escape alone. You must understand, Miguel, two men rescued her."

Mendoza slammed his fists on the desk in front of him. "Two men? Are you telling me two men just waltzed into my underground cells, took my prisoner from three armed guards, and then proceeded to sneak past the dozens of men guarding the compound? All this while dragging a woman beaten half to death?"

"*Sí, Miguel. Dos*! Two men, maybe more. Maybe many more." Carlos pointed to the man beside him. "Luis here, he only stepped out for a moment. Two other guards were still with her. How could anyone know there'd be an attempt to rescue the *señorita*? After the last effort to liberate Miss Taylor failed so horribly, I assumed her *compadres* would not try again."

Mendoza strolled around to the front of his desk. He stepped in front of the two men. "Stop moving, Carlos. You make my head dizzy."

"Sorry, Miguel. Nervous habit." Carlos froze in place like an arctic iceberg.

Mendoza studied the fear on Carlos' face. "Carlos, you must become a better leader to the men. How can they learn if you do not teach?"

"I understand, Miguel. I will do better."

"I would appreciate that, *gracias*." He pointed to the other man. "I am very disappointed in you, Luis. You've been with me many years, have you not?"

"*Sí, jefe*...yes, boss. I have been with you for many years." Luis could barely form a sentence. "*Por favor*, I can explain."

"You think there is an explanation for this?"

"*Sí*. The idea was Marco and Felipe's. We believed it'd be okay to have a fiesta with the *señorita*. We...ah, they...needed a little tequila to make the celebration complete. I went to get a bottle from the pantry. I was only gone a short time."

"This is your excuse? You needed tequila?" Mendoza said.

"It is my explanation." Luis studied the floor. "You must remember, *por favor*, *jefe*, I...umm...Carlos, alerted the others of the *señorita's* escape. We almost had her again until the helicopter came with big guns and rockets."

"*Pinche idiota*," Mendoza snarled.

Mendoza yanked his pistol from the back of his waistband and shot Luis between the eyes. Blood, mixed with chunks of brain matter, splattered Carlos. Wide-eyed and mouth gaping, Carlos stared at the dead man.

"This distresses me, Luis. You should have known better." Mendoza looked at the body, kicking the leg closest to him.

"*Mierde*, *Miguel*!" Carlos rapidly made the sign of the cross. Mendoza pointed the gun at Carlos. "*Par favor*, Miguel, please, think about what my poor wife—your sister, will say if you kill me," Carlos stammered and covered his face. "What about your little nieces and nephews?"

"My sister is the lone reason I do not blow you away right now. She would have to raise your five little *bebes* all alone." He rolled the idea around in his mind for a moment. "Maybe she would be better off."

"*Mierde*. No, she would not."

Mendoza laid the gun on his desk. "I'm afraid you're right, Carlos. For some unknown reason, my sister seems attached to you. I will let you live. Do not fail me again."

"*Gracias*, Miguel." Carlos bowed. "I will do better from now on. You will be proud."

"That's good to know. Clean this mess and get out of here." He waved at Luis' dead body. "Now I must try to fix your blunder."

Mendoza sat at his desk, picked up his phone, and made a call. A man's voice came on the line. Mendoza listened a few moments and his anger flared.

"You did not tell me the IDEA would attempt another rescue. We were not prepared. I have not only lost Miss Taylor, but I still do not know what she has done with the property she stole from me. Is this not what I pay you for? Should you not supply me with this kind of information?"

"Sorry, Miguel, it couldn't be helped." The words, meant to soothe, did little to quench Mendoza's heat. "My person inside didn't know about the extraction until afterwards. John Sanders made those arrangements with his friend at Resolutions. Only two others on the task force were notified. The rest of the team wasn't told until afterward."

"The other two aware of the plan, who are they and can they not be bought?"

"The D.C. Attorney General, and the D.C. Police Chief, who are both major players on the task force. And no, they can't be bought."

"Anyone can be bought." Mendoza leaned back. "What is the reason for all the secrecy? Does Sanders suspect an informant?"

"No, Miguel. He made a spur of the moment decision and had no time to call the team in for a briefing. Don't worry, we're still in business."

"If you slip up again, we may not be." Mendoza began to calm down a bit, but he wasn't ready to let the other man off the hook.

"Don't threaten me, Miguel. I'm already pissed about you roughing up Eve. Part of our deal was for her to not be harmed."

Mendoza laughed. "I agreed not to kill Miss Taylor. I never said I would not have a little fun. She's a delightful adversary."

"You're a bastard, Miguel."

"*Cabron!* A bastard who is making you a very rich man. You would do well to remember who is in charge." Mendoza let the man on the other line think about what he'd said. "Perhaps your usefulness has come to an end?"

"I'm just saying you should have let her go. I would've found another way to locate the flash drive."

"I think you have feelings for Miss Taylor, no?"

The other man paused and then said, "I don't want her hurt,

Miguel."

"Where is she? I want my files *and* Miss Taylor returned. She and I have unfinished business. For some reason, I find myself attracted to the woman's persistence." In spite of what he promised his informant, he planned to kill Eve after he had his fun. He grabbed a cigar. "If you wish to stay alive long enough to spend the money I've supplied you with, I suggest you find these things out. Again, what good is having an informant who cannot inform?"

"I already know where Eve is. I hear she's got the flash drive with her." The IDEA traitor sounded mostly calm, but Mendoza detected an occasional tremor in his tone. "But again, that's just a rumor. There's still a chance the device never left the compound."

"Are you willing to gamble with your life it's still here?"

"No, I guess not. What I do know, for certain, is Eve is recovering at a little neighborhood clinic. The place doubles as a trauma room for Resolutions operatives and is located in a small barrio in northern Bogota. They've got one man on the door, two inside, plus the doctor. They have three other operatives in town who will soon return to D.C. I'm not sure if the fourth is sticking around or not. Your time is limited to get to Eve and the flash drive."

He continued, "If you still want her, I suggest you get a move on. When Eve leaves Colombia, the intel leaves with her—if she still has it."

"Yes, I want her. I will send Carlos immediately." Mendoza motioned to Carlos, who was supervising the removal of Luis' body.

"Make no mistakes, Miguel, Eve will be closely guarded."

"I will keep this in mind." Did the man think he didn't know what he was doing? When Mendoza no longer needed the information the traitor supplied, he would be rid of him.

"There's something else you should know, Miguel. Dillon McKenna is one of the Resolutions' operatives who helped Eve escape."

A fierce roar of anger zipped through Mendoza at lightning

speed, had him breaking into a cold sweat. Hands shaking, he dropped the cigar. "The *cabroncito!* He made me a cripple. I want him dead."

"So I've heard. Word is he shot you when he helped one of your chemists escape a few months back. Well, here's your chance to even the score. He's Eve's guard dog. Take him out, and you've got Eve. A double play."

"Yes, I will see to McKenna," Mendoza spat through gritted teeth. McKenna had infiltrated his cartel and betrayed him. He would kill the man.

"After we get the flash drive back, I want out. I think it's time for me and my inside connection to close up shop."

Mendoza was caught off guard. "You no longer wish to continue our partnership?"

"Not really what I'd call a partnership, but yeah, I'm finished after this last round of information has been put to use. I'd like to spend some of the money you've been feeding me before I get too old to enjoy it."

The informant cleared his throat. "My DEA source thinks you're out of control. You've been killing off too many IDEA agents. The more you kill the more heat Sanders puts on the task force to take out your operations."

"Do you agree with your source? Am I out of control?"

"I'm sure there's some truth to the claim, but frankly I couldn't care less. I'm ready to move on regardless. Miguel, you really don't want to push your luck too much further with the task force. They're getting closer every day to ending you."

"I will not be taken down. This is a fact." He paused to think. "So be it. If you want out, you are out. But not until I get my property back."

"The flash drive?"

"And Eve Taylor. Give me McKenna and there will be an end-of-partnership bonus for you."

"Now that's what I like to hear."

Mendoza slammed down the phone, sat back, and relished multiple visions of revenge.

Chapter Six

Bogota, Colombia

Mac watched over Eve as she waged war against the fever demons throughout the night. She cried out often. Was she in pain or having nightmares? Maybe both? An ache tore at his heart. But what really broke him were the tears trickling down her cheeks accompanied by soft, puppy-like whimpers. *This is how being slowly gutted with a dull knife must feel.*

He stayed by her side, soothing her with soft words, and bathing her face with cool water. Occasionally her eyes, glassy from fever, would flutter open and look into his, almost as if she was studying him. Judging him. Then she'd close them again without saying a word.

Mac fought his mounting frustration, powerless to take her hurt away. Sometime around three in the morning, she stirred. Her head rolled toward him, gaze focusing on him. She struggled to form words.

"Rex?" she whispered.

She wanted fucking Brewer? The man who left her behind? The imaginary knife in Mac's gut shifted upward, piercing his heart. He leaned in closer. "No, Eve. It's Mac."

Eve lifted her head slightly, looked like she was straining to see him. "Mac? You're still here?" She sounded almost happy. Mac's spirits lifted, his heartbeat accelerating.

"I'm right here."

With her good hand, she grabbed one of his. Fear and desperation clouded her face. "Don't let him come back. I won't talk no matter what he does to me, but please don't let him take me again." She clutched his hand tighter. "I hurt. I hurt everywhere. Make it stop."

"Shhh, everything's okay. I've got you. Fucking nobody's gonna touch you again. You're safe. I'm taking you home soon."

"Don't let him...hurt...me, 'kay?" Eve's eyes fluttered. She drifted away, her words fading.

Mac kissed the hand holding onto his with a death grip. "Okay, baby, I won't let anyone hurt you. Sleep now."

Her hand relaxed and let his go. Mac rose, moved to the door, and yelled, "Doc, Eve needs something for pain in here."

A few minutes later, the doctor stood at Eve's bedside, giving another push of morphine through her IV. He hung the next small bag of antibiotics, did a quick check of her vitals, and checked her dressings.

"Agent Taylor's vital signs are improving. Her heart rate is less rapid, her breathing less labored. Both should level out as her temperature continues to drop. Remarkably, her blood pressure has stayed within normal ranges."

Eve shifted beneath the sheet.

"She spoke," Mac said.

"Another good sign."

"I don't think she was really awake."

Peterson said, "Fever often times causes a patient to become delirious. Use the cool washcloths on her. They're soothing and help keep her temp down."

"Copy that. I'm not moving from this chair. If you want to grab some shuteye, now would be the time." Mac wasn't about to leave Eve's side until he was sure she'd be okay—and not just physically. He wanted a glimpse of the strong, confident woman he remembered.

"Mr. McKenna, I'll take you up on your offer. I'll set my alarm in time to hang her next round of antibiotics. If she seems uncomfortable before then, come get me and I'll give her another push of pain meds."

"Thanks, and call me Mac."

"See you soon...Mac."

After Peterson left, Cade stopped by Eve's room. "Any change?"

"Still burning up with fever, but it's leveling out. Hopefully the antibiotics are starting to work." Mac pushed her damp, dark hair back from her forehead.

"Good news." Cade moved to the other side of the bed and laid the back of his hand above Eve's brow.

The innocent act stirred an unfamiliar emotion in Mac. *Jealousy?*

Mac shook off the startling sensation. "Eve woke for a minute. She's gonna pull through."

Cade grinned, stepped away from the bed, and his hand fell to his side.

Damned if Mac didn't feel a sense of relief.

"I hear she's a good agent, a real asset to the task force."

"So I've heard...several times."

"Sounds sarcastic."

"If she's such a fucking good agent, what the hell is she doing here fighting for her life?" Mac gestured around the small room, bare except for the machines, tubes, and a single chair next to the bed.

"I'm not even gonna try to answer that question." Cade's hands went up.

"You're a wise man."

Cade grinned. "Corelli and crew are with the Black Hawk."

"Good. It's just a matter of time until Mendoza finds where we've got Eve. Sanders put out the word she has the flash drive. Mendoza will be turning over stones to find us." Mac settled back into his chair.

"Except it'll be the flash drive, and maybe Eve he's after, not us."

Mac shook his head. "I doubt he's forgotten who crippled him."

"True. If he finds out you were involved in her extraction, he'll want to add your head to his collection." Cade shrugged.

"We're sitting ducks here, and the doc wants us here at least three days, preferably six. It's gonna be a stretch."

"No matter. Mendoza will have a hard time tracking us.

"I'll feel a hell of a lot better when we get Eve out of Colombia altogether."

"Copy that," Cade said.

They both fell silent before Cade broke the quiet camaraderie. "Spoke to Hutch earlier. Eve's partner is coming to see her day after tomorrow. He's going to debrief her while he's here."

Mac's hands knotted into iron-hard fists. "No fucking way."

Cade put up a hand. "Hutch wanted you to have a head's up. He doesn't want you having your 'talk' with Brewer right now. Whatever the fuck that means."

"I know what Hutch meant." Mac curled his hands around the metal arms of the chair, wishing he had Brewer's neck beneath his fingers. "Brewer damn well isn't Eve's friend, and he's certainly not a partner who's worth a shit. A good partner and friend would never have left her behind. Brewer should've gotten her out, or should fucking well died trying. The prick has no right to see her."

"Eve's a DEA agent on the IDEA task force. She knew the risks going in. Debriefing is part of the gig. The woman's doing her damn job, same as you and me."

"Sanders should send someone else to question her."

Cade shook his head. "Brewer wants to see for himself how she's doing."

"He doesn't deserve to know." Mac took a deep breath and tried to release the death-grip he had on the chair.

"I understand he attempted to get to Eve, but Mendoza's men had her surrounded. Both of them being captured would've done no one any good."

"We'll have to disagree on that one. Brewer's a coward who doesn't deserve to breathe the same air as Eve." Mac couldn't hide the anger, frustration, or turmoil pouring over him like a steady summer rainstorm.

"Jesus, Mac, why in the hell did you two break up? I have no clue what happened, but obviously you've still got feelings for the woman."

"I was an ass is what happened."

"So you got a lot of groveling to do?"

"I don't grovel." Mac finally let go and pushed his chair a little farther from the bed. "Wouldn't help anyway. Eve hates me, and I don't trust her. End of story."

☙

Bright streaks from the Colombian sunrise trickled through the thin, worn drapes in the clinic's small bedroom. Eve slept peacefully for the time being. For the second night in a row he dozed in the chair next to her bed all night. Mac's neck and legs were rigid and numb. He stood and stretched his stiff joints.

Doc entered the room armed with a steaming mug of coffee in each hand. Mac nodded his hello. "Damn chairs aren't made to sleep in."

"Afraid not," Peterson said, passing Mac one of the cups. "Try this. It's got one heck of a caffeine kick. Hard to beat the Colombian coffee bean. Won't cure your hurting joints, but it'll sure go far in making you forget them." The doctor sat his own mug on a nearby table and moved to Eve. He examined her gently and skillfully.

"Fuck the aching joints. I'm in it for the caffeine." Mac pointed at Eve with his free hand. "How is she?"

"Fever's dropping." He carefully pulled back the bandages on her shoulder. "This looks good. The swelling's gone down." Doc bent at the knees and leaned in. "Hmm, the drainage is starting to look clearer. All good signs."

Mac took a careful sip of the hot coffee. The effect was immediate. He straightened a little. "After the last round of pain medicine, she's slept solid."

"I added a tranquilizer. All her thrashing around earlier wasn't doing her—or you—any good. How about I sit with Agent Taylor, and you go grab a quick shower? If you run some hot water on your stiff joints, you'll feel like a new man." Mac hesitated. "Mr. Warner is still here, so is Brad Thompson, the young man on guard out front. She should be fine for a few minutes."

"Give me ten."

"Take time to soak under the hot water, Mac. I'm an old man with lots of achy joints. Take my word, you'll feel better."

Fifteen minutes later, Mac returned to Eve's side, hair still damp from his shower. He studied her face, looking for any change, or trace of discomfort. She hadn't moved at all.

Mac shoved his hands in his back pockets and shook off all thoughts of Eve. "I'll take watch now, Doc."

"Shout out if our patient needs me."

Mac's ass hadn't had time to warm the seat when Eve began to stir. Her swollen eye peeked open along with her good one. Recognition and surprise hovered in them.

"Hi there. I'm glad you're back."

"You came. I worried the escape was a dream." She sounded close to normal. The rest had been good for her.

"No baby, it wasn't a dream."

She looked around the tiny room. "Where are we?"

"A small clinic in Bogota." He laid a hand on her forearm.

Panic flickered across her face. "We're still in Colombia?'

"We are, but not much longer." Eve's muscles tensed beneath his hand. "No one knows we're here except Hutch and my team, John Sanders, and a very limited number of the IDEA task force."

She moved restlessly. "What about the doctor?"

"Hutch handpicked him. You're safe here."

Eve twisted a corner of the sheet around her finger.

"I promise." That won him a weak smile.

"Promise, huh?"

"Yep." He offered her a sip of water, and she downed it eagerly. He drank in the sight of her full lips caressing the rim of the glass. God, how he remembered those sweet lips.

"How long have I been off in La-La Land?"

"We found you two days ago. You've been in and out since."

"Am I okay?" She walked her fingertips from her chin to her temple.

"Things were touch and go for a little while, but you'll be fine."

"My team? Any word?"

"Carlyle didn't make it."

"I didn't think so. I saw him go down, and Rex couldn't find a pulse."

Tears welled, and she blinked them away. Mac wondered how one woman could stay so strong. "It's okay to cry, Eve."

"You'd like to see me crumble, wouldn't you? See me all weak and weepy? Well, tough. I've been weak and weepy enough lately, enough to last a lifetime. It's damned embarrassing."

"I'm just saying you don't have to be so brave all the time. You've nothing to be embarrassed about. You stayed strong during a terrible ordeal. Most agents wouldn't have. I admire your stamina."

"Sorry. I don't know why I'm so defensive. Old habits I suppose." She closed her eyes, sucked in a shaky breath. "What about Randi?"

"She made it out fine."

"Rex is dead." A tear leaked down her cheek. "My fault."

Mac hated to see her upset. Even worse, she blamed herself for the failed mission. "Hell, Eve. Your worthless partner isn't dead."

"Rex is alive? Oh my God. I thought I'd lost him, too."

"Brewer will arrive in Bogota sometime today. He'll be debriefing you."

"It'll be good to see him and get an update on Mendoza." She smiled.

"Dammit, Eve, there's nothing good about Brewer. He shouldn't have left you behind."

Their gazes met. Mac knew his flashed anger.

Eve's sparked insolence. "Rex had no choice. I was down, and Mendoza's men were already on me. There were too many of them. Rex would've ended up dead for real if he'd tried to get to me."

"You're defending him?" Mac tried, but couldn't keep the anger from his voice.

Eve flinched. "I'm not defending him. I'm telling you what happened."

Mac sucked in a breath, but the words he didn't want to say came out anyway. "What's the deal? You and Brewer an item? You fucking him?"

"Why would you care? You finished with me two years ago."

Mac had gone too far, but he couldn't seem to stop. "Correction. You walked out on me two years ago."

"No, you drove me out. Get your facts straight."

"The facts? The fact is, I was right. You're in over your head with this job of yours. Here's another fact. You had my replacement lined up less than twenty-four hours after we parted ways." *Less than twenty-four hours after we made love for the last time.*

The pink tint of her skin turned darker. She sputtered, "Your replacement? Listen you arrogant piece—" Eve tried to sit and winced. She slumped onto the pillows, her chest heaving, perspiration gathering on her face.

He shot off the chair and reached out to help.

She flinched before waving his hand away.

Mac went still at her reaction. *She's afraid of me? She hates me that much?* His anger faded to regret. A sudden need to apologize, to take back his hurtful words, overwhelmed him. Rubbing both hands over his face, he took in a deep breath.

"Listen, Eve. I don't want to fight. Let's leave the past where it belongs. In the past."

"Apology accepted."

Now was not the time to revisit their history. Mac let her take a minute to settle and then changed the subject. "You gave us a scare, but you're on the mend now."

"Us?"

"Me and my team. We got you out of Mendoza's compound. You've met most of the guys before."

"I have?" She looked around as if she expected them to pop out of the woodwork.

"Sure, Warner, Corelli, and Beauchamp. And a guy you haven't met. Jake Chapman."

"I see. I'm just another job for you. IDEA called in Resolutions and Hutch sends the famous Dillon McKenna to rescue the poor, helpless little woman. I bet you accepted gratefully, eager to get a chance to finally tell me you were right all along. Well, mission accomplished. You've saved the day and you've pointed out, not only once, but twice, just how right you were. I'll make your day even better by admitting what you're dying to hear. You were right. I'm a piss poor excuse for a field operative. I let my team down. Even got one of them killed. Happy now?"

Mac wanted to reach out to her, but held back. "No, Eve. It's not what I meant at all. Let me expla—"

"Doesn't matter. I'm tired. I don't want to talk anymore." She turned away from him.

"But, Eve—"

"Please. Let me rest."

"Sure. We'll get you out of here in a couple more days."

"I'll be ready." She came across quiet, but firm.

Mac adjusted her covers and sat down. Eve kicked them off and rolled back facing him. She glared at him.

"You don't have to stay. I'm fine. Surely, you have a million other things you'd rather be doing. Maybe you can find a few other damsels in distress to rescue."

Mac set his jaw and muttered, "I'll watch over you." There was no place he'd rather be, and nothing he'd rather do. "I'm not leaving you alone."

"I don't need you. Really, you can go. If I recall correctly, you're damned good at leaving."

Had he heard her right? "What did you say?"

"Never mind. Just close the door on your way out."

"Baby, I'll be happy to close the door for you, but I'm not leaving."

"God, you're still a stubborn ass, aren't you?"

"It's been rumored." Mac settled back. "I'm staying. Get used to it."

Chapter Seven

Mac barely heard the knock on Eve's door above the grinding whir of the window air-conditioner. He stood, instinctively reaching for his gun, and moved between Eve and the door, ready shield her. The knock sounded again. He backed closer to her, his mind and body on red alert.

Cade shouted, "Mac, I've got Brewer."

"She's asleep. He can come back later."

"McKenna, let me in. I'm here to see Eve and I'm not going anywhere until I do."

Eve stirred. "Let him in, Mac. I'm awake."

"You sure you're up to this?"

She waved at the closed door. "He's my partner. Why wouldn't I want to see him?"

"Maybe because he's a spineless prick?"

Eve's eyes narrowed. She raised a brow like a mother would at a misbehaving child. He caught the flash of a half-smirk smile.

"Let him in."

Mac opened the door, but positioned his body to block Rex from entering. "You get five minutes, Brewer. Then I want you out."

"You've got no right to issue orders, McKenna. Step aside."

Towering above Rex, Mac didn't budge.

"Come on, McKenna, don't be an ass."

Before he showed Rex exactly how much of an ass he could be, Cade stepped between them.

"Hey, partner, he's gonna see Eve eventually. Move and let him in. The sooner he sees her, the sooner he's on his way back home, and out of our hair."

Mac looked at Eve. A full grimace replaced her half-smirk. Her eyes were all but pleading with his. *Damn.* He let Rex in.

"Don't forget, Brewer, five minutes." Mac tapped the face of his watch. "Starting now."

Cade silently left the room. Mac stepped to a corner, stood with his feet firmly planted, and crossed his arms.

Rex moved to Eve's bed and looked over his shoulder at Mac, suspicion etching his features. "How about some privacy here?"

"No fucking way, Brewer. You're wasting your five minutes...nope, make that four minutes, thirty-two seconds."

"Mac, please."

Unable to refuse her, he gave in. "I'm right outside the door if you need me." He zeroed in on Rex. "I'm watching the clock." For good measure, he added, "And you."

Mac stomped from the room, deliberately leaving the door open. Cade, standing in the hall, grinned and shook his head.

"That little show of manliness make you feel better?"

"Fuckin' right."

Cade chuckled. "Got a call from Hutch. He wants Beauchamp back in D.C. for briefing on a new case. Corelli's going to deliver him. I'm heading to the airstrip now to see the crew gets off without a hitch. What time do you want the Black Hawk back to fly Eve out?"

"I can't believe I'm saying this, but as long as it's quiet around here, let's give her the full six days recovery. She's still running a fever and could use the extra time to recoup. We'll rendezvous four days from now at 0700 at the air strip for lift off."

Cade looked through the open door, then back at Mac. "Got my vote."

"She'll mend a lot faster once Brewer's ass is out of here."

"You're starting to sound like a jealous ex."

He shrugged. "I am an ex. But according to Eve, I gave up the right to be jealous two years ago. She's made it very clear she wants nothing to do with me."

"If you say so. I'll hang around until Brewer's ready to leave." Cade nodded toward the room.

"No need. I'm not going to give him the ass kicking he deserves. He's safe. For now."

"I'm staying in case he needs a ride back to the air strip. When I leave, I'll be gone about an hour. In the meantime I'm gonna grab a coffee. You need a refill?"

Mac shook his head. "No, I'm good."

Cade disappeared into the kitchen and Mac shifted closer to Eve's door. He'd stay close—in case she needed him, he justified. He peered inside and eyed Rex sitting stiffly in the chair next to the bed. The chair Mac had vacated minutes before.

Rex asked, "How're you feeling, Eve?"

"I'm fine." She touched the sling holding Rex's arm in place. "You okay? I thought you were dead."

"I'm great. It'd take more than a little graze to kill me." Rex grabbed her hand, held it to his cheek. "God, Eve. I'm sorry I couldn't get to you. You were surrounded. I wasn't sure what to do. My head said to go for help, my heart said to try to save you from him."

She smiled weakly, but Mac noted with satisfaction, pulled her hand back. "You would've ended up dead—or worse. You did the right thing."

"Thank you for saying so, Eve. I'll make this up to you somehow."

Mac expected the wimp to start crying next. *Fucking asswipe.*

Eve shifted in the bed. Mac hoped Rex saw the effort behind the move. "There's nothing to make up for. Hey, if you'd been the one down, I'd have left your ass behind."

"I have trouble believing that one."

Eve winked at Rex. "I would have, partner. In a heartbeat."

"In a heartbeat?"

Eve nodded. "Mac told me Randi got out okay."

"She said to tell you hello." Rex rearranged his position in the chair, crossed one leg over the other.

"About Danny, has his girlfriend been told yet?" Eve asked in a whisper. Mac had to lean in closer to eavesdrop.

"How could she not? Lynda works in the communications room. She's dealing like a trooper, but I imagine the reality of Carlyle's death hasn't sunk in. I feel bad about leaving his body behind." Rex grimaced. "I've heard stories of what Mendoza does with his enemy's corpses."

"Maybe we can bring him home after we take down Mendoza. At least the son of a bitch didn't torment me with Danny's body. Mendoza had enough fun telling me about the IDEA rescue team he slaughtered. Did he lie to me?"

Rex shook his head. "Sorry, he told you the truth. Two agents were DEA, the other two, FBI. They didn't reach the compound before they were taken out. I'm not sure how they drew fire so fast."

Eve said, "I'm sure Mendoza expected a rescue attempt and had his men waiting to pick them off. Too many good agents have died. We've gotta end this shit."

Rex took her hand again, and Mac, now leaning against the doorframe, ground his teeth together. Anger settled in his jaw. He glanced at his watch. Time wasn't moving fast enough for him.

"We'll put an end to his madness. The files you downloaded should be enough to do the job. Randi said you didn't make a hand-off to her. I assume you have the flash drive, or hid it on the grounds somewhere before Mendoza's men got to you. Sanders hasn't offered much information yet."

Eve said, "I buried the damn thing when I realized I was stuck inside the walls. I was so sure I was in the clear. I'd already sent Randi on her way to the extraction point."

Rex leaned forward. "Why didn't you put the flash drive in your boot compartment?"

"With my shoulder and knee injuries, I couldn't bend my leg enough to reach the heel."

"Crap."

"Wouldn't have made a difference. The guards took my boots the first day. I never got them back."

"Were you able to get the flash drive out?"

"No. Must still be buried there." Eve picked at a piece of lint on the sheet. "Mac said I wasn't conscious long enough to tell him anything. I don't remember much about the rescue, or what I did, or didn't say to him."

"You sure you didn't make the retrieval? You just said you don't remember much. Maybe McKenna is lying."

Mac went rigid. His hands tightened into fists. He used all the willpower he could muster to not march inside the room and take Rex down a few notches.

Eve's head bobbed up. "That's absurd. Why would he lie?"

"I don't know." Rex shrugged. "Maybe he wants to play hero and turn the intel over to Sanders himself. Or wants to cut a side deal with Mendoza. Who knows why McKenna does anything."

"You're being ridiculous. I was out and nothing but dead weight during the rescue. There's no way I told Mac where I hid the flash drive."

Rex sat back in the chair, crossing his arms, and looking smug. "So tell me why McKenna doesn't want me anywhere near you. There's got to be a reason for his behavior."

"Mac doesn't want you near me because he doesn't like you."

He uncrossed his arms and scooted forward. "I don't like him either. I wouldn't like any man who treated you the way he did. He's a shit, and you're lucky to be rid of him."

"Don't sweat it. Mac doesn't like a lot of people, but he's one of the good guys. What's with all the questions, anyway?"

Mac pushed away from the doorframe and settled his back against the wall, still keeping an eye on Eve and her partner. He took in a few deep gulps of air to ease the tightened muscles in his jaw. He'd love to get Brewer alone for a few rounds, ached with the need. But he had to admit Eve's defensive response gave him enough satisfaction to let things slide...for now.

A charming smile plastered Rex's face. "Damned if I know. I guess I'm just trying to figure out what went down. Everything fell apart so fast at the last minute."

Eve adjusted her legs and rolled to her side. "I've been trying to understand how things went to shit myself. I replayed the op in my head a thousand times in those damned cells of Mendoza's, and since."

Rex's face softened. "You look tired. We'll figure this crap out later. For now, tell me where the flash drive is hidden, and I'll go back in for retrieval."

"I can't tell you." Her voice went low, had Mac straining to hear again.

Rex's eyebrows arched. "What do you mean you can't tell me?"

Eve massaged her forehead. "I mean there's no way to describe where I dug the hole. I'll have to take care of this personally. I'm not even sure I can find the hiding place again. I should've marked the area better, but I was kind of in a hurry at the time."

Rex pulled her hand away from her face. "We'll talk more about this when you're stronger."

"I'm okay." She drew her hand away from his and tucked it beneath her chin.

"Sure you are." He said shakily. "I'm sorry I wasn't the one to get you out."

"Everything worked out in the end. Resolutions sent Mac. He got me out. Sanders got his money's worth."

Rex laughed. "McKenna wouldn't have been my first choice to play your knight in shining armor. I know how you feel about him."

She nodded once. "He certainly wouldn't have been my top pick either. And how I feel about him? Well, I just don't. I don't feel anything about, or for, him. I only know I'm uncomfortable around him. Mac and I are like oil and water." Her gaze drifted downward. "We just don't mix. I wonder how we managed to stay together as long as we did."

"People grow apart, happens all the time." Rex said, "Getting you out of Mendoza's prison cells? I'm the one who left you there. I should've been the one who went after you, but I couldn't get Sanders to agree."

"All that matters is I'm out."

Uncomfortable around him? Oil and water? The words stung. Why should Mac care what Eve thinks about him? He brooded until Eve's speech started to slur. Stepping into the room, he pointed to Rex.

"Time's up. Out. Eve's had enough. You'll finish your debriefing when I get her home."

"For once I agree with you, McKenna." Rex's expression said he'd like to say more, but held back.

"Wait a sec." Eve grabbed Rex's hand. "When you get home, tell Sanders I need to see him when I get back. It's important."

"No problem. He'll be happy to see your pretty face."

"I'm serious. I need to see Sanders ASAP."

"Why don't you let me pass on whatever information is so important?"

"No. What I have to say is for his ears only."

Rex said, "I'm your partner. You can tell me anything."

"Sorry. Not this time." The words piqued Mac's interest. *What the hell's going on? Eve won't tell her partner why she needs to talk to Sanders?"*

Eve's breathing sounded labored. Something wasn't right, but Mac would have to figure it out later. Right now, Eve needed rest.

"Out, Brewer."

"Fuck you, McKenna."

Mac peeked at Eve. She looked even more distressed. He gritted his teeth and let Rex walk away.

Chapter Eight

Bogota, Colombia

Leaning forward with his elbows on his knees, Mac studied Eve. The visit with Rex yesterday had exhausted her, and she'd been sleeping since he'd left. He scooted closer, touched her forehead, and found her temperature nearly normal.

Doc came into the room and hung a new round of piggy-back antibiotics. Mac stood and stretched his neck from side to side.

"Eve's doing remarkably well, Mac. She'll be ready to leave in another day or two. Keep her shoulder dressings dry, change them daily, and make sure she finishes the antibiotics I send with you. The cast will need to stay on four to six weeks, depending on how fast her bones mend. We usually see scaphoid fractures out of the cast earlier. I'd keep the two fingers taped about the same amount of time."

"Doc, I'm only looking after her until we get to a D.C. hospital."

"In that case, Mac, you'll merely need to pass my notes and her meds to the doctors stateside. They'll know what to do."

"What about stuff for the pain?"

"She should do well with a combination of acetaminophen and

ibuprofen. I'll send along some stronger pain pills just in case. But since I set the fracture with a closed reduction, there probably won't be a need for narcotics unless she's extremely active."

"So two more days?"

"She needs the IV fluids and antibiotics two full days. You can depart the next morning."

"Copy that."

"Have you arranged for transport yet?"

"I'll have the Black Hawk crew meet us in three days at 0700 hours. We'll be out of your hair and you can open the clinic to the locals again."

Peterson smiled. "Ah yes, back to normal business...until Hutch sends a new case my way. I haven't seen Cade lately."

Mac stood. "He's in the city scouting for new information on Mendoza."

Dr. Peterson put a finger on Eve's wrist and looked at his watch. "I'm impressed how the young man doing surveillance out front stays so well hidden. If Cade hadn't told me he was outside, I'd never have noticed. Reminds me of my old Delta Force days. I don't miss those times...*much.*"

Mac snorted and moved closer to the door. "Yeah, so many missions, so little time."

The doctor laughed. "I believe you just attempted to be funny, Mac."

"A damned pitiful attempt at humor." Eve said weakly. "Mac, keep your day job."

Mac moved to Eve's bedside. "Finally ready to wake up, baby? How you feeling?"

"Ready to dance the rumba." Eve twirled a finger in the air.

"Good thing. We'll be heading home soon. You gonna be up for the dance?"

"I'm ready now."

"Sure you are."

Eve stretched her head to one side and looked beyond him. "Where's Rex?"

"Had to get back." Mac had to stifle the urge to add a few

more colorful words about Brewer. "He left yesterday, and you've been sleeping since."

"Guess I was tired. Did you throw Rex out?"

"Me?"

"Mr. Innocent?" She pinned his gaze with hers. "Don't pull that crap with me. Did you throw him out?"

Mac sat down, tapping a finger on the metal armrest. "I may have suggested he head back to D.C. and get on with his next assignment." *Screw holding back.* "Then I pointed out to Brewer no one wanted to work with a bastard who leaves his partner behind when things heat up in the field."

Eve sighed. "Jeez, let this go. I would've done the same thing if I'd been in his situation. Get over yourself and leave the man alone. He feels guilty enough without you harping on him."

Mac's heartbeat sped up, his temper rapidly increasing. "The little prick should feel guilty."

"Dammit, Mac." Eve's cheeks flared pink. "Anything that's not your way is the wrong way. Nothing ever changes with you."

His squared his shoulders. "You're only defending Brewer because you're sleeping with him."

"Not that it's any of your business, but I...oh, shit." Eve flinched and sunk deeper into her pillow, her breathing labored.

Mac jumped from his chair. *Damn.* He was forever putting his foot in his mouth.

Beads of sweat spotted her forehead and above her upper lip. "You don't have a damned clue what I—"

Doc cleared his throat and frowned. "That's enough, you two. I don't want Agent Taylor popping her stitches." He looked at Mac. "Do you mind if I examine my patient in private?"

Mac made no effort to leave and the doctor stomped to the other side of the room, held the door open for him. "Out."

Mac saluted. "Yes, sir." Mac softened his voice. "I'll be in the kitchen."

"Thank you."

ଓ

Doc changed Eve's shoulder dressings. "You, young lady, are going to have to settle down if you want this to heal properly. You shouldn't let Mac get to you."

"I understand. But damn, the man makes me so...so...I don't know what he makes me. Pissed, is the best word I can come up with." Eve smiled wanly. "Really, really pissed."

"You have a history?" Dr. Peterson checked her heartbeat, lungs, and extremities.

"Yes, and it isn't a pretty one. The man is a pig-headed fool." She let some of the anger go. "We had a horrible fight the last time we were together."

He paused a moment, lifted a brow. "Takes two people to make a fight."

"True, but I also know two people must compromise to solve the problem. Mac thinks only one person needs to give in. The other person has to bend, never him." Her anger surged again. Mac was pure alpha male. If she remembered correctly, most of the men at Resolutions were the same.

"Then I guess you're justified calling him pig headed."

"Damn right."

"Fortunately, after two more days you'll not have to deal with Mac anymore."

"Very fortunate." *Right?* "Doc, can I borrow a phone? I need to call my SAC."

He pulled a cell phone from his pocket. "Keep the call short. You need your rest."

"Shouldn't take long to update Sanders." Eve rolled the phone in her hand, looking for who knows what. "Is this a protected line?" She wasn't about to beg Mac to let her use his phone.

"It's secure. I'll give you some privacy." He stepped out, closed the door behind him.

Eve tapped in Sanders' number. An overwhelming sense of relief poured over her when he answered. "It's Eve, sir."

"Agent Taylor, I didn't recognize the number."

"I'm using the doctor's phone. Mine's gone, along with my weapons and boots."

"We'll replace your gear. It's good to hear your voice, Eve. We've been worried."

"I'm fine, but we've got one big-ass problem. I wanted to talk to you in person, but I've decided this can't wait any longer. Doc wants me to stay put a couple of days before traveling and this needs dealt with ASAP."

"You on a secure line?" Seriousness replaced his cordial tone.

"Yes."

"What've you got?"

"It's Mendoza. I spent some time digging through his files, trying to find a way past the satellite block he'd put up. I never could forward the data, but I did come across a document hidden so deep I'm surprised I found it. He's not just into drugs and money laundering anymore."

"Christ. What's the bastard up to now?"

"Sir, he's sold some sort of special toxin and prototype weaponry to a group of Afghani terrorists. They're planning a release date at the end of the month."

"There's been no intel suggesting an imminent attack of any kind. We always get a heads up on terrorist activity."

"Like we did with 9/11?"

"Point taken. Give me details."

"Unfortunately, I'm not familiar with all the terminology used, but the sale involves an experimental Air Force chopper capable of getting in and out of an area's Air Defense Identification Zone without detection. If I understood correctly, the transport will be loaded with an airborne toxin with the potential to wipe out millions of people. The drop target is the Pentagon and D.C. area."

"Aircraft able to breach an ADIZ? Holy fuck, there'd be no time to defend the area." The line went quiet for a few heartbeats. "Eve, keep this to yourself. Let me look into things and see what information Homeland Security is willing to give up. If the bird is an experimental craft, they'll have details and know where it's parked."

"What about Rex? I saw him yesterday and felt like a real shit not telling him what I've found." *And not telling Mac.*

"No one, Agent Taylor. Not until I get a handle on exactly what we're dealing with."

"Yes, sir."

"I'll get back to you after I find out what's happening. I'll have details on a new assignment for you at that time."

Eve hung up, uneasiness tugging at her gut.

Damn, damn, double damn. If only I'd gotten out with the files.

ᘛ

"Hey, Doc," Mac said. "I've gotta put in a call to Hutch and Cade to confirm transport details. I might be a while. Mind if I use your office?"

"Sure, no problem. I need to give Agent Taylor one more check and make sure she's ready for an early departure tomorrow."

"Thanks. I shouldn't be too long," Mac said as he pulled the office door closed behind him.

Doctor Peterson examined Eve. "Everything looks good. Bruises are fading, split lip is mended, and your vitals are strong. How's the wrist and ribs feel?"

"Much better."

"Shoulder?"

"Getting there."

"You'll do well once you get home. I do worry about the fever so try to stay on top of it. I'll hang one more bag of IV antibiotics tonight then switch to oral. I'll pull the IV afterwards." He stuffed his stethoscope in his back pocket. "I believe the field dressing you used on the bullet wound saved your life."

"My boss makes us carry the packs when we're in the field. I always thought it was a pain in the ass. I'll never complain again." Eve looked around the room. "Where are my watch dogs?"

"Mac's on phone call in the other room. Cade went to meet the chopper and check details for tomorrow's departure."

"In case I don't get time in the morning I want to say thank you for the repair job. I'm sure I'm not the easiest patient you've ever had."

He patted her hand. "You did just fine, dear. You're very strong. If you're ever this way again, stop by and say hi."

"I'll do that."

"You rest now. I've got some paperwork to prepare for your doctors stateside. I'll be in the front room."

☙

Doc got comfortable in a chair facing the window. He glimpsed outside and saw Brad Thompson standing guard, hidden near the garage. A group of neighborhood boys played stickball a few houses down. "Ah, to be young again, not a care in the world." He opened a notebook and got busy making a few notes about his treatment plan for Eve. He'd scarcely started writing when a knock at the front door interrupted. Doc stood and closed the door to Eve's room, grabbed his gun from a table, and looked through the window to the side of the door.

Two men holding guns stood on the porch. One of the men held a young boy by his shirt and pointed a gun at the kid's head. Doc's heart rate shot up ten-fold. He recognized the man holding the kid. *Carlos Salazar. Mendoza's man. They're here for Eve.* He braced himself and opened the door slowly, weapon in hand.

Doc kept his gun steady on the two men. "What?"

"Step back and put down your gun, "Carlos said. He shoved the barrel of his gun into the boy's temple. "I will kill the boy."

The second man said, "We're here for the woman."

The doctor studied the two men and the young boy. The boy shook and cried, a river of snot running down his chin. Doc did a visual search for Brad Thompson and saw him crumpled on the ground to the side of the front door. *No help there.* The hair on Doc's arms spiked. He didn't see any way to get Mac's attention without risk to the child. *Dammit.*

"Cooperate or the *chico* will not live to play another ball game." Carlos twisted the boy's arm, sending a new torrent of tears down the child's cheeks.

"Enough." Doc set his gun on the table, moved aside.

The men pushed past him. Carlos shoved the kid aside, and the boy took off running.

"Wise decision, *señor*." Carlos whacked Doc on the left temple, taking him down.

Hovering a few beats ahead of unconsciousness, he watched them drag Brad inside and shut the door. They tossed Brad on top of him. Doc winced when Brad's body hit him, bounced off, and smashed to the floor.

Carlos opened Eve's door and peered inside. "Lucky for us, I find the *señorita* in the first room I look. This is a good sign. Keep alert, and let's get her out of here quickly."

The man with him nodded. "Miguel will be pleased you did your job without complication."

"*Sí,* it's good to know I won't be wearing a third eye tonight." Both men laughed.

Carlos took a syringe from his pocket, popped off the top with his teeth, and gave Eve's IV a push of God only knows what. *Probably a tranquilizer.*

She roused and opened her mouth. In the next beat, her eyes rolled upward and closed again. Carlos tapped her left cheek, then her right. Her head flopped from side to side. Doc was too dizzy to move, much less help the woman.

"She's out." With a satisfied grin, Carlos ripped the IV out of her hand, and carried her outside and into the scorching heat of the Colombian sun.

In Doc's office, Mac finished his call and debated if he was ready to go back to Eve's bedside to suffer a little more verbal abuse. A dull thump from one of the other rooms put him on red alert. He closed his phone, tucked it into his back pocket, and slipped silently through the office door, his gun drawn. Two men were dragging Eve outside. Brad and Doc were on the floor, the latter stirring. Mac blew out a breath, relieved he wouldn't have to choose between helping the two injured men and going after

Eve. No contest. Doc and Brad would've drawn the short stick.

Outside, Carlos Salazar, Mendoza's top flunky and second in command, held Eve. *Dammit, how'd they find us?* Mac went rigid and his hand tightened on his gun as he stepped outside.

The man with Carlos opened the driver's door of a dark sedan and crossed around to the passenger side. Carlos tossed Eve in the back and slammed the door. Before they slipped into their seats, Mac landed a kick to Carlos' kidney, sending him to his knees. Mac shoved the piece of shit out of his way, jumped in, and drove off.

In the rearview mirror, Mac glimpsed the second man running back to Carlos and offering him a hand. Carlos slapped him away. Mac slammed the accelerator and sped away.

"Eve! Eve, can you hear me? Aw, crap. Answer me, Eve." Mac gripped the steering wheel and laid the gun on the passenger seat. He dug his cell phone out of his pocket and punched in a number.

Hutch answered on the third ring.

"God-dammit-all-to-hell, Hutch. What the fuck? You said the clinic was safe."

"Slow down, Mac. What happened?" Hutch said calmly. He always managed to stay cool.

"I'll tell you what the fuck happened. Mendoza found us. He sent a couple men. One was Carlos Salazar. You remember Carlos, Mendoza's main toady and overall sleaze-bucket?"

"I know Salazar. Definitely a wormy bastard."

"You want to tell me how Mendoza's men found us in under a week?" Mac pushed his voice a few decibels lower. Maybe some of Hutch's control rubbed off on him.

"I don't know, but I'll damn well find out. We've got a couple of safe houses around Bogota. Head to one. You familiar with the locations?"

"I know where the *safe* houses are located." He loosened his grip on the steering wheel.

"I don't know how Mendoza found you." Hutch rustled papers on the other end of the line. "Maybe someone on the street saw and turned you in. We just received word Salazar was looking for information, flashing big bills around. In a poor neighborhood, the money would be hard to pass up. Any chance you were followed from the airfield?"

Mac rolled the idea around. The day they brought Eve to the clinic had been chaotic, and the ride frenzied. Mac had been focused on her. Still, he'd have spotted a tail. "We weren't followed."

"What about Thompson?"

"Would you have hired him if he couldn't shake a tail? Carlos drives a car the size of a fucking tank even a blind man couldn't miss."

"Brewer's a possibility. I don't know anything about his skills."

"A man who leaves his partner behind during an op has no skills. He's probably an overall waste of breath, suck-ass operative."

"I understand you don't care much for Brewer. Let's leave it at that. Doctor Peterson and Thompson? Where were they when all this went down? What about Warner?"

"Cade's at the air strip." Mac's anger simmered down." I imagine he's back at the clinic by now. When I left, Doc was coming to on the floor, but Thompson was out cold. They were down, but I didn't really have a choice. I had to go after Eve."

"I understand," Hutch said. "I'm sure Doc will take care of Thompson. You take care of Eve. I'll see if I can find how they tracked you down." Hutch cleared his throat and continued. "Try the Zipaquira safe house. The place is hidden well out of the way."

"Copy that."

"When you get settled let me know, and I'll send Cade in with supplies."

"I'll need weapons, food, and clothes for both of us. Have him bring whatever Eve needs from Doc."

"You'll find most of those items at the safe house. I'll get on acquiring the rest. Good luck."

"Thanks." He looked at Eve. She still wasn't moving.

We're gonna fucking need it.

☙

San Carlos Lucas
Mendoza Compound

"Carlos, can one man possibly be so inept? How could you fail me again? Must I take care of getting Miss Taylor and my files back myself? This task cannot be so difficult." Mendoza frowned at the man standing in front of his desk.

He followed Carlos' blood-shot gaze until the *idiota* had finally zeroed in on the man Mendoza had just shot between the eyes. Carlos quickly looked away. Felipe, along with the incompetent Carlos, had let the bitch get away.

Carlos, like usual, rocked from side to side. "No, Miguel. I will get *Señorita* Taylor back and also the files you want. You must be patient. McKenna caught me off guard today."

"Carlos, do you not understand your job is to never be caught off guard? Is this too much to ask? McKenna and Miss Taylor were once together for a long time. Of course, he would protect her with his life. Did I not warn you of this? Of him?"

"*Sí*, you did. I understand the *señorita* is a hard woman to give up." Carlos' gaze drifted back to the floor. He stepped aside, avoiding the blood trailing from the dead man's head. "I think a trick was played on me. I am sure of this. McKenna was supposed to be gone. Filipe and I took down the doctor and guard outside. *Mierda!* How was I to know McKenna was still in the clinic? We were sure we saw him leave earlier."

Mendoza caressed the handle of his pistol on his desk, an ominous warning Carlos should heed. "These are excuses. Excuses are for the weak. You, Carlos, are weak. You've given me no choice. I am calling in a specialist to do your job."

"But, Miguel, you must give me one more chance."

Mendoza enjoyed the panic on Carlos' face, the squeak of fear in the man's voice.

Carlos squirmed while Mendoza deliberated. "I'll give you

one more chance. If you fail, I don't care if you are married to my sweet sister. I don't care if you leave five small *bebes* behind for her to raise alone. I even don't care if God himself comes to me in a vision and begs mercy for you. I will kill you the next time you fail me. Are we clear on this?"

Carlos alternated between bows and nods. "*Sí*, Miguel, we are clear. *Gracias*. I will do better, you will see."

"Stand straight. You know I hate when you grovel." He moved his hand away from the gun, resisted the urge to put Carlos down like a rabid dog.

"I will still bring in a specialist—an assassin, to finish what you cannot. And from now on, you will take orders from him. You will do whatever he tells you to do. If he tells you to cut off your *cojones*, you will sharpen your knife and ask, 'Which testicle first?' And I want you to do this with a smile on your face. Do you understand, Carlos?"

Carlos stared at his crotch. "*Sí, comprende, Miguel, el asesino a sueldo*. I do not like this, but since you leave me no choice, I will do what you ask."

"Ah, but you do have a choice, Carlos. I can kill you now and be finished with you."

"No, no." Carlos stepped back, his gaze on Mendoza's gun. "I will be happy to work with *el asesino a sueldo*."

"Of course you will." Mendoza pointed at Carlos. "You'd better hope my informant can provide me with Miss Taylor's new location."

He held up his hands. "Not to worry, we will find her, Miguel. McKenna too."

"Yes, and when you do, I want you to be sure you and the *el asesino a sueldo* kills Dillon McKenna slowly and painfully. Before you kill him, I want you to make sure he knows you will be bringing Miss Taylor back to me, and describe in detail what I plan to do to her before I kill her." He whispered, "I want him to suffer. Do you understand what I'm telling you, Carlos? I want him to suffer very much."

"*Sí*, Miguel, I understand."

Chapter Nine

Bogota, Colombia

Each passing mile fueled Mac's anger, and it soon reached volcanic level. He punched the dashboard. It wasn't the best idea he'd ever had. A painful sting shot up his arm and settled in his shoulder. On the drive from Bogota City, an overpowering need for revenge threatened to sabotage his concentration. Mac refused to give in. Focusing on Eve and getting her to safety had to come first. Still unconscious in the backseat, she lay on her right side, face flat against the leather.

Mac kept the oversized sedan's speedometer at a steady pace. Relief washed through him when he saw the Zipaquira safe house. He'd come too damn close to letting Eve slip through his fingers back at the clinic. Mendoza's men had put their filthy hands on her again.

He turned off the car and rested his head on the steering wheel. They touched her, and he'd all but handed her over to the bastards. Mac shoved aside his guilt and got out of the car. A grove of rubber trees concealed the small adobe residence. Mac, gun at the ready, made a quick check of the grounds.

He tucked his Glock into the back of his pants and gathered Eve in his arms the way one would carry fine china. He hurried inside and laid her gently on the yellow couch.

The air conditioner chilled the room to excess. Only a house owned by Resolutions would be equipped with central air this far out of the city. Hutch spared no cost. Mac shook out a quilt and covered Eve, who was still dressed in a tank top and boxer shorts. Her goose flesh covered arms and legs were now tucked in. After pulling down the shades in the living area, he worked his way through each room of the house, checking for anything out of order. The rooms were clear, the place immaculate and ready for emergency occupation.

And this qualifies as one big fucking emergency.

Clean towels were stacked neatly in the bathroom closet, the bed linens freshly laundered. Mac found the kitchen well stocked with bottled water and canned goods. Routine protocol. Cade would supply perishable foods.

Mac opened kitchen cabinets and drawers, checking for other supplies. Along with a stash of Colombian pesos and U.S. dollars, he found three satellite phones, a large supply of extended-life batteries, and two customized Colt .45 pistols with enough ammo to hold off an army for a week. *A man can never have too much fire power.* He tucked one of the pistols into his waistband alongside his personal 9mm Glock, and stuffed several full magazines into his pockets.

He went outside, looked around, and moved the sedan behind the house. Mac grabbed a small bunch of bananas off a tree and went back inside. He carried Eve into the lone bedroom, settled her into the bed, and watched her for several minutes. She was still out, but restless and crying out at times. Her fever had returned. *Damn, I wish I had her antibiotics.*

Mac laid a cool washcloth on her forehead and then moved to the kitchen. He stood propped against the counter, peeling a banana when a knock sounded at the back door. Pulling one of his guns free, he inched to the side of the door.

"Yes?"

"It's Cade. Open the fucking door."

Mac unbolted the lock and let him enter. He set his weapon

on the counter and picked the half-peeled banana back up. "You made good time."

"Always do." Cade tossed one of Mac's duffle bags on the granite counter and pulled up a tall stool. "You leave something behind, Mac?"

"Yeah, I may have been in a bit of a hurry when I lit out after Eve." Mac unzipped the duffle and checked out the weapons. "Doc send antibiotics? Eve's running a fever again."

"Yeah and something for the pain, too."

"I sure as shit won't be giving pain meds to her while she's unconscious."

"There's both narcotics and non-narcotic stuff in there." Cade hooked a foot on the stool's rail. "She's out?"

"I'm pretty sure they tranqed her."

"Well the pain pills are there if she needs them later."

"Good to know." Mac shook out one of the antibiotic pills. "How do I give her pills if she's out?"

"No clue." He shrugged. "I've got supplies in the car. I'll grab the stuff in a minute. Hutch says there are clothes in the bedroom closet and the bathroom is stocked."

Mac nodded.

Cade surveyed the room. "Like the freakin' Ritz. All the comforts of home rolled into one neat package."

"Doc and Thompson okay? I hated leaving, but my first obligation was to Eve."

"Thompson?"

"Seriously?" Mac put the pill on the counter, got a bottle of water. He dug out the other pill containers and put them in his pocket. "Brad Thompson, the guy doing a shit job guarding the front door at the clinic."

"Oh, right, Ice Man."

"Ice Man?"

"You ever see the dude's eyes? Ice blue. Damned spooky shit if you ask me."

"Never met him in person."

"Just another newbie in my book. He hasn't got in a full year with Resolutions yet." Cade stretched. "He and Doc are fine. Ice Man took a pretty good hit to the head, but Doc says he's hard-headed, young, and resilient. He'll bounce back."

"I bet it'll be a cold day in hell before someone sneaks up on him again."

"Tough way to learn a lesson." Cade helped himself to a banana, peeled it, and sunk his teeth in. He swallowed and said, "Doc recognized one of the would-be abductors. Carlos Salazar, Mendoza's brother-in-law."

"I got a good look when I pushed him out of my way and grabbed his vehicle."

Cade finished the banana in three bites. "You know the little prick from working with Mendoza. Hell, everyone recognizes Carlos. He's famous for his frequent fuck-ups."

"Oh yeah." Mac grinned. "Mendoza's daily threat of killing his brother-in-law was a joke among the men. Truth is Mendoza's sister would tear him a new ass if he laid a hand on Carlos. I'd say this is one of his frequent fuck-ups."

"No kidding. I bet he's in deep shit right about now."

Mac snorted. "My heart fucking bleeds for him."

Cade chuckled. "I hear you."

"Got any idea how Mendoza and Salazar found us?"

Cade shook his head. "Not yet, but I'd wager it wasn't a lucky guess. I promise we weren't followed. I'm too damn good at spotting, and losing, a tail."

"Damn confident, aren't you?"

"Nah, I'm just that good."

When they stopped laughing, Cade shrugged and his look grew serious. "The clinic's cover is blown."

"About time to relocate anyway." Mac laid out a few knives from the duffle, picked one, and stuck the sheathed weapon into his boot. He added another to his belt.

"Hutch already had Doc scouting for a new place. You know Hutch. The man likes to switch up all his safe houses and resource locations frequently."

"Best way to keep the safe places safe." *Except it didn't work this time.*

"You're right." Cade stuffed a banana in his shirt pocket. "I'll haul in the rest of your supplies and head back. Corelli is on standby to return with one of Hutch's modified AH-6 Little Birds."

"The one customized to transport four passengers inside and loaded for bear?"

"Yep."

"If Eve was in better shape, I'd consider taking her stateside tonight."

"The helicopter isn't taking you back to D.C. right away."

"I agree. She needs a night of rest before heading out." Mac put the remaining knives back in the duffle.

Cade sauntered to a window, pulled back the corner of a blind, and peeked out. "There's more. Hutch wanted me to let you know there's been a change in strategies. I don't think you're gonna like the new plan."

"Talk to me." Feeling the bad vibes coming from his friend, Mac gritted his teeth.

Cade faced him. "Hutch had his pow-wow with IDEA, and all the alphabet-agency heads involved."

"And?" Mac crossed his arms.

"They came up with a new idea."

"Quit stalling."

He moved closer to Mac. "Here's the deal. They want you to go back to Mendoza's compound and recover the flash drive."

Mac uncrossed his limbs and let out a breath. "I'm cool with that. I'm the best pick to get in and out undetected. I planned on paying Mendoza a little visit sometime soon anyway. Gonna whip a little payback on his ass."

"Actually, here's the part of the plan you're not gonna like. You'll be taking Eve with you."

Mac stiffened. "No fucking way. Eve isn't ready for another assignment yet. She's had enough."

"You heard her tell Brewer she couldn't describe where she buried the flash drive. She has to retrieve the device herself. If she can't, they want her to break back into Mendoza's office and download the files again."

Mac got in Cade's face. "Not. Going. To. Fucking. Happen." He shook his head. "There's absolutely no way Eve is going back to Mendoza's compound."

"Hutch tried to tell her boss she may not want to partner with you. Boss man said she'd have to suck it up and do the job."

Oil and water. "Yeah, I don't think she's going to like the plan."

"You'll have to argue this one with Sanders. If you don't take her, they'll send her in with someone else."

Mac stepped back, ran a hand through his hair. "She's not going."

"Run the job past Eve. It's her life, her decision."

"No."

"Think it over, Mac. I'll be back after the final details from Hutch and Sanders come down. May take a day or two."

"There's nothing to think about."

Cade left and Mac thought about calling Hutch and straightening him out on a few things. He decided to wait for his temper to cool off before placing the call.

Hours later, Mac was still playing with the idea of calling Hutch. The safe house had been quiet and Eve had slept most of the day. She responded easily when he woke her earlier and gave her the antibiotics. Whatever Carlos had given Eve was wearing off.

Mac had just finished a check of the grounds when Eve cried out. His mind shifted gears.

Clutching his gun, he went to her.

Chapter Ten

Eve lay tangled in the sheets, her blanket kicked off. She peeked through one eye, saw Mac slip into the room and straighten the bedding. He covered her hand with his, a touch so warm, so familiar, her body ached and her soul longed for more. For just one caress.

"You awake?" he whispered.

She looked around the unfamiliar room, confusion clouding her thoughts. "Mac, what's going on?"

"Mendoza's men found you. I caught them shoving you into a car, put a quick stop to their plan, and brought you here."

Eve tried to focus on Mac's face. "Where exactly is here?"

"A Resolutions safe house outside of Bogota."

She frowned. "Carlos? I remember Carlos coming into my room holding a syringe. Afterwards, everything's a blank."

Mac smiled. "Baby, you've been out a while. Looks like Carlos gave you a tranquilizer before abducting you."

"When?"

"About six hours ago."

Eve couldn't control the trembles racing through her. Mac sat on the bed, the side of the mattress sinking, and pulled her into his arms. Solid and comfortable. Familiar feelings.

"You're shaking."

She breathed in the warm scent of his skin, his clothes. "It's

Carlos. He ranks right up there with Mendoza on the evil scale. I don't want him to touch me."

"You're safe with me." He rubbed her back and his voice vibrated against her cheek.

"I guess I owe you my thanks for saving me again."

He laughed. "No problem. I kind of like rescuing you."

"Of course you do. Gives you another chance to prove I'm not cut out for the job." No longer enjoying his touch, Eve shifted away from him. A sharp pain shot through her shoulder. She sucked in a deep breath, tried to quell the agony.

Mac handed her a bottle of water. He took the pills from his pocket, shook out two, and held them out. "These should help take the edge off the pain."

She shook her head. "No. They'll make my mind fuzzier than it already is."

"Your face is pale. You're obviously in pain." He held the pills in front of her. "Besides, it's just ibuprofen. Non-narcotic."

"Even so, I don't want them. And if I did, I can get them myself."

"Don't be so damn stubborn." He frowned. "You can't even unscrew a fucking lid with that damaged hand."

"You've got balls calling me stubborn. Shock, shock, there's no compromise for the great Dillon McKenna." She wedged the water bottle in the curve of her elbow above the cast and tried to twist the lid off. *Jeez, that hurts!* She threw the unopened bottle across the room.

"Compromise? What're you talking about? I just want you to take two fucking pills to help with the pain."

"Oh, that's right. You aren't familiar with the concept of conceding. You wouldn't give an inch about my promotion to field agent and now you're trying to force pills down my throat I don't want or need."

"I'm right about the pills, and obviously I was right about you not being ready for field ops, or you wouldn't be here now, all broken and bruised."

He retrieved the bottle of water, opened it, and slapped it, along with the pills, onto her night table. The loud whack resounded through the small room. "You took a goddamned bullet to the shoulder. Mendoza had you for a week. You could have died, Eve."

"You're wrong. I'm a damned good agent. Getting shot is part of the job."

She cursed the unwelcome tears beginning to well and turned away, hoping Mac wouldn't notice.

"This line of work is too dangerous." His tone softened. "You were hurt. Don't you understand the thought of you suffering rips my heart out?"

She swiped her eyes and rolled back to face him. He had no right to spring those words on her. Had no right to care what happens to her. "How many new scars have you added to your collection since the last time I saw you? Let's see, two years, so you have what, about six new ones? I guess it's a whole different ballgame when it comes to you—the big, tough, alpha male?"

"Sorry. I'm way out of line. I know you're one of the DEA's best. I'm trying to change the way I feel." His voice trailed away. "Believed I had."

Eve turned away and stifled a cry.

Mac laid a hand on her back, the warmth palpable even through the covers. "Eve? Really, I am sorry."

"Forget it. I shouldn't have brought up the old crap between us. We've been over a long time and the past doesn't matter anymore." She took a deep breath. "Just go away and leave me alone."

"It matters, Eve. You're right. I'm a stubborn ass." Mac stood and backed toward the door, a defeated look on his face.

Why does he still have the power to hurt me? If Eve were honest with herself, she didn't really give a shit about the pills. She was still pissed about the way their relationship had ended.

The door closed behind him, the click echoing in her ears. Her shoulder burned and her hand throbbed. She eyed the ibuprofen he'd left on the bedside table. She'd have taken them when he offered if he hadn't been so damned bossy about it. *Oh, what the hell. I'm being silly, and he knows it.* She took the pills and washed them down with the opened water. *Why do I give a crap what Mac thinks?*

Realization struck her full force, and she let the tears flow.

My God, I'm still in love with Mac.

ଓଃ

Mac wished he could take back his careless remarks the moment he'd seen the hurt on Eve's face. He'd spent a lot of time lately regretting the tactless comments that rolled past his lips without thought. *After two years without her, you'd think I know better. I lost the best thing in my life because I can't control my fucking attitude.*

Did his mother and father have the same argument before she'd gone off and gotten herself killed in a war she shouldn't have been involved in to begin with? If so, it obviously hadn't helped. His mother had still died. His family was still torn apart. Mac's father should have insisted his mother stay home. Afterwards, she might've left like Eve had, but at least she'd still be alive.

An hour later, he pushed Eve's door open, found her sleeping, the water bottle half empty, and the pills gone. He smirked, glad to see she'd come to her senses. The pills were fucking ibuprofen. The way she'd acted, you'd think he'd tried to get her to shoot up crack cocaine.

ଓଃ

Mac made another sweep of the house, checking window and door locks again. After two days, they'd established a routine. He and Eve had a sort of unspoken agreement to avoid conversations that led to disagreements. Which meant they rarely talked. Standing at the kitchen counter, Mac took his Glock apart and cleaned the weapon methodically. He repeated the process with the Colt.

Afterwards, he rummaged through the kitchen cabinets, found a can of soup to heat up, and slapped a couple of ham sandwiches together. He carried the food into Eve's room, hoping she'd accept the meal. A pretty damn pitiful peace offering, but all he could come up with for now.

She was asleep, and he moved a chair next to the bed and plunked down. The woman was something else. Idly, Mac rubbed his chest, thought about what she'd said the first day here, and smiled. He'd acquired exactly six new scars since the last night he and Eve had gotten naked together. She knew him so well.

He fingered a jagged scar at the bottom of his ribcage, and he recalled the way she used to kiss every new one he acquired. God help him, he wanted nothing more than to get naked with Eve and let her make them all better. Then, he'd return the favor. Mac adjusted his suddenly too-tight camo pants before devouring one of the sandwiches and a bowl of soup. When he was full, he relaxed a little, let his eyes drift closed.

Eve cried out, waking Mac from a light sleep. He realized she wasn't in pain, but having a bad dream. He climbed on the bed, held Eve, and soothed her back to sleep. Unable to let go just yet, he gently rocked her. Eve's warm breath glided across his chest. She woke and looked at him longingly, the way she used to. A shimmer of desire sparked in her eyes before she closed them again.

"I love you, Mac," Eve mumbled.

"Eve?" Mac's heart skipped a few beats before he realized she was still asleep, probably still dreaming. Was it possible she still loved him after all this time? Even after the way he'd treated her? Mac suspected, deep in his heart, he'd never stopped loving her. Would never stop loving her. Sadly, he was one-hundred percent certain if they became involved again, he would worry himself sick every time she went in the field on assignment.

Maybe they could work things out, if they tried. She belonged with him. He held her tighter. Something so right had to be worth fighting for.

Didn't it?

☙

Daylight spilled into the bedroom and Eve came awake slowly. Wrapped in Mac's strong arms, everything felt so right, so good. She snuggled closer into the warmth of him.

Eve traced a finger along the small scar above his right brow. It did little to detract from his flawless features. A sexy five o'clock shadow covered his jaw, and the bristly stubble sent shivers through her body that settled in the center of her sex.

His eyes opened and zeroed in on her. A sly, confident smile navigated its way across his lips. Time, along with all their problems, faded away.

Hesitantly their lips met.

If they became involved, she'd only be hurt again. She should've pulled away from him. Instead his tongue swirled with hers and she arched into him. God help her. She wanted him. Delicious tingles raged through her core as his hardness pressed to her thigh.

Beneath the heat of Mac's mouth, she melted as he nibbled past her lips, teased down her throat, and slid a hand inside her shirt.

Mac stilled.

"Mac?" She looked at him. "What's wrong?"

"The bruises, Eve. Your injuries. I got carried away, almost forgot. I can't do this."

"Because I let them touch me? You think I'm dirty now?" She turned away from him, disgusted with the shame in her own voice.

He cupped her chin, pulled her face back toward his. "You're not dirty. Understand this, Eve. Nothing Mendoza or his men did to you is your fault, and nothing, absolutely nothing, could ever make you undesirable to me."

Eve still couldn't meet his gaze.

"Look at me, baby." He relaxed against her and whispered, "I want you right now, right this minute, but I don't want to hurt you."

Eve finally met his gaze. "I guess I'm confused."

"You're still in pain. You've been to hell and back. I'd be a bastard of the worst kind if I let my desire for you overshadow your condition." He caressed the side of her face and she shivered. "Let me just hold you for a while."

"Mac, I appreciate your concern, but I'm okay. I need this." Using her good arm, Eve gently worked her casted arm out of the sleeve. She slipped the shirt over her head, wiggled it off her good arm, and tossed it. "I want you. Now."

Eve wasn't wearing a bra, and she let Mac look his fill. His expression softened, his breathing deepened.

She smiled. "I hope you're gasping for air because you desire me, not because the bruising disgusts you."

"Disgust me? My God, Eve. You have no idea what you do to me. You're beautiful, so damn beautiful. Bruises and all." He fell back against the pillow and sighed. "We're going to have to put a stop to this while I'm still able."

"Not gonna happen." She pulled his head toward hers and saw the resistance, the determination, in his gaze.

If you want him, girl, you're gonna have to do the seducing.

She ran her hand down his arm, gathered his hand in hers. "If you prefer, we can do this without touching the...ah...bruises." She hoped she didn't sound like she was begging—which she was completely prepared to do.

Eve needed to feel the raw heat of his skin against hers. She guided the hand she held to his shirt. "Help me get this off."

Mac removed the shirt, rolled it into a ball, and threw it to the side. He looked at her and smiled wickedly.

Eve glided a hand teasingly across his broad chest. She leaned in, took a deep breath, and moaned as she let it out. The pure male scent of him had her sex weeping with need. She peppered his chest with kisses, and his muscles tightened.

Caressing his shoulders and chest with her bare breasts felt so damned good. "Mac," she said on a whispered breath.

"Dammit, Eve. I'm a weak bastard." He wrapped his arms

around her.

She had a few tender spots still, but his touch was so gentle she didn't care. All that mattered was getting naked with Mac. Her nipples hardened when they rubbed against the patch of thick, dark hair covering his chest.

"This feels so good. Feels so right. God, I've missed you." He murmured against her ear.

His breath sent shivers from Eve's head to her toes. "I've missed you, too."

"Let me make love to you." He kissed the sensitive area behind her ear. A small thrill went through her. He'd remembered the spot, how turned on it made her when he touched her there.

"Yes. Please. Make love to me. Now, Mac." She tugged at his belt buckle, a difficult job using only one hand.

"Slow down, baby." He trailed another round of kisses down her neck, across her chest just above her breasts. "Does this hurt?"

"No."

"Would you tell me if it did?"

"I'm not sure."

Mac licked lightly across her breasts, his touch like a million butterfly kisses, soft and barely there. "Eve. Eve. Let me enjoy this for a while. I want to go slow and easy."

"Slow and easy." She was breathless. Her tone went deep and husky with desire she couldn't control. "I like slow and easy."

"Good."

Mac stroked her stomach, down her hips, and settled at the sweet spot between her thighs. She moaned when he pulled her boxers off, pausing along the way to caress her thighs.

Slow and easy.

He slid a finger inside her. She moaned louder, and he added a second.

Slow and easy.

Eve clenched around his fingers, wanting more, demanding

more. She bucked against his hand. "Mac, please, I've had enough slow and easy, I want fast. Fast and hard."

He twirled his thumb around her most sensitive spot. "It's been too long, baby. Let go for me."

Eve cried out his name, her body drenched in wave after wave of endless pleasure. Like a skilled surfer, she rode down the face of every swell before climbing back up to catch the next upsurge.

"More," she begged.

Mac tore out of his camo pants and briefs in a nanosecond, and positioned himself between her legs. On his elbows, holding the top of his body off hers, he drove deeply into her, hard and fast, the way she'd demanded.

Feeling his slight hesitation, she gripped his shoulder with her good hand and pulled him closer. "Don't even think about stopping."

Mac drove impossibly deeper inside of her.

Eve whimpered in pleasure, climbed to the edge again, and rose to meet him, thrust for thrust.

He growled. "You sure I'm not hurting you, baby?"

Eve struggled to find her voice. "No, everything's perfect. You're perfect. Don't stop."

Mac whispered, "Feels like I've come home. I don't ever want to leave."

When Mac drove her over the edge a final time, he covered her mouth in kisses, smothering her cries of pleasure. He plunged deep inside her one final time, stiffened, and found his own release.

Keeping their bodies together, they rolled to lie face to face. He tucked her close, but avoided any pressure on her shoulder.

"You okay?"

She sighed, long and deep. "Mmmm, best I've been in a long time. Two years to be exact." She rubbed her foot along his leg. "A very long two years."

"I know, baby." He kissed her forehead and groaned. "Ah, Christ. Not only are you still hurting, you have a fever. I should've controlled myself. You're damn hard to be around and not have my hands all over your body."

Eve, touched by his admission, said, "I like your hands all over my body." She circled one of his nipples with her fingernail. "I'm fine, really." *Better than fine.*

She found one of his new scars, leaned forward, and kissed it. "Where's this one from? Looks like a knife wound."

"Good guess. Hutch had me working an extraction, a teenager whose old man held him hostage. After twenty-two hours of negotiations looked like they were going down the crapper, I went in. I entered the apartment just in time to catch the edge of a knife meant for the kid." He rubbed the mark just below his ribs. "Crazy son of a bitch really would've killed his son, his own flesh and blood."

She fingered the scar. "What kind of knife made this unusual shape?"

"Kukri knife."

"I've never heard of a kukri knife."

He chuckled. "A fighting knife with a deep forward curve isn't one you'll see very often in our line of work."

She moved her finger to Mac's other nipple, circled leisurely. "Why didn't the police go in?"

"SWAT tried to approach several hours earlier after the man threatened to kill his wife and they failed. He slit her throat right in front of the kid." His voice faded. "Took the woman's death to make them realize things weren't going to end well if they didn't get some outside help."

"My God, how could he hurt his family?"

"I guess the man was a crazy. D.C. Metro Chief of Police is good friends with Hutch. He called in Resolutions to end the standoff."

Eve's lips found another new scar on his arm. She pulled back, squinting at the spot. "Where's this one from? Looks painful."

"Hey, real men don't feel pain."

Eve pinched his nipple.

"Ouch! Dammit."

Eve grinned. "Just proving a point."

"Okay...shit...you proved your point." He brushed her hand away, cast and all.

"I know. Now tell me where the scar came from."

"Your favorite drug lord and mine, Miguel Mendoza." He ran two fingers along her cast.

"Word is you were undercover a year trying to get your target out." She stroked her fingers across his flat stomach.

"One of his chemists sent an S.O.S. to his family. He wanted out, but discovered the only way you get to leave Mendoza's employment is toes up. The family forked over big bucks to hire Resolutions to haul his ass out."

"You're responsible for Mendoza's limp. He wants revenge." A shudder ran through her body. "He says he's gonna make you suffer, then kill you."

"Let him do his worst. I should've killed the bastard when I had the chance. Unfortunately, things got a little hairy with the extraction at the last minute."

"Why did it take a full year to get the chemist out?"

"I had to work my way inside the cartel and get on Mendoza's good side. Couldn't exactly go in guns-a-blazing until I located the chemist who sent the *I-want-out* message."

"You couldn't just walk into the lab and grab him?"

"Mendoza kept a tight rein on who he allowed access to the lab. The extraction target didn't know me from Adam either. Hell, he wasn't even sure his SOS had been received. Took some time to sort through things and make contact."

"When you did find the chemist, I don't suppose Mendoza let you just waltz away free and clear with his little worker bee."

"That's for sure, but we tried to sneak beneath the radar." He grunted. "The brainiac chemist found the diagrams for an old tunnel system beneath the compound."

"I'm surprised Mendoza didn't know about the tunnels."

"The bastard *knows* they're there. What he *doesn't* know is they're operational."

"Who built them?"

Mac said, "The tunnels were used during the old mining days. I could tell by their condition and the cobwebs I was the first person to use the passageways in years."

Images of rats skittering around her in the cells sparked a wave of panic. Eve's belly knotted. *No. Don't go there.* She refused to dwell on her captivity and forced the memory from her mind. She cleared her throat. "But you didn't manage to get the chemist without incident?"

"We cleared the tunnels okay, but damned if Mendoza wasn't waiting for us outside the compound. Another lab nerd had tipped him off. We were spotted near the walls, and the bullets flew. I shot him in the leg. From the way the blood squirted out of him, I think I nipped an artery. He returned the gesture and got me here."

Mac took her finger and circled the scar. His skin was thick, bumpy, and still had the dark pink color of a recently healed injury. "The chemist and I got away while Mendoza's men were worrying about him. Bad guys lost. Good guys won. End of story."

She smiled. He always had a way of making death-defying missions sound simple. "Mendoza never discovered you used the tunnels?"

"No. And it's a damn good thing because I used the same ones to get you past the security he'd beefed-up after your team infiltrated the compound. He's probably still trying to figure how we got in and out successfully."

"I'm glad you were able to get me out, Mac. I wasn't sure if I had another escape attempt left inside me."

"You tried escaping from Mendoza?" He pulled back to look at her.

"Three times. And three times I failed." She tried not to let on how much those attempts had cost her.

His gaze narrowed and locked on hers.

Damn, did a hiss just escape his lips?

Okay, so maybe she failed at hiding the mental toll the

botched attempts had taken on her.

Beneath her hand, Mac's heart cranked up a few notches to beat double-time, punching his chest wall. He rubbed his face several times, and hugged Eve tighter to him. He let out a deep, controlled breath. "My God, woman, you're amazing. I've missed you. I've missed us. More than anything in my life."

"I've missed you, too." She wanted to wilt in his arms. "There are so many problems between us, Mac. Where do we go from here?"

Mac patted his growling stomach. "How about the kitchen?"

"Kitchen?"

"I say we eat before we make any life-altering plans. You slept through the last gourmet meal I fixed you."

"You cooked for me?"

"I know my way around a stove." He gave her a quick kiss. "Come on, let's get you fed."

"I want a shower first." She held up her cast. "Hopefully I won't get this soaked."

A mischievous grin lit his face. "Need some help? I wouldn't want to see you ruin the cast."

Eve scowled. "Forget it. I want to get clean, not engage in shower sex."

"Your loss. Yell if you change your mind and decide you need my shower expertise."

Mac rose from bed, flashing Eve one hell of a great view of his firm backside. He bent over and lazily pulled on his camo pants before heading to the kitchen. Snippets of the Hard Buns infomercial flashed through her mind. Apparently they were going to put off talking about what just happened between them. Eve was more than happy to go along with the plan. Now, all she had to do was put the images of the hot, steamy sex they'd shared out of her mind and concentrate on something else.

Like remembering all the past showers they'd shared. Mac's soapy hands caressing her. Slick hands exploring and probing every inch of her body. More than the spray of warm water had kept her hot and panting. Oh, yeah, he was definitely an expert in the art of shower sex, and she turned all tingly and breathless just thinking about his skills.

Eve shook her head and concentrated on wrapping her arm with one of the plastic cast covers Doc sent . If she didn't block out the past with Mac, she'd never get through the present with her heart intact. Being with him was one giant disaster waiting to happen. She'd not been able to resist him earlier, but she couldn't let things spiral out of control again. Taking a few hesitant steps, she entered the shower, and let the warm water wash the memories away.

Twenty minutes later, she sat at the kitchen table, pilfering through Mac's duffle bag full of weapons, her mind no longer thinking of hot and steamy sex with him. Well, sort of. Now, she was only half-thinking of Mac and sex. The other half of her brain zeroed in on the cache of weaponry spread before her.

"Where did these come from, Mac?"

"Cade. He brought food and medical supplies too." He pointed at her. "I see you found the stash of clothes."

"Perfect fit." She smoothed her pants. "Jeez, Mac, there's a small arsenal here."

"You know how a man feels about his weapons. We don't leave home without them, and of course, you can never have too many."

"Yeah, boys and their toys." She lined up a few of the handguns and studied them. "You really think you need all of these?"

"I'm willing to share my toys." He winked at her. "Take what you want."

Damn him. Even his winks are sexy. "Thanks."

Like a kid on Christmas morning and Santa was her new best friend, Eve dug through the bag. She took an instant liking to a small Glock. The weight was perfect for her hand.

"Good thing Mendoza and his dick-brained sidekick broke my left wrist." She held up the cast. "Would've pissed me off if I couldn't use my shooting hand."

"That would've sucked all right." Mac answered.

She snorted. "Cute, Mac, real cute."

The smile he'd stifled was of the pat-the-little-woman on the head variety. He'd never take her job seriously. Screw him, she decided while tucking the Glock into her waistband.

Eve picked up a sleek satellite phone and shoved it into a back pocket. She found a small knife, held it for inspection, and turned it in her hand. "This sure isn't one of the kukri knives you were talking about. Blade's nice and straight."

Mac glanced over his shoulder at the trench knife she held. "Good for close range fighting, but not my first choice of knives."

Mac pulled a large K-bar knife from an ankle sheath and made a few air swipes. Flashes of light reflected off the shiny blade. "This is a first-rate knife."

Eve maneuvered the smaller knife around in her hand. "I don't know. I'm kind of partial to the feel of this one."

She burrowed a niche inside her cast and carefully slid the trench knife inside. The knife was small enough to hide beneath all the gauze and plaster of Paris.

Zipping the duffle closed, Eve studied Mac as he arranged slices of crisp bacon alongside mounds of scrambled eggs on two plates. He added two pieces of toast to each and sat one of the plates in front of her.

Mac said, "Eat."

"Don't have to tell me twice. I'm starving." She had a fork in her hand in less than a second.

He added a bowl of sliced bananas to the table. Eve savored the sweet aroma of the fruit and the strong smoky smell of the bacon and eggs. Halfway through her food, she began to slow down.

Sex, shower, and food. Life doesn't get much better.

Even if I have no business sharing the excellent things life has to offer with Mac.

Chapter Eleven

Mac had made love to Eve and now he was feeding her breakfast as if they were a normal couple spending a lazy weekend morning at home. All he needed was the fucking Sunday morning comics to complete the picture. She looked relaxed, almost content. For a short moment he'd nearly forgotten the woman was being hunted by an out-of-control, psycho drug lord.

He leaned above Eve's shoulder, his arm brushing hers, and set a plate of food in front of her. A whiff of the sweet lemon fragrance of shampoo, mixed with Eve's own special scent, kicked Mac's libido into the red zone. He turned away. Eve needed to eat. His horny-ass needs could wait.

"Wow, I didn't realize how hungry I was. This is so much better than Doc's food. Especially the bananas. They're delicious." She forked a piece, wrapped her lips around the fruit, and chewed.

Damn, how did she manage to turn eating a banana into a sexy art form? Whoa, boy. Don't go there. Talk. Talk is good. Talk will take my mind off this out-of-control lust.

He pointed toward the kitchen door. "There's a grove out back. This place used to be a big banana and rubber tree farm before a fire took most of the trees. Hutch bought the property for Resolutions after the fire."

"So, Hutch picked the house and land up at a fire sale?" Eve looked at him, her eyebrows slightly raised. *She expected him to laugh?*

"Oh, you're being funny."

"At least mildly amusing." Eve shrugged. "Tough crowd."

"I'm sure it'll hit me later just how funny." Mac leaned against the counter. "Any pain this morning?"

"No. I feel pretty damned good actually. Wrist doesn't hurt anymore." She wiggled her fingers below the cast. "Swelling's down enough I'm getting movement back. I'm half tempted to unbind my pinky and ring finger."

"Not a good plan. Doc said leave them taped till the cast comes off. I'm glad you're feeling better."

Eve said, "Amazing what being totally worthless will do."

"Or partaking in a round of great sex."

"Truly great sex."

"I'm glad we agree."

"Time for rest is over. I plan on going back to the Mendoza compound to finish my mission and retrieve the flash drive. It's time." A flash of regret skittered across her face a second before she lowered her chin.

"What's that about, Eve?"

"What?"

"The guilty frown?"

"I have no idea what you're talking about." She sounded innocent, but he was on to her. She was hiding something.

"Fine, we'll discuss your little secrets later. For now, just tell me where the flash drive is and I'll make the retrieval."

Eve gawked at him as if he'd grown a third arm. "Not gonna happen."

"You sure as hell can't make the extraction. You're in a cast and still running a fever." Trying to talk sense into her was a waste of time, but he had to try. "Your wrist may be better, but I think it's going to take a little bit longer for your shoulder to be back at full speed."

"Wow, I feel special. I'm well enough to fuck, but not do my job?"

Mac bared his teeth, reached for a bit of composure. "If you were completely healed, I'd turn you over my knee and paddle your ass." Instead he cradled her face in his hands, turned her head from side to side. "You've taken a beating, baby. Beneath the fading rainbow of bruises and dark circles under your eyes, you're ghostly pale."

"Thanks for reminding me how appealing I am." She slapped his hand away.

Mac pulled her from of the chair into his arms and kissed her. He ran the back of his curled fingers over her soft cheek. "You know that's not what I meant. You're always beautiful to me. But you need more time to recuperate."

"No, I don't. I'm ready to finish the job. The flash drive has the final pieces we need to nail Mendoza and get his evil ass off the streets." She pushed away, her hands still resting on his chest. "The IDEA task force has waited a long time for that piece of evidence. Too many good agents have died trying to get it."

"I said I'll make the extraction." He fought his gut reaction, tried not to get angry. She wanted to do her job. He respected her determination. *The eternally stubborn woman.*

"Sorry, Mac. I can't let you. Besides, I couldn't begin to describe where I hid it."

"I figured you wouldn't let me get the flash drive for you."

"You figured right." Eve shrugged.

Mac shrugged right back at her. "I've got a news flash for you, Eve. I'm going back to San Carlos Lucas with you."

"This is an IDEA operation. My assignment. And Rex's. We can do our jobs."

Mac smiled. "Not anymore, baby. Your boss hired Resolutions to get you back into the Mendoza compound. More specifically, he wants me for the job."

"Why would I need you?" Her face reddened. "Rex and I had no problem getting past the compound walls before."

"Are you kidding? Your team lost a man, you were captured, and almost died yourself." He wanted to shake some sense into her. "You call that no problems?"

"I meant we infiltrated the compound without incident. I'll make sure we get out safely this time."

"It's gonna be harder." Mac wished she would listen to reason, but he knew Eve, and nothing he said would change her mind once she made it up. "After you and your team breached the compound, Mendoza doubled his security force. Chances are good you won't be able to retrieve the hidden flash drive. Getting back inside the study—if you need another go at his computer—will be a bigger challenge. I'm the only guy who can get you past all the extra security."

"Oh, pa-leeease! What have you got that I don't have?"

He looked at his ever-present-around-Eve hard-on and smiled sheepishly. "Well, baby, if I need to expla—"

Eve punched his shoulder. "Mac! I'm serious."

"Okay, okay." He rubbed his shoulder in an exaggerated manner. "Seriously? I know where the secret tunnel into the compound is. Remember? The in and out Mendoza has no clue about."

"You can tell me about the tunnels. If helping makes you feel manlier, you can deliver us to the outside entrance. Rex and I will go in alone from there."

He shook his head. "That's not the way this op is going down."

"I'll talk to John Sanders."

"Don't bother. Your SAC called in Hutch and personally set up this operation. This is Sanders' brainchild."

"Then I'll set him straight." She pulled out of his embrace. He let her go, hoping she'd see reason if he let her have a little space.

"Talking with your boss is not going to help."

"But, I don't—"

"Face the facts, Eve. I'm in, and Brewer is out. I'm your partner for this gig."

"Partner? No. I don't think so." She moved away and paced.

"Brewer won't be going on this mission."

She frowned. "He's my partner, I won't leave him out."

"Brewer is going to have to learn to do without you from now on. After this assignment, you're going back to tech support and research." Mac wasn't sure why he spewed such bullshit. The words just popped out.

"I beg your pardon?" Eve's face flushed red, and she looked pissed enough to chew his face off.

Mac bit back a groan. He'd stepped in a pile of elephant turds this time, but he wasn't about to turn back now. "We're together again. I haven't changed my mind about you being in the danger zone. I can't be worrying about whether or not my woman is safe. I told you this when you transferred into field work."

Damn. Like Eve said, he was a stubborn fool. Mac kept his stare glued to hers, waiting for the shit to hit the fan. Until now, he'd really believed he'd changed. He'd at least meant to change. The reality was two years without her hadn't made a difference. He still feared she would die if she kept taking dangerous field assignments. Sure, he was chauvinistic and had a bit of trouble shaking the alpha attitude. Tough shit. He had to protect Eve, had to protect his woman. And whether she realized it, or not, she was his woman.

"We're back to this, Mac? Are you out of your mind? I don't understand how a man living in the twenty-first century can still think like a man from the Stone Age. I want a job where I can make a difference in people's lives. Getting rid of a man who sells drugs, murders, and deals with ter—God only knows what else, is making a difference."

He crossed his arms. "My mom wanted to make a difference. She decided to use her nursing skills to help change the world. I have to admit she was right, in a way. When the land mine her transport hit blew her to pieces, I'd say there was a fucking big difference—in my world and in my family's."

The old hurt still rankled. Mac hated to think about those dark days, but maybe hearing the way his life had crashed and burned, would help Eve understand. "I was thirteen. Mom should have been home with me, not out trying to save the world. Dad and I were never the same after she died. My dad should've protected her, should have kept her safe."

"How? By not letting her do a job she loved? By locking her in the house and throwing away the key? Is that what you want to do with me?"

"I can't lose you like I lost my mom. The pain cut too deep. Can't you understand? Don't you know what losing you would do to me?"

"Sure, Mac, I understand. I'm sorry about your mother, but I'm not her. I'm not going back to a desk job." She slipped her hand into a pocket. "Not even for you."

"Fine. We'll get the flash drive and afterward, you can partner with Brewer again. Let him worry about you from now on. I'm finished."

"Fine." Eve shot lightning bolts of anger in his direction.

Mac shot them right back. "Fine."

"Damn you, Mac. You'll never change."

Eve stormed from the kitchen into the bedroom and slammed the door behind her. The bang left his ears ringing.

ꕥ

Eve tossed the borrowed Glock on the night table.

She flopped onto the un-made bed, pulled out the satellite phone, and poked in Rex's cell number fast and furiously.

"Hello."

"Rex?"

"Eve? Where are you? I heard the clinic was attacked and Mendoza tried to kidnap you. I've been worried sick. Sanders won't tell anyone where you are."

"Settle down. You sound like an old woman."

"I'm worried about you."

"I'm fine. Really." Eve shouldn't take out her frustration on her partner. She softened her tone. "Mac got me out of another scrape. We're at a safe house."

"McKenna saves the day again. Great."

Rex sounded strangely disappointed. "Are you upset Mac interrupted my abduction? Seriously?"

"I'm glad he was there for you."

"You don't sound glad." Did Rex somehow know about Mendoza and the Afghani terrorists? Did he think she was holding out on him? No, there was no way Rex knew about the terrorists. Sanders had sworn her to secrecy, and her boss would keep quiet, too. Eve had almost blurted the secret to Mac, but managed to bite back the words before she spilled her guts.

"You sure the house you're in now is safe? Wasn't the clinic supposed to be secure?"

"This place is an old abandoned banana and rubber tree farm outside the city. A fire wiped out most of the trees a few years ago and Hutch bought the property. No one would ever think to search here for me. I'm safe."

"If you're sure. I trust your judgment."

"I am." Eve stared at the closed door, wishing the man on the other side believed in her enough to let her do her job.

"Eve, you still there? Are you all right?"

"I told you I'm fine. I'm good." *Mad as hell, but fine.*

"You looked pretty rough when I saw you at the clinic."

She let out an exaggerated sigh. "I know. Everyone keeps telling me."

"You know what I mean. I'm talking about all the bruises and cuts. Jesus, Eve, you've got a bullet hole in your shoulder and you're wearing a cast from your elbow to your fingers. You should be in a hospital recuperating, not running from Mendoza."

"I don't need a hospital, and let's just think of the cast as an extra weapon. If Mendoza gets close, I'll use this bad boy to crack him upside the head." She knocked on the cast.

"Extra weapon? Are you kidding? Dammit, Eve, I'm serious."

She envisioned the small trench knife burrowed neatly inside her cast. "I'm serious, too. Stop worrying."

"I'll stop when I see for myself you're okay."

"What about you, Rex? How's your wound?"

"The bullet hit the fleshy part on the underside of my arm. I'm not sure it even qualifies as a wound."

"Good news." Eve had decided Sanders wouldn't share information about the terrorist plot yet, but she had no idea how much he'd told the task force about her upcoming mission with Mac. "Has Sanders mentioned anything about getting the flash drive back?"

"No. He says the problem will be dealt with, but he hasn't bothered to give me details." An awkward moment of quiet passed between them. "I told Sanders you needed to get with him soon like you requested. You want me to come get you? You could recoup in D.C."

"Thanks for relaying the message, but I spoke with him on a secure phone." Eve had to tell Rex about her new mission—with Mac. *Just say it.* "I'm not coming home right away. Sanders is sending me back to Mendoza's for the flash drive."

"You're up for an assignment?"

"Sure, I'm good to go."

"Then I guess I'll see you in San Carlos Lucas."

"I'm afraid not, Rex." *Oh man this sucks.* "Sanders wants Mac to go in with me this time. Since he succeeded before, he thinks Mac can get me in and out undetected a second time."

Eve didn't tell him about the secret tunnels. She was all kinds of angry at Mac, but she didn't feel she should share the information.

"What? You've got to be kidding. I'm your partner. Not McKenna."

"I don't like this shit any more than you."

"This is just fucking great. Sanders keeps me in the dark about where you are, doesn't tell me about the new mission to Mendoza's, and now he's letting McKenna partner with you. What next?"

"I wish my orders were different."

"Yeah, me too." Rex sounded resigned to the plan for barely a moment before his voice flared with anger again. "This is such bullshit!"

"I know." What else was there to say? She agreed completely with Rex.

He sighed heavily. "Listen, I want to meet you in Bogota, or maybe in San Carlos Lucas, before you go back to Mendoza's. Tell me where you're at."

"I don't exactly know where I am." Her location hadn't been an issue until now. "I was out cold when Mac brought me here. Mendoza's men drugged me."

"You've got to have some inkling."

"Not much. I know I'm somewhere outside the city, at a farm along the base of the mountains. A banana and rubber tree farm. I told you about the fire." Eve tried to recall the trip here and came up empty. "Doesn't matter anyway. We're leaving first thing in the morning."

"Get directions from McKenna and call me back."

"No. Mac would never agree to you coming here." Not to mention the minor detail she couldn't ask Mac for directions because she had no intention of ever speaking to him again.

"Do you think Sanders would change his mind if we talked to him?"

"He isn't going to change his mind." Mac was right about that. She and Rex would just have to accept the facts.

"But—"

"Mac and I are partners for this mission."

Chapter Twelve

Mac couldn't believe how quickly he'd managed to fuck up things with Eve. He shouldn't be surprised. The morning had gone so well—at least until he pissed her off. If he lived to be a hundred years old, he'd never understand exactly what compelled him to pull the alpha male bullshit.

"I can fix this. I just need to figure out how. I'll work on changing Eve's mind right after I figure out why I'm fucking talking to myself."

It'd been a long day and his patience was worn thin. He'd spent a few too many days stuck inside small houses with Eve. She hadn't left the bedroom since they argued, except to grab food and water. He heard her marching in her room while he stayed busy wearing down a path in the floor of the small living room.

Mac's sixth sense, honed from years of working special ops, went on alert. He stopped pacing and brought his gun up. A sharp bark echoed from the front yard. There was nothing to bark at in the middle of nowhere, shouldn't even be a dog around this far out. Something was going down. Mumbling a string of curses, Mac moved toward the window. "What the fuck?"

Holding his Glock steady, he pulled back the blinds. The

barking came to an abrupt halt and a small patch of bushes swayed near the edge of the driveway. But the rubber trees weren't moving at all. The wind wasn't blowing Jack shit outside. A flash of light shimmered through the leaves. It had to be—*Gun!*

Before he had time to warn Eve, the first shots exploded through the window. Glass shattered around him and he dove for the floor, rolling behind the couch. Small pieces of glass embedded in his arms and upper torso, and stung like a bitch.

Hearing gunfire, Eve crouched and scooted into the living room clutching her Glock. The shooting stopped.

"Mac? You in here?"

"Stay down, Eve." His voice came from behind the couch. "We've got at least two shooters in the front. There's probably more covering the back."

Shards of glass scattered around the room and long streaks of blood striped the floor. Her pulse raced and her belly cramped. Had Mac taken a bullet? "Are you hit?"

"I'm fine."

Before she could ask about the blood, another onslaught of bullets drilled through the window. Mac rose to his knees and returned fire while Eve scrambled behind the couch, pumping a steady flow of bullets through the window beside him. The shooting halted. Except for Mac and Eve's deep breathing, eerie silence flooded the room. Mac sat on the floor, his back against the couch. She mirrored his move.

He wiped his forehead, leaving a thin trail of blood. "I'm not sure why they quit firing."

"I imagine they're trying to decide if they hit one of us."

He frowned. "More like *hoping* they hit one of us, preferably both. You all right?"

Eve looked at the hand holding her Glock. "I'm okay, but I'm going to have to find an easier way to drop a magazine and reload. Slapping a new one into the grip with the cast and broken fingers is no picnic in the park."

"Hit the grip on your knee to drive the magazine in."

She pictured the movement. "Good idea."

"All my ideas are good."

"Naturally." His arms were bleeding and blood dotted his tee shirt. "You've been hit!"

"No. I rolled across broken glass. The cuts are superficial. We need to leave before these guys call for back-up." Mac grabbed the duffle full of weapons and slung the bag on his shoulder. "Let's work our way toward the back door."

Irritation nipped at Eve when he positioned her behind him, standing between her and the window, and guided her toward the kitchen. *Mr. Protector doing his thing.* Reaching the kitchen, Mac motioned for her to crouch and move to the refrigerator. He followed closely behind. She bit back a low growl.

"Stay here while I check the back door."

"Mac, you're bleeding, and I'm not helpless. I think I can manage to check a doorway."

"I told you these are only small cuts from the broken glass. I don't think I'll drop dead from blood loss any time soon. After all, I am a big, tough alpha male."

The smart ass had borrowed her tease from the day before. Not replying, Eve stayed hunkered next to the refrigerator. He'd never take her seriously. If they got out of this mess alive, she would kill him.

"Don't look so glum, Eve. I'm joking." Mac retrieved the smaller duffle bag with supplies from the kitchen table, and slung the strap over his shoulder with the other one. Staying low, he crept to the door, lifted one of the blind's slats, and peeked out.

"Looks clear, but you know what they say."

"Looks can be deceiving." *So can men.*

He tucked his pistol into his waistband and pulled a loaded HK rifle.

Keeping her head down, Eve made her way to him.

"I still don't see anything, but I know they're there."

His voice, barely a whisper, had her straining to hear. Eve moved behind him and signaled she was in position.

He carefully cracked the door open and a low squeak echoed. Bullets whizzed past them. "Fuck this." Mac flung the door open, and they returned fire. "I had a good idea they'd be out there, the bastards."

"Sounds like one shooter back here. Let's beat feet before his friends out front decide to join him." Eve spoke above the gunfire.

"You go first. Head toward what's left of the banana grove. I'll cover you."

Eve hesitated, decided now might not be the best time to lecture him about his annoying habit of over-protectiveness. "What about you?"

"I'll be right behind you. When you're deep into the trees, lay down cover for me."

"I'll be waiting," Eve said.

Mac pulled the gun from his waistband and handed it to Eve. "This should give you a little more time before you have to do the one handed re-load." He started shooting while she tucked the second gun into her waistband.

"Thanks." She patted the gun.

"Always happy to help." Mac stopped firing, pulled her close, and gave her a quick kiss.

"Stay safe for me, baby." He opened fire. "Okay, on my signal, haul ass."

In spite of the toe curling kiss, she made good time reaching the cover of the banana grove. Anxious for Mac to join her, she leaned against a tree, solidly planted her feet, and began firing.

With Eve covering him, Mac easily cleared the back door and sprinted toward her in record time. She stood with her feet apart, a firm one-handed grip on her gun, and a determined expression on her face, firing at the enemy. Reality punched Mac square in the gut. She was beautiful even in the middle of a fire fight. And natural. Like she belonged in this deadly line of work.

He shook the notion away. The concept was fucking crazy.

Mac took a stand next to her at the same instant one of Eve's bullets found its mark. The man went down with a strangled cry, followed by silence. Seconds later, more gunfire exploded.

Mac reloaded the HK. "Here come the shooters from the front yard. Let's get a move on."

"Definitely a good plan." Eve pushed away from her spot next to the tree, and Mac fell in place behind her.

They ran, returning fire. Less than a minute had gone by when Eve paused, spun around, and with a firm grip on her gun, took out a second man with a dead center shot to his forehead. *Holy fuck. She's a better shot than I am.*

One of Mac's rounds hit the remaining shooter. The fight ended, leaving a metallic scent and a small rising fog of gun smoke behind. Mac hustled to Eve's side and, seeing how winded she was, slowed their pace to a lazy jog before coming to a complete halt.

Gasping, he bent over, hands on his knees. "Three shooters are down. I think that's all there were. I'm going to swing back and get the car. Why don't you take a breather?"

For once Mac was grateful she didn't argue or make a disgusted face at him. Five minutes after he left, he returned without the car.

Eve looked up. "Where's the vehicle?"

"The bastards disabled the engine. We're going to have to keep moving on foot." He slapped at a fly buzzing past his head. "Or wait for backup to arrive."

"We move." She shot from the sitting position she'd taken. "Mendoza will send other men. I'm surprised only three men came to begin with."

Eve's face had turned ashen. He couldn't blame her for wanting to avoid Mendoza's men after what she'd been through. "I'd like to know how the fuck Mendoza's men found us. Any clue?"

Eve shook her head.

"This is one of the safest houses in the Resolutions' system.

There's no way anyone could have known the location." Mac had a few ideas rolling around in his mind. "There are no leaks at Resolutions. No one on the IDEA task force knows where you are this time except Sanders. He'd never tell."

Guilt flashed across Eve's face.

"Hiding something again, Eve?"

She started walking.

"Eve?"

"It's nothing."

"Let me be the judge. Now is not the time to keep secrets."

"I talked to Rex this morning. I informed him we were going back to Mendoza's compound without him. I wanted to be the one to tell him."

Mac stopped, grabbed her arm, and brought her to an abrupt standstill. "You did what?"

"I told him he wasn't going back to San Carlos Lucas with me."

"What else?" Mac stared at her, his posture achingly stiff.

"I don't like what you're thinking," she said.

"You don't know what I'm thinking."

"Yes, I do. You've got that look in your eyes."

"Which one is that?"

"The one I don't like." She wiped the sweat trickling down between her breasts. His gaze followed her hand.

"You don't like a lot of them."

"Well, I especially don't like this one. It says you're thinking I told Rex where we are, and he led Mendoza to us." She spat the words as if they were distasteful. Hell, maybe they were.

"You're saying you didn't tell Brewer about the safe house?"

"I told him, but I didn't give him the location. I don't even know the location."

He sucked in a breath. "Exactly what did you tell him?"

"Nothing much. I said the house was outside the city."

"And?" There was more, Eve's face gave her away. He had a bad feeling about her conversation with Rex.

"I mentioned the place had been a big rubber and banana

tree farm before a fire destroyed most of the groves."

"Dammit, Eve." Mac wished Rex was right here, right now, so he could choke the bastard. "How fucking hard do you think it'd be to discover which farm on the outskirts of Bogota was burned out?"

"No, Mac, you're wrong. Even if Rex did figure out our location, he wouldn't tell anyone, especially Mendoza. Rex is my partner. He wouldn't betray me."

Mac shook his head, didn't bother trying to hide his disgust.

"Rex has been on the task force since the beginning. He's been my partner for two years. He wants Mendoza's cartel taken down."

"Mendoza isn't finding where we're at on his own." Mac paused for a moment and mentally hammered out a few details. "Someone is feeding him info. Besides Hutch, only Cade, Sanders and Brewer are aware of our location. If I had to guess who the asshole is doling out information, I'd choose Brewer."

She frowned. "Then you'd choose wrong."

"Would you stop and think about this? Mendoza found us at the clinic right after Brewer's visit and the safe house after you talked to him on the phone. Coincidence? Uh-uhh, I don't think so."

"You are so unbelievably wrong." Eve moved away from him, presenting him with her back.

A horrible realization occurred to Mac and his face flushed hot with anger. His hands balled into tight fists at the same time his stomach muscles knotted. He ignored the churning acid lodged in the back of his throat.

"Son. Of. A. Fucking. Bitch. Brewer leaked the details about your mission to Mendoza's compound. No wonder the op ended in one giant goatfuck. Mendoza had been tipped off and was waiting to ambush your team. Your partner's a traitor."

"Rex was part of the team. He was shot." Refusing to look him in the eye, Eve shook her head rapidly. Her shoulders stiffened.

"Take off the blinders."

Eve rounded to face him, her eyes narrowed. "You don't understand. Danny died. Rex would never, and I mean never do something that would've led to that. No one on the team would. Sanders and the D.C. Attorney General personally handpicked the task force. It's solid. I refuse to believe one of my teammates would turn."

"Then you're a fool, baby."

"Oh God, Mac, if you're right, that means someone I trusted totally is responsible for Danny's murder and the other agents we've lost."

Eve's shoulders slumped. The need to comfort her overwhelmed him. He reached for Eve and she backed away, hugging herself.

"Now, that person is helping Mendoza get to me."

Chapter Thirteen

San Carlos Lucas
Mendoza Compound

Mendoza sprawled in the chair behind his large desk, shining his gun with a cloth. He thought about Eve Taylor, the woman he wanted. The defiant bitch made his loins burn hot and his temper flare red. He would soon have her. He would keep her on all fours, train her like a dog and savor the game. The DEA agent was nothing like the spineless whores he usually dealt with.

Sí, *Eve Taylor will be a challenge. One I will win. I always win.* Bit by bit, he would break her strong, disrespectful will and bring her to her knees. In the end, she would beg for mercy. Once he had the information he wanted from Eve and he'd done his worst, he would take her to his bed and have his way with her. Only after he'd had his fill—if it was even possible to tire of such a woman—would he put Eve Taylor out of her misery. That itself would be a treat.

In the meantime, he had to settle for the whoresome females available in San Carlos Lucas and Buenaventura. Having them wouldn't cure him of his desire for Miss Taylor, but might go a long way toward venting his irritation.

A sharp knock at the door interrupted his frustrated

thoughts.

"Miguel, it is me. The specialist you summoned has arrived." The voice was muted through the door, but understandable and recognizable. *Carlos. My sister has no clue how much restraint is needed to let the* idiota *live.*

He set his gun on the desk and stood. "Come in."

The men entered and Mendoza marched circles around the so-called specialist standing before him. The man, who'd returned from Bogota minutes ago, appeared tired and disordered. A bandage covered a two-inch area above his left temple. Letting out a deep breath, Mendoza stopped in front of him, and crossed his hands behind his back. He stared into the man's bloodshot eyes.

The man didn't blink.

"What is this, *mi amigo*?" Mendoza pointed to the bandage.

"McKenna nicked me. A lucky shot. The men with me were not so fortunate." The specialist raised a hand, molded it into the shape of a gun, and pretended to fire off two shots. After blowing away the imaginary smoke from his index finger, he lowered his hand. "The woman killed both of them."

"I expect Carlos to fuck up. He's a moron." Mendoza pointed at the man. "But you? I had much higher expectations. You disappoint me." Mendoza jabbed his finger into the man's chest. The man stood firm, never flinching. Exasperated, Mendoza threw his hands up. "I am surrounded by incompetents. I paid you *mucho pesos* to do this job. You have failed me. Do you have anything to say?"

The man shrugged. "Sometimes shit goes wrong. Don't worry. I won't miss a second time, Mr. Mendoza."

"Sometimes shit goes wrong?"

The man nodded. "It's a fact."

Mendoza slipped behind his desk and plopped in his chair, irritated and angry. He drew his gun and fired. The blast echoed through the room, and the smell of death filled Mendoza's nostrils. The heavy thud of the specialist's body hitting the floor was followed by the ping of the ejected casing bouncing across the desk.

Carlos stepped back and whispered, "I'm glad *el asesino a sueldo* fucked up this time, not me." Carlos quickly made the sign of the cross on his chest and opened one eye at a time.

"You no longer take orders from this man."

"Mierda!" Carlos eagerly nodded. "Dead men don't give orders."

Mendoza pointed at the lifeless heap lying on the floor. "Quit cowering and clean this mess up. I have things to do." He wanted to get back to thinking about what he'd do to Eve Taylor once he had her.

Carlos kicked the body. "*Sí*, Miguel."

Chapter Fourteen

Bogota, Colombia

Mac and Eve made their way toward the dense tropical foliage at the base of the mountains overlooking Bogota. Scratches stung her face where razor-sharp leaves had slapped her. Mac had picked up a machete from the garage. Once they were several hundred feet into the jungle, he put the blade to good use slicing a path. She wasn't sure if the gesture pissed her off or made her want to pledge her undying appreciation.

After battling an endless supply of mosquitoes and oozing a few gallons of sweat, they came across a well-hidden grotto located near a small waterfall. Eve was exhausted, itchy, and every inch of her body ached.

Mac tossed down his duffle bag, walked a slow circle around the area. "Looks like a good place to rest."

"Not on my account. I'm fine." She leaned against a tree, swatted at another flying pest. She was afraid if they stopped too long, she might not be able to get moving again. More afraid he'd think her weak. "Let's keep going."

He grimaced. "I'm glad you're fine, but I'm whipped and would like to rest, if you don't mind."

"Oh. Sorry. I jumped to the conclusion you were going all

alpha male on me again."

Eve gave him a once over and a short pang of guilt raced through her. His face and arms gleamed with sweat. He dropped the machete and sucked in several deep breaths. Scratches from the sharp branches and fronds of the jungle added fresh blood to his dried cuts from the broken glass. Looked like the physical exertion of swinging the machete back and forth had exhausted even Mac's well-toned body.

He's human after all. Good to know.

Eve stretched her neck, turning her head from side to side, and concentrated on calming her labored breathing. "Sure, taking a little break is okay with me."

"Thanks for giving your permission." He stood and ran a hand through his damp hair. "By the way, you're really not fine. You're pale, and the dark circles under your eyes are growing deeper. Even your breathing is ragged and labored." He slid his backpack off and let the bag drop to the ground. "You're exhausted."

"You're not looking so hot yourself."

Mac ignored her retort. *He must really be worn out.* She stepped closer. He removed a thin blanket from his backpack and spread it on a carpet of moss. It looked pretty damned inviting.

"Sit, Eve."

She didn't hesitate. "Could you toss me a water?" She dug a pill from her pocket and popped it.

Mac's eyes went wide.

"It's ibuprofen. No biggie." Unless he was the one trying to shove it down her throat.

Before Eve changed her mind or spit the pill out, Mac passed an opened bottle of water to her. She took a long, deep swallow. A throaty moan escaped and sent a wave of heat through him. The woman was fucking sex on a stick. But damn, now was not the time for his libido to crank into full gear.

He pointed to the bottle. "Finish. You can't afford to get

dehydrated again."

"You think?"

"Sorry." From the bag, he took two pieces of cloth then trekked the few feet to the waterfall, and dipped them in the water. He used the first to wash himself and handed Eve the second.

She ran small circles over her face, neck, and chest. "God, that feels good." She shifted into a sluggish, languid drawl that turned his insides soft and his dick hard. "How long will we stay here?"

His mind zeroed in on her, and he swore sex oozed freely with every word spoken. Mac cleared his throat, wishing he could clear all visions of Eve naked and under him from his mind.

"I don't think anyone followed us from the house."

After dipping the cloth in the water again, he cautiously washed around her wound. Blood stained the bandages, putting a damper on lust-filled images.

"Dammit, let me check the sutures."

Mac removed the light layers of gauze. "A couple of stitches have come loose. I'll reinforce them with Steri-strips. I'm sure there's some in the duffle."

"It's probably past time for them to come out anyway. Use a Band-Aid."

"The way you move, Steri-strips will work better." Using a 4x4 of gauze, he gently cleaned the wound with an antiseptic from the bag, dabbed it dry, and applied Steri-strips. He added a clean bandage. With the back of his of hand, he touched her forehead and then, unable to resist, ran his fingers down her cheek.

"Looks like your fever is creeping back up. The ibuprofen you took should help." He tossed her the repellent. "We can both use another round of bug spray."

"Thanks."

"Let's lie down. I'm beat."

"Me, too."

He winced when his back hit the blanket. "Guess I should pick some of the glass from my arms first."

"Let me help. Pass the antiseptic, and I'll clean your cuts. You don't want them infected."

"I can handle this. You need to rest."

"Give me the fucking bottle, Mac."

He started to open the lid.

"I've got better control of my fingers now. Let me have a go." Mac handed her the antiseptic and scooted closer. It took a couple tries, but she managed to open it. Meticulously, they removed the glass shards from his upper body.

"I don't think any of these cuts are deep enough to worry about, but here's a shit load of them."

"You don't have to tell me. I feel each and every one." On cue, he flinched with the next piece of glass extracted, reinforcing his words.

Eve cleaned his cuts. When she finished, Mac tossed the medical supplies aside and lay back, dragging Eve with him. She offered no resistance. Even stranger, she snuggled into the curve of his arm and rested her head on his shoulder.

"You doin' okay? You're awfully quiet."

"I'm fine, considering my partner and best friend has been deceiving me for two years." She lifted her face, looked at him. "Jeez, sounds like I'm throwing myself a pity-party."

His heart beat faster and he smiled at her. "You're allowed. In fact, I'll bring the cake and pointy little hats."

"Guess I'm having a hard time believing Rex could be responsible for this mess. If he is, how could I not have known? What kind of operative misses something so important?"

Mac raised a hand to her cheek. "Maybe you should wait to see what Hutch and Cade find out about the attacks before you beat yourself up too much."

"Yeah, hang on to those party hats. I'll wait for proof before I accuse Rex of betraying me and the rest of the task force."

He gazed at her until her eyes gradually shut. Softly stroking her neck, he listened as her breathing faded to whispers. He didn't realize how tense she really was until she relaxed in slumber. When Mac was sure she was sleeping sound, he pulled his backpack closer. Quietly he took his satellite phone and tapped in a number. Hutch answered before the first ring completed.

"Mac, where are you? I got word earlier the safe house was breached."

"No shit, Hutch. We barely got out alive." Mac tried to keep his voice low, but didn't bother trying to hide his anger. "What the fuck is going on? How does the bastard keep finding us?"

"I'm not sure where the leak is, but I'm guessing someone at the IDEA is the culprit. I spoke with Sanders, who agrees, and he's started pulling information on all task force team members. He's digging deep into employment and military records, personal histories, and obtaining detailed bank records. He'll work his way up the ranks until he finds the leak."

Mac said, "Tell him to save himself a lot of work and start with Rex Brewer. I don't trust the chicken-shit little bastard. He knew our location both times Mendoza's men found us. I'm betting Eve was set up at Mendoza's compound. Naturally, Brewer had that info, too."

"I'll let Sanders know and do a little looking into Brewer's past myself. Give me a status update. Where are you now? How's Eve?"

"Eve's tough. She'll be fine. We're about three clicks north of the safe house and another mile into the jungle cover. It's time to call the chopper back to Bogota and pull us out. After Eve rests, we'll head to the airstrip for a lift to Mendoza's compound."

Hutch said, "It'll be dark soon. Why don't you stay put until morning? Give Eve more time to recuperate and Sanders more time to find his leak."

"Copy that. We'll dig in and move out at first light." Mac yawned, and a heavy tiredness crept through him. "I don't want anyone except Resolutions operatives to know where we are. Until Sanders finds the leak, I'd prefer he not even have the information."

"I agree. I don't think Sanders will have a problem with the need-to-know status either. Give Cade a head's up when you get close to the airstrip. That'll give Corelli time to get the chopper fired up and ready for immediate evac." Hutch sounded preoccupied. *Already rolling around a few plans in his head?*

"I'll radio you when insertion is complete."

"Good luck, Mac."

"Thanks. Until we find who's broadcasting our location, we'll need all the luck we can get." Mac cut the signal and slipped the phone back into the backpack. He looked at the woman sleeping in his arms. Why couldn't he keep from worrying about her? Afraid she'd end up dead like his mother? Eve in action, even injured, was a force to be reckoned with. Skillfully, she'd picked off two of the shooters today and managed to keep a good pace through the thick jungle. Damned if she didn't manage to do so with a fever and a body that screamed exhaustion.

Eve was right, she wasn't his mother. His mother had been a nurse, a woman with no combat training. Eve was a trained DEA field operative. His thoughts drifted to the night two years ago when Eve had told him about her promotion to field agent. Instead of celebrating with her, he'd quickly doused the excitement and pride twinkling in her eyes. Mac remembered, all right....

"Mac!" She'd waved her new DEA badge in his face. "I finally got my transfer from legal to field work. You're now looking at the newest special agent in the D.C. office of the DEA. How's that for news? I'll be working for John Sanders on his IDEA task force."

Mac's heart had frozen on the spot. Fear had grabbed him by the throat, and he remembered his mouth had gone so dry he couldn't form words, much less speak. His mind had glazed over in immense disappointment and anger.

"Mac? You gonna say something?" The pleasure had already started fading from her voice and face.

"That's nice, Eve. Now go back and tell Sanders the answer is no." Finding his voice, he'd struggled to keep the tone low and even.

She'd looked at him like he'd lost his mind. Maybe he had. "Are you crazy, Mac? No way am I turning down this transfer. You know I've been trying for a year to get this promotion. After all the hard work I've put in, I've earned the position."

"The work's too dangerous."

"Jeez, Mac, you're beginning to sound like my brothers. I told you how overprotective the Alpha Four are. I left Iowa to escape their smothering shield and have no intention of letting you pick up where they left off."

"Choose me or choose the job, Eve. You can't have both."

The memory of her last words sent a stabbing pain to his heart, left him feeling like all the blood had been squeezed from his body.

"Then I choose the job." Eve had muttered the words, almost sent him to his knees.

And just like that, it was over.

When Mac had taken the assignment to rescue Eve from Mendoza, he'd gone in thinking he'd changed and could handle Eve constantly putting her life on the line. He continuously faced danger during his own missions and survived. Besides, it wasn't really his any of his business. Eve wasn't his anymore.

She'd been trained by the DEA and had two years of experience under her belt. How hard could her job be to accept? How hard could making a change be? Apparently a lot fucking harder than he'd ever dreamed. Maybe a little more work on curbing the chauvinistic attitude was necessary.

Using his thumb and forefinger, he massaged the bridge of his nose between his eyes. *Fuck. Doesn't matter if I've changed or not. After we complete this mission, I'll be done with her, won't have to witness the risks she takes.*

Eve sighed in her sleep, snuggled closer, and tossed a lazy leg across his thigh. Who was he kidding? He didn't want to lose her again. Mac didn't want to spend his life without her. Being together like this was a second chance, a gift. One he planned to keep.

Life with Eve could be good.

The pulsating trickle from the nearby waterfall lulled him to sleep.

☙

Eve's desperate cries jarred him awake. Clawing him, she twisted and struggled in his arms. He tried to draw her closer. She fought him.

"Eve, wake up. You're all right, you're safe."

Eve stilled and pushed away. "Sorry, Mac. I had a dream. No, I had a nightmare."

He drew her trembling body against his and lazily rubbed her back. "I know, baby. Everything's okay now."

"Yeah." Eve didn't sound like she believed him.

"You want to talk about the nightmare?"

"Not right now." She shook her head.

"Then try to get some more sleep. We've got about four hours until we leave for the airstrip. Cade and Corelli will meet us there."

After a moment of silence, she said, "Mac, what if you're right?"

He smoothed her hair and planted a kiss on top of her head. "About what?"

"About me not being cut out to be a field agent. Maybe I will end up like your mother. My parents are gone, but my brothers would be heartbroken if something happened to me."

Heartbroken didn't begin to describe what Mac would suffer if anything ever happened to Eve. Just thinking about the possibility made his heart skip a beat.

Mac studied her in the near darkness. He ran the back of his fingers down the side of her face, savored the softness of her skin. Her bruises and spilt lip were history. This woman had stood against Miguel Mendoza. *And* survived.

He waited to speak until his voice wouldn't crack. "I'm sorry I ever said you weren't ready. I was wrong, baby. You're a damn good operative, the DEA is lucky to have you. I saw you in action today. You took out two bad guys. A lot of men couldn't have held up to the abuse you've taken and still kept moving like you did through this thick jungle." He added with a smile, "Who needs GI Joe when you've got a rough and tough Eve?"

She laughed. His matched hers. When the laughter died, Mac looked deep into her dark eyes. He took her chin his in hand and leaned forward to take her lips, praying she wouldn't resist.

Eve scooted closer and kissed him back. Relief flooded his senses.

She pushed him away. "I should still be mad at you."

"But you're not," Mac teased and drew her back into another mind-numbing kiss. Kisses he'd never grow tired of. His body hummed with desire.

Eve ran her hand over the zipper of his pants, slid it open on the third pass, and worked her hand inside. She gripped his erection, and he growled with a sexual hunger only Eve made him feel.

"Wanna help me out here?" Eve purred.

Mac undid the button and pushed his pants and boxers down.

She stroked him until he thought he'd explode in her hand. "Stop, baby. I want to be inside you when I come."

He rolled Eve onto her back and drew her good arm above her head. He ran his hand down the soft inside of the arm he'd just positioned, past her side, and across her stomach until he reached her other hand. Slow and easy...hard and fast would come later.

He ran a finger from the tip of her injured fingers to bandage covering her shoulder. "You doin' okay?"

She looked at him with greedy eyes. "Touch me again."

With a careful caress, he pushed her shirt up and over her head. Mac studied the soft mounds of her breasts. He lowered his head and feasted until her nipples pebbled. Her soft moans fed his arousal, and he hungered for more.

Mac removed her camos and panties and worked his way down her stomach, stopping long enough to give a little attention to her belly button. She squirmed when his head dipped lower. He found her, worked her.

Eve twisted, as if trying to get closer. Any closer and she'd be inside his skin.

When his mouth replaced his fingers, she opened her thighs wider, and gave him more room to work his magic. She grasped his hair and came, calling out his name. Mac was undressed and inside her before the quivering and explosions slowed, before she caught her breath. Relentless and driven, he pushed her body to a whole new level of gratification before giving in to his own release.

Afterwards, when their breathing slowed, Mac remained inside her, holding her close. The flutter of her heartbeat against his skin touched him somewhere deep within his soul. He didn't want to let her go. Couldn't let her go. He'd never get enough. "I could lie like this forever, Eve. You and me, face to face, heart to heart."

"We're good together, Mac. We've never had a problem in the sex department." Her whispers were barely audible above the noise of the waterfall.

"It's more than sex." He pulled her closer. "I love you, Eve. I always have, always will."

She didn't reply.

"You're not quite ready to admit you love me," Mac spoke for her. "It's okay."

Eve wasn't sure she'd heard him right.

There were so many types of love in a man's world. They love grilled steaks. They love fast cars and sports. They love movies with car chases and lots of shit blowing up. How should Eve take this declaration of love? Did it come from his heart? From his soul? Or was she just another thing to love? A thing he could keep in a neat little house surrounded by a picket fence? *Well I'm not anyone's thing.*

She searched his face and realized Mac still loved her from the depths of his heart. It was evident in the way he looked at her, the way he touched her. But how much was he willing to sacrifice to have her? Was he willing to give up his absurd need to protect her?

Eve did love him. But was she ready to admit this? Was she willing to risk her heart again?

"Loving each other? Well, I'm not sure love's enough for two people who can't seem to be together longer than a few hours without fighting, unless of course, we're in bed. A relationship can't survive on sex and fights."

Mac's grin went impish and his brow arched.

"Mac, I'm serious." She shot him what she calculated to be one of her best frowns ever.

"I know, I know. But you walked right in to that one, baby." He held her tight. "We can figure all this out after we get the files back from Mendoza's compound. We'll find a way to work things out."

"There's nothing I'd like more, Mac." Unless working out their problems only involved doing things his way.

"Trust me, Eve, we'll figure this out."

Trust the man who had broken her heart? Easier said than done.

☙

Mac made love to Eve twice more before the waterfall had lulled them to sleep. The early morning dawn came, bringing a light drizzle. It'd been too long since he'd slept all night with her in his arms. Her breathing, still so familiar after all this time, relaxed him, allowed him to shut out the rest of the world. Eve hadn't returned his declaration of love. She still had doubts. He didn't.

He'd have to find a way to convince her he could change. Hell, he'd have to prove it to himself. Changing turned out to be more difficult than he'd ever imagined. Feeling the warmth of her in his arms, how could he not want to do everything in his power to keep her safe? To protect her from the Mendozas of the world.

Mac woke her. Before they left the makeshift shelter, he had plans for them. She stretched and ran her hand over her face several times.

"Time to go already?" She purred, sounding sleepy and sexy at one time.

Mac stood and pulled her into a tight hug. He inhaled Eve's scent, her musky woman's smell made more intense by the rain.

"Come with me." He covered her cast in the plastic cover Doc had sent.

She looked at her arm then at him, a question in her gaze. "Where?"

"To clean up by the waterfall. Maybe play around a little."

"Waterfall sex? Nature's version of shower sex?"

"Mmm...waterfall sex. Sounds good to me. I've always been a big fan of nature, you know."

Eve didn't resist when he led her toward the water.

For a while, Eve blocked out the rest of the world and pushed aside her worries. Worry was a waste of time, serving no purpose except to make you weak and dependent. The events of the past two and half weeks had threatened to undermine the hard-earned independence she'd labored for since the day she'd left her family's farm in Iowa and the four older brothers who'd raised her. Eve was ten when her parents died in a car accident. Turned out to be the same day her fun-loving brothers turned into overbearing, overprotective caretakers who smothered her with their well-meant safekeeping. *The Alpha Four*.

Eve graduated law school and soon she was on her way to D.C. where she'd landed a job with the DEA. She was on her own and could finally breathe without her brothers watching her every move. Then she'd met Mac.

He'd turned her world upside down, and she quickly fell in love. They were together until the day John Sanders promoted her to field agent and offered her a spot on the recently formed IDEA task force team. Mac demanded she not take the job. She demanded he grow up. According to Mac, fieldwork was too damn dangerous for *his* woman.

In the end, Eve called his bluff. Turned out he wasn't bluffing. She never heard from Mac again until he rescued her from Mendoza's cells.

Now they were together again. But for how long? They'd made love with a passion she'd never find with any other man. She didn't kid herself, though. Once the mission ended, in spite of his declaration of love, they'd probably go their separate ways. *Am I out of my mind? I barely survived the first time Mac drove me away. I'll never survive losing him a second time.*

"Earth to Eve. Earth to Eve."

"Sorry, I'm just wool gathering."

"Anything you want to share?"

"No, nothing important."

With a warm hand on her back, Mac guided her the few feet to the plunge pool created by the waterfall. Skillfully, he shed their clothes, and with them, her caution.

In the quiet morning light, they took turns counting and kissing each other's scars, the ritual both familiar and comforting. Counting and kissing led to lovemaking.

Yeah, I'm crazy and keep coming back for more.

☙

An hour later, a very sated Eve navigated her cast through the sleeve of her T-shirt while Mac returned their supplies to the bags. Sitting next to her while she finished dressing, he checked and re-loaded the guns, including hers. An inkling of irritation struck like lightning, but she let it slide. For the most part her pain was gone, but with her arm in a cast, letting him help seemed easier.

He passed the loaded Glock to her, and she slipped it in her waistband. A repeat performance and her second gun was ready and tucked away. Mac dug around in the backpack and brought out a bottle of water.

"You want one?"

"Hey, I'm impressed, Mac."

"Impressed?"

She grinned. "You *asked* if I wanted water instead of *demanding* I take it. Has an alien taken possession of your body? Have they come to take you back to the mother ship?"

"I can make nice when I'm in the mood or...." He dipped his head in close and a whisper tickled her ear. "Or, when I have the right motivation."

"We made nice most of last night. And, I have a feeling you got just the right kind of motivation you needed." Flashes of Mac running his strong hands and kissable lips from one end of her dripping body to the other sent shivers through her. Her nipples tightened. "I have to agree, we made lots of nice last night. The motivation was definitely the right kind." Mac shook the water bottle. "Yes or no?"

"Yes. Thank you." She unscrewed the lid and smiled.

"You ready for the hike to the air strip?"

"Yes."

"Let's head. Maybe after we clear the jungle we'll get lucky and catch a ride."

For about a half mile, they followed the same trail Mac hacked away the day before. Then they veered to the west and Mac began clearing a new path. Eve trailed behind and enjoyed the view, awed by every powerful, muscle-flexing swing Mac took.

Drizzle morphed into a downpour that soon slowed into a thick mist. Eve pushed sweat and rain-dampened hair from her face as she navigated the slippery ground and thick foliage. She forced her body to keep up with Mac. Eve grew stronger every day, but the hike was rapidly becoming one huge energy suck.

Two hours later, they reached the road leading into the city. The sun came out, warming the air into a sticky, humid consistency. She worked to draw a breath without coughing. "I can't believe one tiny, little bullet hole in my shoulder has fucked me up so much."

"Tiny hole?" He snorted a laugh. "You sure that hole isn't in your head?"

"I don't like to harp on minor details."

"Apparently."

Eve swiped moisture away from her face with her forearm. "It took a lot longer getting out of the jungle than getting in. I started to think we were lost."

"I didn't want to exit anywhere near where we entered...just in case." Mac gave her a Mr.-Know-It-All grin. She wanted to tell him where to shove his smile, but curbed the impulse and focused on keeping a rapid pace.

Staying close to the dense tree line, they hiked another thirty minutes. An old, battered pickup truck crawled toward them, engine spitting. Mac stepped from the trees and flagged the driver. The vehicle ground to a stop, brakes groaning with age.

He waved his arms in large circles. "*Paren! Por favor, Paren!* Stop! Please, stop!"

"*Que necesita transport?*" the old man asked.

"Yes, we need a ride."

The man eyed Mac, the rifle slung over his shoulder, and nodded. Mac helped Eve climb into the rusted bed of the truck. He propped the duffle bag behind her. Reclining, she sighed deeply. If they weren't on the run, she would've peeled off her borrowed boots.

"Feels good to sit." Eve stretched her neck, rubbed the fingers dangling from her cast, and sighed.

"You've had a long couple of weeks." Mac did a fair amount of stretching, too.

"The old guy wasn't fazed by your rifle."

Mac laughed. "Everyone in Colombia carries some sort of fire power from the day they're big enough lift the weight of a weapon. Loaded for bear is the norm in a country overrun with drug cartels, paramilitary militias, and rebel guerilla groups. He would've been more suspicious if I wasn't carrying."

"Point taken."

Mac held out the last water.

"Only if you'll share."

In three long gulps, Mac drank half. He handed the water to Eve and she finished it off, pleased he continued to play nice.

"We'll get more water onboard the chopper. Knowing Cade, there'll be plenty. Speaking of Cade, I better call him with our ETA."

"Have fun. I'm gonna lie back and enjoy what little breeze is coming my way."

Mac called Cade, who picked up immediately.

"What? You sitting on top of the phone?"

Cade laughed. "Damn near. How's the hike? Eve keeping up?"

"Our hiking days are finished, and Eve kept up just fine. She could out-hike your ass any day."

"Is that a little pride I hear in your voice?"

"Go to hell."

"Right after you."

"We're about forty-five minutes away, assuming our transport holds together. We'll be in an old battered pickup, moving slower than molasses in the Arctic."

"What color is the truck?" Cade asked around a garbled laugh. "Wouldn't want to open fire on the wrong vehicle."

"Funny." To be on the safe side, Mac answered, "Not really sure what color this piece of junk is. Could've been gray, or white at some point in time. Doesn't matter, you'll hear it coming long before you see us. This truck inspires a whole new elite class of clunkers."

"Sounds like a WWII tank."

"No shit. Try riding in the damn thing. I've got four new loose teeth."

Cade chuckled. "Unless I hear differently, we'll have the chopper locked and loaded, ready for liftoff the second you and Eve are onboard. Heads up, Mac. This place has been quiet all morning. Too fucking quiet for my liking."

"Copy that. See you in few."

Eve winced with every bump and pothole the old truck hit. He smoothed back errant strands of hair from her face. He couldn't tell if her skin was heated from the sun's hot rays, or the fever refusing to leave gracefully.

"Mac." One simple word, spoken so softly.

"Shouldn't be much longer."

"Beats walking," she said with a half-smile.

"I guess." He stretched his legs, laid his weapon across them. "You have any idea how long fevers usually last?"

"Depends on what's causing it, I guess. I think around day three, antibiotics should be working. My meds should be kicking ass by now. I think I still have a fever, but nothing like before."

He caressed her forehead. "I guess I do worry about you too much."

"No shit?" She mumbled.

"What did you say?" Mac leaned closer to hear above the roar of the truck.

"I said, how much longer?"

"Not long. Hang in there, baby."

"I will."

He'd hang in there, too and hopefully the ceasefire between him and Eve would hold until they completed their mission.

Chapter Fifteen

The airstrip came into view and Mac sought his teammates. Gears ground as the truck screeched to a teeth-jarring halt near the helicopter. Mac's head snapped forward with the jolt.

He spotted Cade standing in the doorway behind one of the mounted miniguns. His face intense, Cade had an assault rifle slung on his shoulder and held a pair of long-range binoculars. A smart man would steer clear of Cade in combat mode.

Corelli sat buckled into the starboard pilot seat, helmet and radio mic in place. His hand rested on the control stick, his focus guarding the starboard side of the helicopter.

Mac stood, tossed the backpack and duffle from the truck, and grabbed his rifle. He dug out some of the cash he'd taken from the safe house, and passed a few bills to the old man through the driver's window. Eve climbed down and jogged to the helicopter, Mac following close behind. He tossed the bags through the open door, helped Eve inside, and boarded the chopper in one smooth, quick movement the way he'd done so many times before.

"Let's get this bird in the air, Corelli," Cade yelled into his mic. He faced Eve and smiled slyly. "Good to see you walking on this time."

"As opposed to being carried inside, unconscious, and

drooling?" She smiled.

"You got it," Cade said with a wink and a nodded greeting to Mac. "Nice truck, Mac. Thinking about buying the hunk of junk?"

"Beat hiking the whole way." Mac relaxed as the chopper rose from the tarmac, shifted, and cleared the area.

"Special delivery from your boss." Cade tossed Eve a bag. "Sanders said the things in there might come in handy."

Eve pulled out a pair of boots and replaced the borrowed pair from the safe house. "Much better fit." She lifted a Glock exactly like the one Mendoza's men had taken from her. "The man knows what he's doing." She took a sturdy bra out next, looked it over, and shoved it back inside the goody bag.

Cade passed her an envelope. "He sent this, too."

Eve read the note then dug the bra out again. She felt the side seams and grinned.

Mac said. "What's up?"

"New flash drives hidden inside. Might come in handy if I can't find the one I hid."

"Sewn in the bra?" Mac said.

"IDEA is always coming up with new crap for us to try."

"That's a nifty spy toy." Cade's eyes held a lazy gleam. "Wanna model it for us?"

Mac let loose a stream a string of curse words.

"Turn around, boys. I want to put this on."

"Hey, with your arm in a cast and all," Cade offered, "I'm happy to give you a hand."

"You fucking try, and I'll rip off your head." Mac shifted. "I'll help."

"You guys act like cavemen. I can do this by myself. And no peeking."

"You heard her, Cade."

"Really, Mac." Eve grunted and groaned a few times, but soon said, "Okay. You can turn back."

"You need an equipment check, Eve? I'm your man," Cade said and ducked as Mac sailed one of the discarded boots past him. "Just sayin'."

"Enough fuckin' around, Cade." Mac wiped his brow. "No Beauchamp this trip?"

"What you see is what you get, Corelli at the controls, me on weapons. You...or Eve, can take one of the miniguns if need be."

"Beauchamp still in debriefing?" Mac asked.

"No, he's moved on to another op. Hutch wanted him back on assignment ASAP since his last mission didn't end well. Like getting thrown from a horse, you gotta get right back in the saddle."

"I remember. He lost a hostage. Bad scene."

"Majorly bad, but Beauchamp has his head on straight. The Resolutions' shrink stamped him fit for duty. Good thing, too, he's got his work cut out this time around. Some gazillionaire's daughter is being held for ransom and Beauchamp's the unlucky bastard who gets to extract her rich little ass from the bad guys."

"What about Chapman?" Mac's footing shifted with the jarring of the chopper.

"Chappy is flying co-pilot on Beauchamp's op. He's still training and will stay with the transport until Beauchamp grabs the kidnap victim."

"Which basically means he's bored shitless right about now?" Mac laughed.

Cade smiled. "You got it. Poor schmuck. Sucks being the new kid on the block."

"Cade, you were the poor schmuck once upon a time."

"Hey, I was born experienced. I've never had to waffle through newbie status."

"Of course you were. What was I thinking?"

"Stop with the jokes. I don't understand why everything is so damned funny with you guys." Eve looked at Cade, then Mac. Slowly, she shook her head, her expression one of disgust.

"Hey, you gotta loosen up, or this job will take you down. Black humor, Eve. Helps relieve the stress." Mac studied her face. "You and your team never joked around in a tense situation?"

"Sure, we did. Danny Carlyle died because we made light of the situation." Her face darkened with something unreadable.

"Carlyle died because Mendoza got the drop on you and your team."

"We were too busy making fun of each other to see the ambush coming. Danny lost his life because we didn't keep our heads in the game."

"You and your team did your job. You can't second guess what you can't change."

Eve went quiet and buckled her harness. She'd let Carlyle's death weigh her down. Mac had learned firsthand how guilt ate away at your soul. Guilt had consumed his dad after his mother's death. He knew he should've protected his wife. Clearly women needed protection. But Eve didn't want to be shielded.

Mac moved to the front of the helicopter to check on Corelli. "Nice ride."

"This baby may be smaller than the MH 60K, but it packs more power. Hutch has some damn fine toys in his toy box."

"He does," Mac agreed. "What's our ETA to San Carlos Lucas?"

"A little over an hour, but I'd like to do a bit of recon before we land. Since Eve's extraction, Mendoza is bound to have the troops mulling around in full force. He's not gonna want to be caught with his pants down twice in a row."

"Copy that. Where you planning to put this bad bird down?"

Corelli flashed him a grin. "It definitely won't be where we touched down last time. The site is one hot zone I don't care to revisit anytime soon."

"Good plan, Corelli."

"I've got a couple places for insertion mapped out. We'll get a better look on recon, decide from there."

Mac smacked his shoulder. "Okay. Holler if you need anything beforehand."

Mac moved to the back and found Eve dozing sideways in her seat, her head against the headrest. She'd tied her shoulder length hair into a ponytail. Small wisps had escaped from the tie and fluttered in the gusts of warm wind created by the helicopter's movements. A faint sweat-bead necklace circled her throat just above the collar. Her heartbeat visibly pulsed at the base of her neck. Mac fought the urge to cover her soft, bare skin with kisses.

"Mac, you planning on standing there gawking at Eve all day?" Cade startled Mac from his daydream of helicopter sex with Eve.

"What? No...no...I was just thinking." Mac double-checked Eve's seatbelt, grabbed two bottles of water, and took a seat next to the one Cade had settled into. He unscrewed the top on one and tossed the other to his friend.

"Eve looks a lot better than last time I saw her." Cade said. "But, she went lights out the second her head hit the seatback. You sure she's ready for this op?"

"Fuck no, I don't think she's up to this. Eve seems to think she is. John Sanders thinks she is. But if I had my way, her ass would be in a hospital. Her temp still hasn't stabilized. That can't be a good sign."

"You two have a rough night?"

Mac smiled when he recalled every single detail of the night they'd spent together. *No, far from rough.*

"Hey, Mac, you want to keep your mind here in the present? You gotta get your shit together before we go boots on the ground."

"Yeah, yeah, I'm here. I'm ready to take on Mendoza. I can't wait to get my hands on him."

"You need to keep in mind finding Mendoza and killing him is not our mission. You've got to stick with the plan or Hutch will have your ass for breakfast."

"I'll do my job."

"Good to hear. In and out with the package, that's the deal."

"But if Mendoza gets in my way, all bets are off. I'll take the bastard down."

"Understood."

"You got it."

"So, Mac, what exactly is the plan for extraction? I assume Mendoza's grounds will be swarming with guards on both sides of the wall again."

"We'll go in underground again. You'll hang back while Eve and I head to the grounds to dig up the flash drive. We get back to the tunnels and you cover our butts. This plan should minimize the risk to Eve."

"If Eve can't find where she buried the flash drive?"

"Then the op will take a bit longer. We'll break into Mendoza's study and download the files...again. Then we get the fuck out. Hopefully all in one piece."

"I hate to sound pessimistic, but what if Mendoza's changed the password Eve used last time? If someone busted into my files, I'd change it first thing."

"That's what a normal person would do," Mac said with a snort. "Mendoza is cocky enough to think we can't get into the compound again." Mac rubbed his neck. "But, if I'm wrong and he did make a change...well...I guess we're fucked, and we haul ass to the LZ."

"Hutch says there's no new intel on Mendoza or a new password coming from IDEA's contacts. I assume if there's an update, Sanders would fill us in. Chances are good the old password is valid."

"We're not hearing new intel because IDEA's got no one left on the inside. Still, our luck may hold."

"Speaking of lucky, what's the deal with you and Eve? How lucky did you get last night?"

"You pervert, that's none of your business." Mac's face heated.

"Damn, not willing to share details. You got it bad."

"The thing is, Cade, I'm not sure I can handle Eve's job. Finding her all bruised and busted in Mendoza's cesspool tore my insides out. I practically lost control when I heard her screaming before I even got a glimpse at what the bastard had done to her. I could've really fucked up the extraction. I'm better off not knowing where she's at and what's happening. Especially when she's on missions."

"You haven't thought twice about her since you broke up? You've had no contact with her for two years and your life was better? You never worried about her?"

Mac had no answer.

"I rest my case." Cade smashed his empty water bottle and tucked the container under his leg. "You're gonna have to trust Eve's instincts. She's a first rate agent and doing a damn good job of hanging in there before you got her out of Mendoza's. That takes balls."

"I know all that crap. Doesn't make things any easier to handle. Having a set of balls won't keep her safe. Didn't help my mom, not one fucking iota."

"I know you don't want to hear this, but Eve's not in the same situation your mother was. Eve trained for the kinds of operations she's assigned."

"Training can't protect her from the Mendozas of the world."

"You're right," Cade agreed. "But the Mendozas of the world are everywhere. How many people are murdered by gangs, or druggies, in the U.S. every year? How many die during robberies and muggings?"

"I get your point."

Cade shook his head. "I don't think you do. You think life was a picnic for Eve when you were on the job? Asking Eve to give up her work isn't fair unless you're willing to do the same in return. You're an adrenaline junkie. Are you willing to sit behind a desk all day?"

"Eve and I will have to come to some kind of compromise."

"All fine and dandy, but you gotta have a two-way compromise."

Mac sighed and hung his head. "I get what you're saying. Now all I gotta do is figure in my head how to get past the fact my mom died while saving the world. I realize the chances are slim Eve will suffer the same fate. I gotta tell you, convincing myself to ease up isn't so simple."

"Exactly the reason I'm staying single. Relationships are not well-suited to this line of work."

"Falling in love isn't an option, Cade. It just happens. Trust me on that. I tried to put Eve out of my mind for two years. The task wasn't possible."

Cade's face hardened. "Falling in love? Not gonna happen. I'm single and staying that way."

"You may eat those words one day."

Mac moved to the seat next to Eve and laid his head back, letting the repetitious whump-whump-whump of the rotor blades drown his worries.

Chapter Sixteen

San Carlos Lucas
Mendoza Compound

Mendoza's informant sauntered through his front door and into the living room. He flopped onto one of the massive couches, grabbed the decorative throw pillows, and tossed them to one corner.

"*Cómo éstas, mi amigo. Bienvinido. Mi casa es su casa.* It has been a while. I did not think you liked to be seen around the compound. Too many waggling tongues, you say."

Mendoza pushed himself up with his cane, moved to the bar across the room, and poured shots of tequila into two crystal tumblers. He handed one to the man who'd been feeding him IDEA information.

"You're right, I don't trust your staff to keep quiet about my...well...let's just say...my association with you. I have good news I wanted to deliver in person."

"I wondered what you were up to, coming here unannounced. It is good news, no?"

"Excellent news, Miguel. I think you'll be pleased."

"Tell me, *mi amigo.*"

"You no longer need to look for Eve Taylor. She's coming to

you and bringing McKenna with her."

Mendoza said, "This is good news, very good news indeed."

"Gets better, Miguel. If Eve and McKenna are returning to the compound, they're coming for the flash drive. Which of course means the IDEA doesn't have info to use against you. The damned files never left the grounds."

"*Gracious a Dios!* You are right. I was sure such was the case, but could take no chances. I began moving some of my operations to new locations—just to be safe." He leaned forward, elbows on his knees. "You are absolutely sure about this?" If true, the files on his new business venture and his Afghani partners remained safe.

"I'm sure. I seriously doubt Eve is coming to San Carlos Lucas for a friendly visit with you, her all-time favorite drug lord and abuser. And Miguel, try not to let Carlos fuck things up again."

"*Sí*, I will make sure. This gives me great pleasure knowing I don't have to depend on the incompetent, *idiota* to find Miss Taylor and her *amante*. After trying to reclaim her for almost two weeks, I have very little faith in his ability to do anything right."

The other man snorted. "Carlos has no ability. He's more trouble than he's worth, Miguel. You should rid yourself of him."

"I would like nothing better, but you see, then I would have my sister to deal with. I can assure you, my sister is not fun to deal with. She can be such *la putita* at times."

"Familial ties are a messy business."

"*Sí*, this is so true."

"What do you plan to do with Eve after she arrives?" The informant asked.

"Do you really care? You'll get your payoff regardless."

"You're right. I like the money. When this is finished I plan on enjoying every fucking penny." He shrugged. "But once we were good friends, and I hate seeing her hurt."

"You should know by now, men in our line of work have no true *amigos*. Friendships are not good for business."

A flicker of regret crossed the informant's face.

"You get Miss Taylor to cooperate with me, and perhaps I will not to kill her. I will, however, enjoy her. I deserve this, no? She has been an annoying problem for me since she first came here. I will teach her to be obedient. If she learns to please me, I shall keep her for myself. If not, I will give her to Carlos to do whatever he pleases."

"I think Eve would prefer death over Carlos."

"*Mierda!*" Mendoza laughed. "I see your point. Perhaps you would like to have her if I decide not to keep her."

"No offense, but I'm not a big fan of leftovers. Not even a fine piece like Eve."

"Ah, yes. I believe they called this, 'sloppy seconds' in an American movie. You Americans can be so crude at times."

"What will you do with McKenna?"

"McKenna?" Mendoza rubbed his ruined leg. "I plan to kill him very painfully. I may even choose to let him watch me play with Miss Taylor first."

"That's one sure way to torture McKenna. Be careful, Miguel. The man won't be taken down easily."

"I remember."

"You should inform Carlos."

"I have many times, but will once again warn him. Speaking of Carlos, please excuse me one moment while I call the *pendejo cabron*! I need him to prepare for our guests' arrival. Do you know when we should expect them?"

"I would guess sometime later today, tomorrow morning at the latest."

Carlos arrived within five minutes. He bowed slightly to their guest, and then said to Mendoza, "You wish to see me, Miguel?"

"Yes, I do." Carlos shook. The weakness repulsed Mendoza, yet at the same time, gave him pleasure knowing he had the power to put the fear of God in his men. "Stop quivering like the coward you are. I'm not going to shoot you." *Yet.*

The exchange drew a laugh from the informant, still relaxed on the couch.

"I appreciate your generosity, Miguel." Carlos said.

"*Sí*, I'm sure you do. I have a job even you will find hard to fuck up, Carlos. I want you to prepare the men for the arrival of Miss Taylor and McKenna."

"But, Miguel, I have not located their whereabouts yet." He pointed to the informant. "Is this why he is here? He knows where they are?"

"Our friend has just informed me the two are returning to the compound. I want the grounds secured. You will double the guards. McKenna and Miss Taylor must be inside the walls before we take them. There is to be no chance of escape this time. Do you understand this, Carlos?"

"*Sí, Miguel.*" The man rocked from side to side.

"I want our people in San Carlos Lucas on alert and watching for anything out of the ordinary. I should be notified immediately of helicopters, or small airplanes landing in the area. They are to keep watch for any strangers who may show up during the next forty-eight hours."

"I will see to the arrangements, Miguel."

Mendoza nodded, satisfied. "When Miss Taylor and McKenna arrive, I want them taken alive. What I do not want, Carlos, is for you to fuck up. This really is your last chance to prove you are not the idiot you appear to be."

"I can do this, Miguel. You can rest assured, the *señorita* will soon be yours and you will have the satisfaction of torturing and killing McKenna."

"Let's hope so, Carlos, because sister or no sister, I will kill you if you fail me this time."

Chapter Seventeen

Mac switched into battle mode as Corelli landed the Little Bird effortlessly in a tight clearing eight kilometers from Mendoza's compound. The rotor blades breathed their last breath and stopped circling.

Cade gathered the two backpacks loaded with supplies they'd need for the mission. "Nice landing, Corelli."

"I've got the magic touch." He rubbed his hands together. "I could land any aircraft on a bumble-bee's ass if needed."

"Cocky son of a bitch, aren't you?"

Corelli shrugged. "Just being honest."

"Don't you think you should share some of the credit with Hutch?" Cade needled him. "You know, the man who added all the expensive modifications that make flying the aircraft so easy?"

"Hey, this baby is one sweet ride with all the add-ons, but you still gotta have talent to squeeze into the miniscule space I just put down in."

Spreading his arms, Cade conceded, "You win. You're the best at tight vertical landings I've ever seen. But I do worry one of these days you're not going to be able to see around that big head of yours and you, and your perfect landings, will be history."

"Knock it off. Let's review the plan one more time." Mac stood and pulled on one of the two backpacks. "Cade, Eve, and I go in, get the flash drive, and meet Corelli back here. We'll radio when we've got the goods and are on the move. Corelli, you'll find someplace safer to wait this one out—it's too much of a hotspot here right now and you're minus a gunner."

Corelli looked through binoculars, his head turning in long easy movements. "Ah, now we're talkin'. A damned nice mountaintop to the south looks like a good place to sit and wait. From this point the flight will take about seven minutes."

Mac, keeping a watchful eye on things, said, "Sounds like a good holding spot. We're also gonna need a new extraction point since I imagine we've been spotted at the current landing zone."

"Mac's right, Corelli, even with the quiet ride of this little baby, I'd bet my left nut we were seen."

"Cade, you've got to have a set of balls before you can gamble with them." Corelli winked.

"You may be the pilot jock, but I'm the man with the big *cojones*," Cade shot back.

Mac said, "This LZ is hot and no longer a feasible area for withdrawal. We can't fucking sit here jabbering much longer."

"I'll find another extraction point." Corelli pulled out a map and the three men studied it. Corelli pointed to an area. "This one's doable. When you give me a call, I'll head there. The new LZ is bound to be safer. Being a bit closer is another plus. If you're under fire on exit, you won't have far to run."

"Good. I like safer and closer," Mac said. "Exactly what's our location now, Corelli? We're about what, twenty kilometers out of downtown San Carlos Lucas?"

The pilot nodded. "We're about twenty-four clicks outside city center. The Mendoza compound is about four clicks south of here. On a good day you could hike from this point to Mendoza's in about hour and a half. But rain poured like piss out of a bucket all night and jungle conditions are gonna slow you down considerably. It could take up to three hours. From what we saw on our short aerial recon, you've got a good scattering of Mendoza's men to work around—or through."

"Eve's still not at full speed. Gonna be a tough haul for her." Cade gathered his weapons.

"It'd be better to eliminate Mendoza's men on the way in, not have them slowing us down on the way out." Mac put the diagram away. "I'll handle Eve."

"I don't need handled, Mac. Not by you or anyone else," Eve said, sounding pissed.

All three of the men turned. She unbuckled her harness and stood.

"You're awake. Good timing." Mac wished he could back-peddle.

"Yeah, I'm awake, but you're obviously too busy planning how to take care of the little woman to notice. I can keep up without your help." She glared at the other two men. "Or anyone else's."

Cade and Corelli jumped from the helicopter, started the outside check of the chopper, and Mac sensed, wanting to stay far away from the unavoidable confrontation he and Eve were about to have. He rubbed his face, wanting to join them.

"Dammit, Eve, I didn't mean I needed to take care of you, I just meant—"

"I know exactly what you meant." She added a sheathed K-bar knife to her belt, grabbed one of the assault rifles Cade had brought along, and tossed the strap over her good shoulder. "Let's finish this. The quicker this mission is completed, the sooner our partnership is finished. It's too hard to be around you."

"Wait, Eve. Listen, I'm sorry if I offended you. I know you can keep up."

"You want to smother me. I can't handle the alpha shit anymore. I can't change what happened to your mother, and I damned well can't live my life trying to make up for her death. Let's be honest, we just aren't meant to be together."

Mac grabbed her good arm. "Eve, don't write me off yet. We can work through this. We'll talk later."

"Not gonna happen." She pulled away.

Eve hopped from the AH-6J and stood with both feet apart in front of Cade and Corelli. "You two don't have to worry about me not pulling my weight. I'm good to go."

She spun around and stomped off toward Mendoza's

compound.

"Shit, Mac, I think you've gone and pissed your lady off big-time. Gonna make this job all kinds of fun." Cade smiled sheepishly.

"He so fucking did." Corelli leaned against the helicopter. "I almost wish I could hike in with you guys."

Cade swung the other pack on his shoulder and snapped a brazen, animated salute at Corelli. In spite of his anger, Mac couldn't hold back a quick chuckle. He took off, caught up with Eve, and took the lead.

Eve didn't acknowledge him and stayed a good ten paces behind.

Talk about a major pride buster. Damn this is going to be long op.

Cade edged up to Eve. "Listen, about what I said back there? I only meant you're not at full speed because of your injuries."

"Don't sweat it, Cade. I know what you meant. I'm not angry with you or Corelli. I'm just frustrated with your alpha pal up there."

"He can be a pain in the ass." Cade swiped away a kamikaze mosquito.

"You two wanna cut the talk and stay alert back there?" Mac whispered over his shoulder.

"Copy that, sir," Cade said and then flipped him off.

Eve bit back a laugh. *Yeah, Mac can be an ass.*

Two and a half hours later, they'd worked their way through the thick foliage to the hidden entrance of the underground passageways. Eve pulled at her sticky shirt, letting air inside. Once she let go, the material suctioned to her skin again. "Damn it's hot."

Mac added, "Too fucking humid to breathe, but we made good time."

There was a distant movement to their left and Eve slipped behind some bushy fronds. Mac and Cade faded into the shadows along with her.

"The area is crawling with Mendoza's men," Eve whispered.

"Going in through the tunnels will be risky, but scaling the wall would've been impossible."

Mac said, "Mendoza fucked up once. He's gonna want to avoid any further breaches."

They silently took out several of the guards and hid their bodies in the undergrowth. After reaching the hidden entrance, they dug in for a quick surveillance of the area.

Cade brushed his ankle. "Fuck me. If one more goddamn fire ant bites me I'm going to shoot the little fucker."

Eve couldn't help smiling.

Mac studied the area through small binoculars. "Hold off on shooting them for a while longer. I think we can make a clean run to the entrance after the next guard passes by. The two-man patrols are averaging about six minute intervals."

Eve said, "Mac, you know the tunnels. How do you want to handle this?"

"You and I go first. We'll move the greenery and the mossy rock away from the opening. The sucker's big, but lightweight."

"Mac, the *sucker* is a boulder."

He and Cade gave her stereotypical masculine smiles, irritating the shit out of her. Eve half-expected one of them to pat her on the head.

Mac said, "We won't have a problem with the entrance. Cade, when we're in, you follow and cover our tracks. We'll secure the entrance afterwards. If any of Mendoza's men come by, we stick with our K-bars or hand to hand like we've been doing. We don't want to draw any attention with gunfire. Once Eve and I reach the opening, our view of the outside will be obstructed, so give us a signal if you need a hand."

Eve acknowledged Mac's plan with a nod. Cade followed suit. They all made a quick weapons check. Eve stuck her fingers inside her cast and stroked the small, hidden knife she'd secured from the safe house.

Two of Mendoza's guards clambered by, chatting and smoking cigarettes. They stopped in front of the bush hiding Eve. She inched deeper into the thick foliage. Holding an index finger to his lips, Mac stood a few feet away.

Right. Like I'm going to do a wild dance and draw attention to myself. He's in his protect-the-little-woman mode again. If she'd blinked, she'd have missed the quick grin that raced across Cade's lips. Cade was catching on.

The taller of the two guards dropped his cigarette and stamped on the butt. He took out a banano and lighted the tip. Eve recognized the smell—rolled marijuana laced with cocaine—a favorite of Mendoza's crew. Laughing and grabbing for the new smoke, the second guard flicked his finished cigarette into the bushes they were hiding in. When the butt landed on Mac, burning a small hole in his sleeve, and most likely his skin, he gently pushed it off, never flinching.

The two guards stood in place, their backs to her, passing the banano between them. So much for a clean run to the tunnel entrance.

Mac signaled Cade. Before Eve had a chance to react, they'd jumped behind the guards, locked their arms around the men's necks, and gave them a quick twist. The guard's spinal cords snapped. A clean kill.

Mac and Cade hid the bodies in the thick overgrowth.

Eve whispered, "The banano smokes explain a lot about the level of intelligence of Mendoza's men. The bastards have fried what little brain cells they had to begin with."

The comment won her a quiet laugh from both Mac and Cade.

"Ready?" Mac winked at her.

Eve winked back. She could be condescending, too. "Let's do this."

Mac and Eve dashed to the hidden opening. Carefully, they pressed back the shrubs. Eve took a deep breath and prepared to push the large rock out of the way. It slid easily, caught her off balance, and her butt landed on the ground.

"A hollowed boulder? You could've told me before I fell on my ass."

"What, ruin the chance to see the expression on your face?" Mac grinned.

She smacked his arm. "Ha-ha, I'm glad I could amuse you."

"I love a woman with a good sense of humor."

Mac and Eve startled at the sound of Cade's feet shuffling across the path and went silent. Cade used a leafy branch to cover their tracks. Once Cade cleared the entrance, he helped Mac repositioned the greenery and pull the hollowed boulder back in place. Mac flipped on a small flashlight.

Cade glanced around their surroundings. "Damn. We must be standing in the entrance to hell."

"Mendoza's hell," Mac agreed.

Cade said, "Get the monster-size rock moved?"

"You little shit," Eve snapped with a tight smile. "You knew the hunk of stone weighed zilch. Now I understand the over-inflated egos the two of you had when I questioned whether or not the damned thing could be moved."

"Sorry. Mac's plan. He's the little shit, not me."

Mac said, "Back stabber."

Cade thumped his chest. "And damn proud of it."

"There's way too much testosterone in this little space for me. Back to work, guys. Let's get inside the compound so I can finish the mission Mendoza so rudely interrupted."

Flashlight in hand, Mac led the way, Eve in the middle, Cade bringing up the rear. The tunnels were dark and grew warmer the deeper they went. Stale, humid air filled Eve's nostrils and reminded her of the pure evil she'd encountered here. A streak of fear gripped her insides, threatened to twist them in knots. *Don't panic, don't panic, don't panic. I can do this.* She took a deep breath, exhaled. Several deep breaths later, she'd shaken off most of the anxiety.

Cade said, "So many tunnels and chambers."

His comment brought her the rest of the way back from the edge of a full-blown melt down. "The compound wasn't always Mendoza's personal paradise. I read something about mining being one of San Carlos Lucas' main industries decades ago. I'm not sure what they mined here."

"This was a silver mine," Mac said. "The mines dried up, the coca plants grew, and like most of Colombia, the drug trade became the area's main source of income. Mendoza deals all major drugs, but the rumor is he's about to gear his operations to specialize in cocaine."

And dealing arms to terrorists. Sanders should've let these men know exactly what we're dealing with here. Or let me tell them. Eve couldn't stop the sharp stab of regret that hit dead center in her chest.

"The chemist I extracted was the head lab geek who created a new strain of coca plant capable of yielding four times more cocaine than the old variety."

Eve rubbed the side of her neck, soothed away knots of tension, and let go of the guilt. *Get your head back in the game.* "I guess you validated the cocaine rumor."

"If Mendoza's cartel wasn't the leader of the pack before, this little move will push him to top status," Cade said.

Mac's chemist was *that* chemist, the lead chemist and probably the one who developed the deadly toxin. "Jeez, Mac, no wonder Mendoza hates you so much. You took his top dog."

"Nah, he hates me because I put a bullet in his leg, making him Mr. Gimpy for the rest of his soon-to-be-short life. Best shot I ever fired...at least until I put a bullet between his beady little eyes."

Eve said, "I wouldn't mind a chance to take Mendoza out."

Cade said, "It's gonna feel good when Mendoza goes down, no matter who fires the kill shot."

"We've lost some good men pursuing this bastard." A sadness Eve couldn't fight crept through her. "Shutting him down can't come fast enough for me. The information I downloaded is enough to take him out once and for all. His business associates, too. Growers, suppliers, lowly dealers. Even a few dirty customs and law enforcement officers." *And let's not forget terrorists.* She wanted to tell Mac and Cade everything. "I also got names of his murder victims, kill dates, locations, and even why Mendoza had them executed."

Mac said, "The murdering son of a bitch played God with a

lot of lives."

Isn't that what she and Sanders were doing? A man should know exactly what he is fighting for, what he might die for. Shouldn't he?

"He kept records of his hits? Seems risky," Cade said.

"Risky, cocky, whatever. He kept specific, play by play records, not only of the killings, but of the torturing beforehand. I'm sure he gets his rocks off every time he reads them." Eve pushed back a wisp of hair that had fallen in her eyes. "The bastard probably has written details about me."

Mac hissed. "Fucking bastard. Death is way too easy for the son of a bitch. But he's got to die."

For once they agreed.

Chapter Eighteen

Eve wiped away a trail of sweat rolling down the side of her neck. A fly whizzed past and the buzzing echoed in her ears. Mac kept a steady pace. The way he navigated, his small flashlight doing little to alleviate the darkness, amazed her.

They came to a large vertical grate blocking the tunnel. Mac held up a hand. She and Cade stopped. Mac took his backpack off, pulled two bottles of water and handed one to Eve. Cade grabbed one of his own. The sloshing of the water in the bottles seemed loud in the stillness of the tunnel.

"Right up ahead, we'll reach the main underground area." Mac pointed to his right. "To our far right are prison cells, to the left, the stairwell to the grounds. Straight ahead, the stairway leading to the interior of the villa."

Eve didn't remember the stairs that led outside, but knew she'd been dragged up them to the living quarters. The dark hall leading to the cells was familiar also. She'd never forget the smells of the musty, decayed air. The scent of death.

Focusing on Mac's words, she fought another small surge of panic threatening to erupt. Her chest tightened and she looked first to Mac, and then to Cade.

"You okay, Eve? Gotta be tough being back here," Cade said.

She worked through the panic one more time. In control again, she answered, "I'm fine. Thanks. I'm just trying to visualize the areas Mac is talking about. My mind's a little fuzzy."

Not a total lie. Eve tried to get her bearings straight. In the snatches of weak light Mac's flashlight offered, Cade had seen her panicked look. If he'd seen, Mac had probably noticed, too. If he did, Mac chose not to mention the short episode.

Eve shook the iron grate. "How do we get around this? This is the right passageway isn't it?"

"Oh, ye of little faith." Mac put a hand on each of her upper arms and moved her aside. He pulled a small rock from the wall, took a key from underneath, and stuck the odd shaped key into a small crack in one of the metal bars. A slight twist, followed by a snap, and the grate swung open. Mac replaced the key and rock.

Mac toed a similar rock on the other side of the gate. "This has a key, too." He pointed to the bar he put the key in. "This crack has an identical one on other side. You'd have to get pretty damn close to tell this is a keyhole, not a break in the metal."

Eve ran her hand around the crevice, leaned in closer. "This explains why they don't think the tunnel is usable. The grate seems planted solid into the rocky sides of the walls and non-functioning. What great craftsmanship."

"The chemist told me it's been here fifty years or more. Said there were other passageways with hidden locks, but this was the only one he found. Who knows, maybe the others were destroyed."

Mac faced Cade. "Hang loose, but keep your guard up. Give us about an hour to work our way around all of Mendoza's guards and dig up the flash drive. If for some reason we have to go inside the villa and download another, we'll need more time. If we're not back in about two hours, you'd best come running."

Cade said, "There's nothing I love more than hanging out in dark, hot tunnels that smell like piss and death warmed over."

"Yep, every man's aspiration, and you're one of the lucky few who actually get to live the dream." Mac handed Cade his flashlight. "If you trek back to the entrance of the tunnel, you'll be able to call on the sat phone. Give Hutch an update, let him know we're in, and will radio from the chopper once we're airborne."

"Copy that." You two keep a heads up. Good luck."

"Thanks," Mac said. "Time to play, Eve. Ready?"

"Oh, yeah."

It took about ten minutes to reach the point where the mouth of the tunnel opened into the long hallway with access to several chambers. Leaning, backs against the wall, they watched and listened.

Mac nudged her. "Clear. Let's head left and take the stairs outside."

"I'm right behind you."

They were almost to the stairs when the stifled voices of men approaching had Eve pausing. They darted into a recessed doorway. Hidden in the concaved area, Eve moved back and Mac scooted closer. He stood solid, his back to her front, with a gun in one hand, his knife in the other. She hadn't even seen him draw the knife from the sheath. *He's good.*

Through her thin shirt, the firm muscles of his back nestled against her breasts. Her nipples pebbled on contact. *Great. Did Mac notice*? Her heart pounded against his spine. *Yay, me! Show Mac what he does to my libido.* Occasionally she peeked around his upper arms to scan the dimly lit hallway. Her Colt remained pressed to her side, ready for anything.

Two of Mendoza's men passed. Eve held her breath until they were out of range. "Why do bad guys always travel in pairs?"

"Normally I'd say for moral support, but these guys have no morals." Mac slid his knife back inside the sheath.

They stepped from their hiding place and, without a sound, hurried to the stairs leading up and out of the underground. They reached the door and slipped onto the grounds.

Eve paused just outside the door and let her eyes adjust to the light. She studied the area, tried to get her bearings.

"You okay?" Mac stood close, the vein along his temple pulsating.

"Couldn't be better. Don't you ever get tired of asking?"

"Never."

"Of course you don't. Now all I have to do is try to remember where I hid the flash drive."

"You're kidding? Aren't you?"

She focused on a vaguely familiar spot. The right spot.

"Yeah, just kidding."

☙

Mac followed Eve as she moved with a practiced grace he could only admire. And admire, he did. Damn, she was easy to look at.

He followed her as she scrambled to a cluster of breadnut and mango trees. Chewing on her bottom lip, Eve skimmed the area and said, "Somewhere around here is the mango trunk I marked." Her gaze settled on three large fruit trees standing side by side.

"That it?" Mac stayed close and kept an eye out for trouble. The place seemed too quiet, too easy to get to. His fingertips tingled. Mendoza's compound had been breached twice in less than two weeks. There should be more patrols this close to the house. Not a good sign.

"I'm looking for one with a piece of bark bent back and a V shaped mark on the trunk. Should be right about here. Yes! This one."

At the base of the tree, Eve fell to her knees and brushed away the leaves and rocks covering a small mound of dirt. Mac stayed alert while she used her K-bar knife and dug up the clear zip-lock bag that held the downloaded flash drive.

She held the bag and examined the contents. "Looks intact."

"Good. Now let's blow this place. I don't want to push our luck."

"Hold on." Switching from her kneeling position, she sat, and held her right leg up to Mac. "Grab my boot, Mac. With this cast on, it'll take me forever. I didn't get the chance to use the hidey hole last time."

Mac hesitated for a few moments before taking the offered boot. Keeping a firm grip with one hand, he asked, "Now what?"

"There's a small hidden compartment in the heel. Use your knife, pry the flap open, and place the flash drive inside. Leave it in the plastic bag."

Mac complied. "Handy little compartment."

"It is."

"You don't want to stash the drive in the bra Sanders sent?"

"This will work."

"Ok." After he inserted the flash drive, Mac used the handle of his knife to hammer the heel back in place. He lowered her foot and gave her a hand up. "Finished. Now can we get the fuck out of here, Eve?" The tingling in his fingertips increased. Mental alarms were going off.

Mac turned at the same time one of Mendoza's minions stepped from behind a flowering bush to the left of him. Before the guard had time to yank his AK-47 from his shoulder, or yell a warning, Mac pulled the man against his chest, and slit the guard's throat.

He wiped his knife on the dead man's shirt and tucked the K-Bar back into the sheath. Soundlessly, he laid the body down, and pushed it under the same bush he'd emerged from. Mac and Eve spread leaves around the body and over the blood soaked ground, leaving behind no trace of the kill. He expected to see horror written on Eve's face. Instead he saw steely determination. The woman constantly amazed him. They hustled back toward the underground tunnels.

They reached the entrance, ready to head underground. Mac positioned his side to her back, guarding their retreat—and her. Uneasy vibes got stronger by the second and he doubted he'd be able to shake the feeling of impending disaster until they touched down on American soil again.

Eve turned the door handle and pulled. The door burst open, knocking her against Mac. From the shadows, six armed men surged forward.

Mac dropped to one knee and raised his rifle at the men. Eve propped her hip against Mac's shoulder. She shuddered violently then went still, seemingly frozen in place.

"Oh...my...God. This can't be...real," she mumbled. Her head tipped to an odd angle and her gaze clouded over.

The last man stepped from of the shadows and stood in front of the other five. "It's fucking real, doll face. It's me in the flesh."

Eve held her gun in a white-knuckled grip and pointed it straight at his head. As if hypnotized, she drifted toward him, leaving Mac a few steps behind.

"Eve, stop!" Mac's gut churned, and he swallowed the acid rising in his throat. "Dammit, Eve, what the fuck are you doing?"

Mac stopped and pointed his assault rifle at the man. At least five guns shifted in his direction.

She stopped a mere foot in front of her target. "Danny?" Eve whimpered.

Danny grabbed her wrist, the one holding the Glock. "Hey, doll face. Watch the gun. Don't want to ruin my good looks, do you?" He lowered her hand, the gun still in her grip.

Mac wanted to tear the guy's head off for touching her.

"You won't need the gun, Eve. You and McKenna can't shoot your way past us." Danny pointed a thumb in Mac's direction. "Tell him to put down his weapon and you pass yours over."

Eve didn't move. Danny squeezed her hand until she loosened her grip. He retrieved the Glock and then tucked it into his waistband. He slipped the rifle she had on her shoulder off and handed it to a guard.

Eve's mouth opened but no words came. Her head shook slightly, her expression blank.

Mac had to force his knees not to buckle. He tightened his hold on his rifle. "Eve? Baby, you're scaring the shit out of me."

"Danny?" She said brokenly. "I saw you go down, a bullet to the chest. You had no pulse, Rex checked. You were dead. How...how is this possible?"

"Do you believe in magic, doll face?" He laughed. "Not Eve Taylor. You were always too smart to fall for any bullshit."

Danny? No wonder Eve's in shock.

"You're alive." Hesitantly, she touched Danny's arm.

Danny brushed her hand away. "Back off, Eve. In case you haven't figured things out yet, I'm one of the bad guys."

Eve shook her head. "What'd they do to you? You were shot."

"I wasn't hurt, much less killed. Had my trusty Kevlar vest on."

"You had no pulse."

"Wrong again. I plastered a bit of rubber facial putty—the kind funeral homes use, around my throat. The shit blocks your pulse. Pretty good stuff, but I got to tell you, the crap itches like a son of a bitch."

"You faked your death?"

Mac ached for her. The woman had truly mourned this piece of shit standing before her, had even blamed herself for his death.

"Like I said, you can't pull the wool over your eyes. The plan was pure perfection. I needed to sneak under the task force radar so I could disappear. It's time to enjoy all the money I've made off our good friend, Miguel." He glanced away. "There was also the minor detail of Sanders beginning to wonder how Mendoza and his cartel kept slipping through the cracks. And here I was, hoping I could work this gig forever."

"You've been feeding information to Mendoza? Why?"

"Why? Well, I make a shitload more money working for Mendoza than I could ever make with the DEA, IDEA, or any other alphabet agency. More money than I ever dreamed of. I couldn't retire on the measly pension the government pays."

Since the conversation began, she stood in one place, as if in a trance. But she shifted, and Mac thanked God she was coming back.

"You were part of the team, Danny. Me, Rex, Randi, we were your friends. How could you betray us?"

The other man smiled. "A man can do all kinds of things for the right price."

"You make treason sound so simple."

"Far from simple, Eve. We planned on Brewer getting away

so he could tell Sanders about my unfortunate demise. Randi, the slippery little bitch, wasn't supposed to survive, but Mendoza's men fucked up. And you? Another part of the plan that didn't quite pan out."

Danny looked at Mac, then back to her. "I never meant for you to be hurt. Mendoza told me he wanted to keep you for his own. I guess he's tired of his Colombian whores. I really did think he'd treat you better than he did. With the money he has, I figured you'd learn to like him."

"Do you hear what you're saying, Danny? Randi was supposed to die?"

"I never did like her."

"You sold me to Mendoza as if I'm some piece of meat? How do you sleep at night?"

Mac said, "Men like him have no conscience, Eve. Isn't that right, Carlyle? You're no better than Mendoza." Mac's jaw tightened until his teeth threatened to crumble.

Danny ignored Mac. "I swear, Eve, you weren't supposed to get roughed up. How could I have known you'd hide the flash drive and go all G.I. Jane on us? You should've told Mendoza where you hid the damned thing."

"What about your family and your girlfriend? How could you let them think you're dead?"

"I have no family. Lynda will be fine. She'll forget all about me in no time and move on with the rest of her life."

"You're responsible for all the IDEA agents who have been killed during the last two years? What's the going rate these days for selling out your friends? Your country? How do you justify so many deaths, Danny?"

Danny shrugged. "Some sacrifices are necessary."

She lunged at Danny. "You bastard, you're a monster."

He pushed her away. "I've been called worse."

Eve said, "I can't believe I called you my friend, or wasted a single tear on you."

"Eve, I really am sorry Mendoza and his men hurt you."

"You're sorry, Danny? You and your bastard friends have

been trying to kill me since Mac rescued me from Mendoza's cells."

"When McKenna busted you out, we couldn't take a chance you'd retrieved the files and taken them with you. Rumor was you were thinking about selling the info to a rival drug cartel instead of turning the goods in to Sanders. You had to be stopped."

"Bullshit, Danny. I'd never sell out. That's your style." Her hand clenched into a fist. Mac was glad anger replaced her shock.

"When we learned you and McKenna were coming back to the compound, we were finally sure you'd left the intel on the grounds. Mendoza was one happy bastard. We just had to sit back and wait for you to show."

"McKenna, I've always wanted to meet you in person." Danny jerked his chin at Mac. "I must say I'm a little disappointed. The way Eve brags on you—at least until you two parted ways—I kind of expected you to be an eight-foot tall god of some sort. You're a mere mortal like the rest of us."

"You're no man. You're nothing but a fucking murderer and a coward." Mac glared.

"Such harsh words, McKenna."

Mac sized up the situation and the man standing in front of Eve. She still had another gun in her waistband. If she would just step a few feet back, Mac could take Carlyle, and together they had a decent shot at taking out the other five men. As if Carlyle had read his mind, he yanked Eve in front him and pulled her weapon.

"Don't even try, McKenna." He held Eve's Colt to her head. "I'll kill her and Mendoza's men will drop you like a fly in nothing flat. Lay down your piece, nice and easy, and kick it here."

Eve struggled against Danny, but he seized her injured arm and she winced. "Don't, Mac. Keep the gun and shoot the son of a bitch," Eve pleaded.

"Now, doll face, is that any way to talk about an old friend?"

Danny chuckled and tightened his grip.

She paled.

"Let us go, Danny. You can give yourself up and cut a deal. Sanders will work something out with you." Eve stared at Mac, but her words were meant for Danny.

"Gee, now there's a great quandary. Spend the rest of my life behind bars, or spend it on a nice sunny island somewhere, sucking down fruity drinks decorated with little pink umbrellas, and lounging next to the hot bod chick of the day. What option do you think I'll choose?"

"Then take your blood money and run. Let Mac and me go." Eve practically spit the words.

Mac was proud she didn't show the fear he was sure she kept buried deep inside her.

"Not a likely scenario, doll face."

"Danny, Mendoza will kill us."

"I don't really have much of a choice here, Eve. Besides, Mendoza's not going to kill you. I think he has a thing for you. If you're real nice to him, he'll keep you around."

"Keep me around? To use for his whore and punching bag?"

"At least you'd be alive."

"What about Mac? He'll kill him."

Danny shrugged. "A casualty of war."

"Fuck you, Danny." Eve stomped on his foot, twisted, and shook loose.

Eve stepped forward. Something hard whacked her shins and she tumbled to the ground, her legs helter-skelter. A blinding burn hit her on impact. A scuffle arose behind her and instinctively she knew Mac had bolted toward her.

Danny fired his gun in the air and Eve stilled. She prayed Mac had done the same.

"Stay back, McKenna. Unlike Carlyle, I will put a bullet between the lovely Miss Taylor's eyes without hesitation."

Mendoza. Tremors shot through Eve, her belly churning with every quiver.

Ignoring the pain, she flipped into a sitting position, queasiness bombarding her insides. She fought the out-of-control pounding in her chest making her lightheaded.

Barely hanging on to what little control she had left, Eve let loose a quick sigh of relief. Mac had stopped moving forward. He looked at her, clearly torn by anguish and concern. She wondered how he would've handled this situation if she wasn't involved. She had a pretty good idea and it involved a lot of shooting and dead bodies.

"Now drop the gun," Mendoza said.

Mac laid his rifle down and held his arms high, placing his hands on top of his head. The guards frisked him and removed his two handguns and knife.

"See how easy disarming a man can be, Carlyle?"

Chapter Nineteen

Miguel Mendoza laughed and glared at Eve. She sat awkwardly on the damp ground, rubbing her shin. He stroked the intricately carved ivory handle of the cane he'd used to trip her.

"Ah, *querida*, what is it about you I can't seem to resist?" He poked her with his cane.

She stiffened and thrust her chin upward. "Fuck you, Miguel."

"Be patient. We will soon get to that part of my plan." He circled her. Eve studied him and searched for a way out.

"I love a woman who is all fire. I've never wanted to break a woman so badly in my life. Even now, sprawled on the ground beneath me you somehow manage to stay insolent and ready to strike."

"I'll kill you, Miguel," she hissed.

"See, this is why you make my blood boil like lava, like a volcano waiting to erupt. Since the day you were brought to me, I've been a patient man, showing remarkable restraint. Your wound and fever kept me from having you immediately. After all, what fun would there be in taking a woman in such a weakened state? I want you in full fighting strength when I bed you."

Eve said, "That will never happen."

Mac struggled against the men holding him.

Mendoza pointed his gun at him. "Pulling the trigger would be too easy a death for the man who has taken so much from me. You will soon receive the punishment you so rightly deserve."

"I think from the look on your face, you would kill me if given half a chance." Mendoza limped a step closer to Mac. "I have no intention of giving you the opportunity to strike."

And Mac would strike like a viper. There's something Eve would love to see.

"You've got that right, you fucking son of a bitch. I'll kill you the first chance I get." One of Mendoza's men yanked Mac's arm, and he cursed through gritted teeth.

Eve cringed and slapped away the hand Danny offered. Mendoza laughed as Eve scrambled to her feet. Mac moved forward to help her and Mendoza struck him.

"Miguel, leave him alone!"

"You brought McKenna with you this time, no? This is in very poor taste to bring an *antiguo amante,* old lover, to the home of your soon-to-be new lover. Or is McKenna a gift for me? A peace offering?"

Eve pushed past Danny and stood defiantly before Mendoza. She kicked his cane. "I'd shove that fancy cane up your ass, Miguel, but I'm afraid you'd enjoy it way too much."

"Ah yes, you are indeed feisty. You'll be a hellcat in bed."

"Go to hell!"

"That is no way for a lady to talk, but I will let your insolence slide this time." He said to his men, "Bring him closer." He circled Eve and stopped to face her. "Now, Miss Taylor, I know you would not be back in San Carlos Lucas unless you've come to retrieve the information you left behind." He held out a hand. "You will kindly hand me the flash drive."

"I have no idea what you're talking about, asshole."

Mendoza slapped Eve, snapping her head back.

Damn that hurt. She heard Mac grunting as he struggled to break free. Heartache and frustration blanketed Mac's face.

Mendoza said, "Mr. Carlyle, you hit the jackpot on how to

make McKenna suffer. Tormenting and causing Miss Taylor pain is the best way to exact my revenge. Just look at him squirm. *Querida.*" Mendoza pointed toward a still livid Mac, shaking his head. "This unnecessary violence upsets McKenna very much, does it not?" He signaled his men and one of them gut punched Mac. He doubled over, straining to catch his breath.

Eve felt as if she'd taken the hit to her belly.

"See, this is not good for McKenna. I ask you again, what have you done with my property?"

When Eve refused to answer, Danny stepped between her and Mendoza. There was an almost pleading quality to Carlyle's eyes.

"Miguel, you gotta calm down. You're pissing Eve off, making her more defiant. And, Eve, doll face, can't you just answer the man? Give him what he wants?"

Neither replied.

Danny pushed Eve into a sitting position, his gaze morphing into one of determination. "I'll handle this myself." Carlyle knelt in front of her and grabbed her right foot. He examined her new boot. Eve kicked his right knee, causing him to fall on his ass. He jumped back up.

"This is what you call taking care of business, Carlyle?" Mendoza and his men roared with laughter.

"Dammit, Eve. No wonder Mendoza slaps you around so much. You can be a real pain in the ass. Now give me your fucking foot."

"Danny, don't do this." Her voice cracked.

"There's no going back for me, doll face."

She kicked him again, but he managed to evade the hit this time. He took her right foot, unlaced her boot, and removed it. Danny stood next to Mendoza. He withdrew a pocketknife, flipped open the hidden compartment in the heel, and removed a plastic bag. He held the flash drive for all to see.

"Well, well, what have we here? Oh, yeah, this is me—Danny Carlyle, taking care of business." He smiled cunningly at Mendoza. "Aren't you the lucky one, Miguel? Looks like she used the hidey-hole in the heel this time."

Mendoza made no attempt to hide his anger. "If you had knowledge of this, why did you not show me the first time we had Miss Taylor as a guest in our cells?"

"No need. I checked her boot myself while she was unconscious and came up empty. I decided it wasn't a big deal since the flash drive wasn't there."

"Check this and be sure you destroy it." Danny tossed the device to Mendoza, then knelt and put Eve's boot back on and tied the laces. "With your shoulder out of commission, you couldn't get to the heel last time. You were out of time and had to ditch the drive real quick like. Right, Eve?"

Eve stood and inched away from Danny. She kept her back stiff, and her head high. She didn't want to breathe the same air he did.

"Giving me the cold shoulder, huh? No skin off my back," Danny said.

"This woman likes to ignore those who are superior to her." Mendoza grabbed a handful of Eve's hair, yanked her head back, and stopped her from moving away from him. "*Querida*, must you be so disrespectful of your friends? No worry, you will learn soon."

Carlos plodded from the inside of the door, huffing and puffing, sweat running in rivers down his face. Several men with weapons, followed close behind.

Mendoza said, "You are sweating like the pig you are, Carlos."

"Hey, Carlos, catch your breath, man." Danny taunted him. "You need to get that beefy bod of yours in shape, my friend. How do you expect to chase after the good guys in your condition?"

Carlos winced and glared at Mendoza. "You should not let him speak to me this way, Miguel."

"Why would I stop him?" Mendoza snickered. "He's right *mi gordinflon poco amigo*, my chubby little friend. Carlos, you are in terrible shape. Why does my sister put up with you?"

"This is your sister's doing, she cooks well...and cooks too much."

"With you, it's always someone else's fault. What did you find, Carlos?" Mendoza let go of Eve's hair and she staggered forward.

Carlos scowled first at Eve, then at Mac. "They must have come alone. I did not find anyone else on the grounds. My men and I have searched the house, the tunnels, and grounds thoroughly."

"Then how did they get in?"

"We have not determined this yet, Miguel."

"It is really not a hard task to guard against intruders." Mendoza looked him in the eye and waved the gun he held. Carlos immediately began rocking side to side. "Have you doubled the guards as I requested?"

"*Sí*. You can rest assured, Miguel, we have things under control."

"*Idiota*, Carlos, I never rest assured with anything if you are involved. Let's move into my study."

Bypassing the doorway that led to the tunnels, Mendoza and his men pushed Mac and Eve indoors and into his study. "Carlyle, I want you to find out if the IDEA sent Miss Taylor and McKenna here alone. I'd hate to think anyone else is roaming around, unescorted on the grounds. Sadly, I'm not sure if my men are capable of finding any unwanted visitors."

Danny blew out a disgusted breath. "I see what you mean. I'll make a call and get back to you."

Who was Danny calling? Was he working with someone else? Eve's mouth went dry. Two traitors?

"Show our guests to their quarters." Mendoza said as he ran fingers down Eve's reddened cheek. He whispered, "I look forward to spending some quality time with you, *querida*. You have much to learn. Maybe I will even let McKenna watch. I think he would enjoy that very much, no?" He pulled her earpiece, found her mic, and yanked it free.

Carlos said, "Miguel, I realize you would like to have your

revenge for the problems these two have caused you, but should we not just kill them? Rid ourselves of them and the trouble they bring?"

"You call being a cripple a problem? What about the money I lost shutting down several areas of my business on the *outside* chance the IDEA might have my files? You have the *cojones* to call this a problem?"

Mendoza inhaled long and deep then exhaled slowly. His breath skated across Eve's neck, and she cringed.

"No, I do not wish to kill them—yet. I'd like to play first. What better torture could I offer McKenna than to take his woman for myself?"

He pulled Eve close and looked to Mac, who'd resumed his struggle. "*Por favor*. Pay close attention now, McKenna." Mendoza took Eve by the arm and yanked her against his body. He ground his hips into hers then kissed her with brutal force.

She screamed and squirmed, trying to pull away. Laughing, Mendoza let her go. Eve wiped her mouth, glared at Mendoza, and spat in his face.

Mendoza punched her, knocking her on her butt.

Mac thrashed violently. He took several more hits to his stomach, but didn't stop trying to get free.

Eve quit squirming. "Stay the fuck back. I'm fine, Mac. Mendoza hits like *el hijo de puta débil!* A pansy-assed son of a bitch."

Mendoza's eyes blazed. "You dare to call me a weak son of a bitch?"

He raised his cane and the carved, ivory-balled handle connected with her temple. Eve crumpled to the floor, fought to stay alert.

With an animalistic howl, Mac broke free and knocked two of the guards against each other. He'd almost reached her before the butt end of an AK-47 slammed into the side of his head.

Mendoza grinned with enthusiasm as Mac joined Eve on the floor.

The dark realm of unconsciousness still tried to suck Eve in.

Mendoza nudged Mac with his cane. Getting no response, he kicked Mac's ribs, then bent and retrieved his mic and ear bud. If she'd had the strength, Eve would have fought back for Mac...for herself.

"Carlos, drag these *amantes* to the cells. I have other business to attend and will deal with them later. This *punta* has cost me enough money. He knelt next to Eve. "I want you fully rested and alert so you will enjoy, and appreciate, my games."

He tossed the communication devices to Carlos. "Be sure to sweep the grounds again for intruders. I want everyone on alert. These radios are not for decoration. Someone is on the receiving end."

Carlos slid them into a pocket. "*Sí*, I will get the men searching right now."

Two of the guards grabbed Mac under the arms and another tossed Eve over his shoulder. Mendoza's cell phone rang, and he hurriedly motioned for Carlos and the guards to stay.

"*Hola.*" He listened attentively. "*Sí, sí.* Bring him to me now."

He glowered at Danny. "We have another visitor."

Danny raised an eyebrow. "Who?"

"My men say they do not recognize this man. They are bringi—"

The study door opened and two guards dragged a beaten and bloodied man into the room. They dropped him with a thud, facedown at Mendoza's feet.

Mendoza toed the body. "Flip him on his back so I can question him."

"He is unco...ah, uncoci...*inconsciente.*" One of the guards stuttered in broken English.

"Unconscious, you fool. The word is unconscious. And keep your head up when I speak to you."

The guard's head bobbed vigorously. "*Sí*, unconscious. The man is unconscious."

"Let me see," Mendoza said.

Eve stretched, trying to get a look at the body. The guards

flipped him over. *Damn.* All she could see was a bloody heap. A couple inches more and she would've succeeded. Mendoza's men had beaten the man to a pulp.

Mendoza said, "No, I do not know this man. Do you recognize him, Carlyle?"

"I do, and I'd fucking like to know what the hell he's doing here."

"He is of no use to me in this condition. Take him to the cells. I will also see to him when I return."

"No, wait," Danny said "Take Eve and McKenna, but let me try and wake this one. I want to know why he's here. The sooner the better."

Mendoza said, "As you wish."

Eve blacked out.

Chapter Twenty

The offices of Resolutions, Inc.
Washington, D.C.

A brisk knock on Robert Hutchinson's office door mercifully interrupted the study of his monthly expense reports. A task long reputed to be the biggest waste of time by executives throughout the world, no matter how necessary they were for tax records. You have to keep the IRS happy. The door flew open and Resolutions' office manager, receptionist, assistant and keeper-of-all-things-sacred, Spice Winters, bounced into the room.

Hutch had been told many times Spice resembled a forest pixie. If there really were such things, she was one. A boundless whirl of energy, she was a tiny thing with a full head of fiery red hair, an oval face, and over-large eyes that truly did twinkle.

Spice planted her feet in front of his desk. "Hey, boss. SAC Sanders and another man are here to see you. SAC Sanders looks mad. Like a junk yard dog on Sunday."

"A junkyard dog on Sunday?" Hutch couldn't help but grin at one of the many Southern idioms Spice used. "Who'd you say is with Sanders?"

"No clue, but I can tell you he's a geeky looking, white shirt with pocket protector, suit wearin' type of techie dude. They don't have an appointment. Want me to tell them you're busy?"

He shook his head and pushed away the expense report. "Not necessary. There's a lot going on with McKenna and Agent Taylor in Colombia, and we've got a few other matters to take care of privately. John wouldn't be here if his business wasn't urgent."

"You and Sanders investigating covert operations on the sly? That's like spies spying on spies. Way. Too. Cool."

Hutch held back a laugh, decided it was bad enough to let a grin slip when things were so serious. "Spice, send them in, would you?"

"I'm on it, boss." She sprung away with more energy than the Energizer bunny and returned with their guests.

Sanders' said, "Hutch, this is Agent Anthony James, head of the DEA's Forensic Accountants."

Hutch stood and shook Sanders' hand, then the other man's. Agent James was young, maybe younger than Spice. The kid had to be a genius to be a department head already.

"Glad to meet you, Agent James. Have a seat, please, both of you." Hutch motioned to the leather chairs in front of his desk.

Agent James dropped into one. "Good to meet you too, sir. If you don't mind, call me Tony."

Hutch nodded. "Have you heard from Agent Taylor or McKenna and his team? Or do you have some news about our *other* project?"

"Hutch, you can speak freely. I brought Tony in to search for a leak on my end of things. He's pulled the accounting and bank records of all the IDEA and DEA agents. Got three hits for large cash deposits. One turned out to be nothing, just the receipts from the sale of a sail boat, paid in cash, but a clean deal."

Hutch studied Sanders and then Tony. "The other two?"

Sanders gestured toward the accountant. "I'll let Tony take this one."

Tony cleared his throat, withdrew a small PDA from his

pocket, and hit several buttons. "Sorry, I need my notes."

"No problem," Hutch said.

"I found no explanations for the other suspicious deposits. Between the two employees, each had several accounts totaling more than a half a million dollars in recent deposits. Digging deeper, I traced transfers from those accounts to larger off shore accounts. All deposits were made over the last two years and the amounts of the transfers equaled in excess of twenty million dollars. That's just the money in the Caymans and Swiss bank accounts. There are more accounts I'm still running." Tony's attention never left his PDA.

Hutch said, "Who do the accounts belong to?"

Sanders answered, "DEA Special Agent Danny Carlyle and his girlfriend, Lynda Turner. Carlyle was part of the IDEA task force. They—"

"Whoa, partner." Hutch leaned forward in his seat. "Let me stop you here for just a second. Wasn't Carlyle killed in San Carlos Lucas during the failed mission a few weeks ago?"

"Yes, sir, he was. Apparently Lynda Turner decided to keep their little side business going, and has continued selling classified information to Mendoza."

"Poor woman must really be choked up and grieving for her lost boyfriend." Hutch grunted with disgust.

"Yeah, I'm sure she's torn up." Sanders returned the sarcasm, a good dose of anger added in.

Hutch asked, "What else do you know about Lynda Turner?"

"She's the DEA telecommunications specialist who's been fucking over my task force for two years. Sad thing is she's good at her job, maybe the best we've ever had in her department."

"Obviously." Hutch didn't want to think about how he'd feel if one of his agents betrayed him.

"With her training she could easily access agency calls coming in and going out."

"Your lines aren't secured?" Hutch raised his brows.

"From outside sources—yes, but internally, if you've got the skills Turner has, you can access almost any phone inside our system. Communications is her specialty. Covert audio, visual, and surveillance solutions. She's up to date on all the latest technologies." Sanders looked away.

"In other words, she tapped your phone?"

Sanders rubbed his forehead, took an exaggerated breath. "I'm embarrassed to admit this, but yes, she did. Last night, after Tony brought me all the data he'd found, I had a sweep of her work area, Carlyle's, and my office, done. The techs found all kinds of gadget goodies. Apparently, she's had free reign on all my calls. We're not sure how she avoided detection during the Agency's random in-house sweeps. We do them frequently. No one but me knows when one will take place."

Hutch asked, "Exactly how random are these surprise checks?"

The accountant sat quietly, only moving his head to follow the conversation.

Sanders said, "Very random and at my total discretion. When the mood hits, I pick up the phone and call—ah, well shit. She pulls the tap when she hears me order a sweep. Dammit all to hell."

"There you go," Hutch said, surprised Sanders missed that one. "You don't think anyone else at either the DEA, or IDEA is involved?"

"I'd like to say no, however, it came to my attention early today that Special Agent Rex Brewer didn't report to duty this morning, and we haven't been able to make contact with him. Cell phone goes straight to voice mail."

"Eve Taylor's partner?"

Sanders said, "I'm afraid so."

"McKenna may have called this one right."

"We were unable to find anything suspicious in Brewer's work area, and there's been no questionable activity found on his bank accounts." Sanders looked to Tony who remained quiet.

"Brewer wouldn't necessarily need to have any listening devices if he was working with Carlyle and Turner. They could've handled the money." Hutch picked up a pen and began clicking the top open then closed. "But I'm not sure why he'd trust anyone with his cut of the cash."

"True. Carlyle's area came up clean and we know about his involvement."

Hutch said, "I read the reports several times on the failed mission to retrieve Mendoza's files last week. Wasn't Brewer the agent who declared Carlyle dead?"

"Where are you going with this, Hutch?"

"I'm just wondering—did Brewer take Carlyle out? Maybe he wanted more money for himself? A fight for control? Possibly a love triangle involving Carlyle's girlfriend?"

Sanders answered, "Carlyle was taken down by enemy fire. To be honest, I'm still hoping Brewer's clean. He's been with DEA for several years, and he's a damned good agent to boot."

"Money can drive a man to do strange things. So can love."

Sanders uncrossed his leg. "I don't want to believe Brewer turned on his team."

Hutch dropped the pen on the desktop. "Well, right now things aren't looking good for your man."

"No, they're not."

"There was another agent on that mission—Randi Ford, I believe. Did Agent Ford see anything out of the ordinary with Brewer's actions during the mission? Perhaps Agent Taylor did? She was in charge after all."

Sanders shifted in his chair. "Seems neither Agent Ford or Agent Taylor noted any discrepancies in Brewer's behavior."

"Doesn't mean he's not guilty."

"Doesn't mean he is." Sanders sounded a bit on the defensive side.

Hutch's liked the way John Sanders supported his agents. He was a good man. Damn shame someone on his team had turned traitor.

"Tony." Hutch gestured toward the forensic accountant. "I'm assuming, once you saw the bank deposits, you didn't discuss the financial findings with Sanders on the phone?"

"Of course I didn't."

Hutch said, "Did you discuss the information with anyone else?"

"No, he wouldn't have." Sanders spoke for his man. "Tony knows how important this is. He called me and asked to meet at the coffee shop across the street."

"You don't think Ms. Turner found that suspicious?"

Sanders shook his head. "It's not unusual to have coffee with my department heads away from the office."

"What did she have to say about all this when you confronted her?"

"We haven't interrogated Turner, yet. I presumed you'd want in on the action."

"Damn right I want in. I gather she's put my operatives and your agent in grave danger."

"That's a given," Sanders said.

"Then let's have a little chat with the telecommunications expert from Hell. Where's she being held?"

"She's not. I've got two agents on her and have her busy researching a surveillance op needing a set-up in two days. The agents shadowing her have orders not to approach unless she tries to leave the building. I'm confident Turner doesn't have a clue we're on to her game."

"She doesn't suspect a thing?" Hutch was impressed.

"Nada. We're in the process of obtaining search warrants for her home and Carlyle's."

"What about Brewer?"

"I've got people on that, too. However, I'm hoping we'll find him and straighten this out before I have to use the warrant on him."

"I'm going to call McKenna and warn him he and his extraction team are most likely walking into a trap." Hutch reached for his phone.

"You cancelling the op?"

"No, just giving them the heads up they've been compromised. The team may alter their plan, but they won't abort." He smiled. "Remember, we're the resolution to your problem."

"The reason we hired you."

Hutch grinned and rose. "If you want to head back to your office I'll catch up after my call with McKenna. Just tell me when and where."

"One of the IDEA interrogation rooms will do. Let's say about an hour from now. That'll give us both a chance to make a few calls."

ଓ

Hutch turned off his SAT phone, tossed it on his desk, and yelled for Spice. Frustration had him stretching his neck again, trying to work the tension loose. The muffled crackling of each vertebra popping in and out of alignment echoed in his ears. Seemed like he was always stretching some damned muscle these days.

Spice poked her head in his office. "That you yelling, boss? Didn't you have the darn intercom put in so you wouldn't have to crow like a rooster in a henhouse anymore?"

"Spice, come in and have a seat."

The tiny woman looked surprised. "My goodness, you've got the stress thing going on big time."

"How do you know? Psychic powers?"

"Nope. Good old-fashioned powers of observation. Stop rubbing so hard," she admonished him. "You're leaving a river of red streaks on your neck."

Hutch laughed and the tension drained from his joints. The woman lightened his mood like nobody else. "You got me there. I'm frustrated and madder than hell."

"Why, boss?"

Hutch gave her the short version. Spice sat on the edge of her seat, small hands balled into tight fists, eyes wide. Her lips pressed together in the shape of an O, and when she began to bob up and down in her seat, Hutch couldn't take any more.

"Spice, now you need to relax."

"I'd like to go a couple of rounds with those traitorous cockroaches. I'd tear them limb from limb and then I'd stuff my foot down their throats until my toes come out their assholes."

"Sounds like a pretty brutal scenario. I didn't know you had such a violent streak."

Her face reddened. "Don't you be making fun of me, Robert Hutchinson."

"I'm not." At least he struggled not to. "I want you to keep trying to get McKenna or Warner on the SAT phone. Maybe try the chopper's radio." He opened a desk drawer and grabbed a second phone. "Use this. I've got to meet Sanders at the IDEA offices. It's time to pull the plug on Lynda Turner's little side business."

Her brows drew down into a fierce frown. "I'd be glad to help with taking her down a few notches."

Visions of Spice ripping Lynda Turner apart danced in his mind. A smile tugged his lips. "I know you would, but getting ahold of McKenna and team takes top priority. If you reach anyone, patch them through to me."

"If you're sure you don't want me—"

"I'm sure."

ω

Hutch studied Lynda Turner, sitting alone in a conference room typing on a laptop. He and Sanders watched the live feed from a video surveillance camera mounted in the conference room.

"A busy little bee without a care in the world," Hutch said.

"Unless you notice how straight and stiff she's sitting in the chair." Sanders pointed in her direction.

"Or the way she keeps chewing on her lower lip and eyeing the surveillance cam. Your girl knows something's up."

"It's possible. Once I had her moved from her office to this conference room, she may have started feeling a few all's-not-right-in-the-bee-hive vibes. She knows I'm coming to see her and she's aware there's a cam in there. Hell, she installed it."

"I'm ready if you are."

Sanders nodded. "Let's get this over with."

They left the surveillance area and entered the room where Lynda worked, Sanders first, Hutch following close behind.

A friendly smile materialized on Lynda's face when she saw her boss. She stopped typing and dropped her hands to her lap. "Hey, boss. Research on the new surveillance op is almost complete, and I don't anticipate problems with the setup."

"Lynda, I'd like to introduce you to Robert Hutchinson, head of Resolutions, Inc."

"I've heard of you, Mr. Hutchinson." She offered her hand. "Nice to meet you."

Hutch ignored her outstretched hand and took a seat.

She looked to her boss. "Sir?"

"We know, Lynda."

"Know what?"

"About you and Carlyle."

She glanced around the room. "Oh. You...you know we're dating? Sorry, sir. We kno...knew it's against policy, but we couldn't help the way we felt about each other."

Hutch smacked the table. "Goddammit! This isn't about your love life, agent. It's about fucking over your boss and so-called friends."

She stammered, but made no coherent reply.

"It's over, Lynda." Sanders sat next to her.

"I really have no clu—"

"Enough with the fucking lies," Hutch said.

Lynda gasped and gripped Sanders hand.

He shook it off. "He's right. Enough with the bullshit. We know about your arrangement with Mendoza."

"You know what we've done?" Her gaze swept downward, settled on her hands.

"We do. We're not sure exactly how deep this goes. Who else is involved besides you?"

"Just me and Danny." She choked on Danny's name and

tears began pool in her eyes.

"We figured as much." Sanders kept his tone even.

She shifted in her seat and relief washed over her face. "I think I'm glad you know. This whole thing hasn't gone the way we planned."

"Is Agent Brewer involved in this mess?" Sanders said steadily, showing no anger, no condemnation—no emotion at all.

"No. At least not that I know of. Danny doesn't tell me everything. He said we'd never get caught. He promised." Tears began to fall in earnest. "No...no one...sup...posed to...be hurt."

Sanders' expression hardened. "Do you have any idea how many good agents I've lost because of you and Carlyle?"

She shook her head. Her sobs slowed. "Danny couldn't stop Mendoza from killing them. Their deaths were not our faults. The last four agents on the mission to rescue Agent Taylor weren't supposed to die either. Everything was a big misunderstanding. They were supposed find an open grave with two bodies, assume the dead were Agent Taylor and Danny, and turn back. The rescue team didn't buy into the ruse, even though Mendoza's men mangled the bodies and dressed the male in Danny's clothes. They even threw Agent Taylor's boots in the grave for good measure."

"The excuses go on and on. Nothing is your fucking fault." Hutch shook his head.

Sanders added, "Do you believe that load of crap because I'm sure not buying any of this bullshit."

She winced.

"You make me sick. You worked with Agent Taylor. Goddamn you, you worked with all the agents you helped Mendoza kill." Sanders scooted his chair away from the table.

Her sobs came in torrents.

Hutch was pissed. Pissed for the four IDEA agents killed during the rescue mission and all the others before them. Pissed for the two unknown people in the grave meant to take the place of Carlyle and Taylor. And most of all, pissed Mac and his team were now exposed and at risk.

"I didn't want to help him."

"Then why did you?" Sanders' question seemed almost a plea. "You've dirtied my house!"

Lynda pulled a clean hankie from her pocket. "I'm in love with him, sir."

Hutch fought to keep the disgust out of his voice. "You were so in love with him, the minute he died you jumped right in and continued the business of selling out to Mendoza? You never missed a beat passing intel to him. Now you've all but pulled the trigger on my operatives and Agent Taylor." Refusing to sit at the same level as Turner, he sat on the conference table, placed an elbow on his thigh, and leaned toward her. "I'd say your grief must be overwhelming."

"I don't understand." She went silent for a minute and another big hiccup took her breath away. "Oh, God, is Danny dead? Has something happened to him?"

Hutch grunted in disbelief. The woman had said the IDEA rescue team was supposed to believe Taylor *and* Carlyle were dead. *Is it possible?*

Sanders shifted and leaned forward. "Danny's been dead since Mendoza ambushed Agent Taylor's team in San Carlos Lucas. Why play dumb?"

"No, you're wrong. Danny's not dead. He and Mendoza faked his death. Danny wanted out of his deal with Mendoza. He wanted to retire."

Sanders' control began to show signs of splintering. "Agent Carlyle *wasn't* killed during the mission?"

"No. He still tells me what information I need to gather and send." She blew her nose. "I'm supposed to wrap up odds and ends here. Wipe our personnel files, you know, stuff like that."

"How does he contact you?" Sanders said unsteadily. Looked like his calm had finally dissolved into anger.

Hutch was impressed the rage had taken this long to kick in.

"Throw-away phones, sir. I use a new one every day."

"I don't understand." Sanders rubbed his neck. "How could you sell us out?"

"I had to. Danny said it was the only way we'd have enough cash to be able to spend the rest of our lives together. He claimed if the government paid him what he was worth and gave him a decent retirement fund, we wouldn't have to do this." Her gaze drifted, she slumped in the chair. "We were going to an island to disappear." Her eyelids closed.

Hutch said, "I'm afraid, Ms. Turner, the only place you'll be spending the rest of your life, is in a cell. That's if a jury doesn't put you out of your misery by lethal injection."

A shudder, one that may have measured on the Richter scale, racked her body and a final tear ran down her cheek.

Chapter Twenty-One

San Carlos Lucas, Colombia
Mendoza Compound

Mac's head throbbed in cadence with the marching band stomping through his brain. Damn, even thinking hurt. Other body parts checked in sporting different levels of pain, ranging from slight aches to total numbness. His face, sticky and wet, stuck like glue to the floor. Mac, not sure if he had the strength to lift his head, lay still trying to recall what in the hell happened.

Had he been hit by a car? Been caught in an explosion? Nah, he would feel more mangled. Instead of trying to remember what happened to him, he switched his focus to more important things. Like figuring out where the fuck he was.

Wherever Mac had ended up, was dark, hot, and humid. The room stank of stale sweat and old urine. The lack of heavy breathing or movement around him meant he was most likely alone. A need to solve the puzzle propelled him to roll onto his back. Bones crunched and popped, a reminder he was still alive. No one pounced on him or spoke. *Yep, I'm alone.*

The coppery smell of blood hit him full force and instinctively, he dashed his hands over his body. No blood.

Good, the smell came from the room, not from him. He stretched his arms, twisting them from side to side, and ran his hands across the floor, concentrating on the feel. Concrete or packed dirt, he decided, but couldn't be sure which.

Carefully he sat up, riding the waves of dizziness assaulting him. His hands drifted to his head, and he checked for bumps. He flinched when he found a large swollen area. With a little deep breathing, the spinning slowed. Once his eyes adjusted, he realized the room wasn't as dark as he thought. He rose to his hands and knees, moving his head forward then back, working out the kinks. He drew in another large breath of stale air, but air just the same.

The cobwebs began to clear. Memories came flooding back, causing his chest to tighten painfully like a fist, one finger at a time.

Eve. Where the fuck is she?

Eve's mind spun like a Tilt-A-Whirl. Begging to stop the ride, she searched for the off button, her brain coming up empty each time. Through the blur, she heard voices. No, not voices. One voice, straining with panic and concern. The sound so familiar, she ached to answer. But words wouldn't form, lips refused to move. She willed her hand to her throbbing cheek, found the side of her face swollen. *Damn you, Mendoza.*

Eve stilled the instant large hands traveled over her body. Not a rough touch intent on hurting her, but a gentle caress meant to search and sooth. After a thorough check, strong, solid arms gathered her close. *Mac.* He buried his face in her hair, and she savored the warmth of his breath tingling against her scalp.

"Eve." He sighed deeply, turning her damp skin into a mess of goose bumps. "Come on baby, wake up." His whisper tickled, and his familiar scent lured her into a calm place.

She tried to open her eyes. They weren't cooperating, but least the spinning in her head had slowed, and she no longer felt stuck in a scene from *The Exorcist.* She rolled into Mac's heat and wrapped her arm around his waist. His embrace felt so damn good. She didn't want him to ever let go.

"You're going to be fine. I love you, Eve." He smoothed back her hair and tilted her head upward, a new gentleness in his touch. "Time to open your eyes and help me figure a way out of this place."

Mac loved her? No, he'd said that before. Surely he confused sex with love. If Mac loved her, he'd find a way to control his urge to protect her. They both knew they were parting company when they completed the op. *I've misunderstood his words...or dreamed them.*

Eve stiffened and pushed away. Fine lines etched the corners of his eyes, his brows arched and he frowned grimly.

"It's about time." His face relaxed. He ran the back of his hand over her cheek again, carefully circled the area that hurt the most. "You've got one mean-ass bruise to add to your collection, but no apparent broken bones. How do you feel?"

"Other than my lip and face pounding like a jackhammer on steroids? Not so bad. You?"

"I've had better days." He rubbed his head. "Lucky for me, my head's the most indestructible part of my body."

"Any idea how long we've been here?"

Mac glanced at his watch. "Less than thirty minutes."

Eve twisted her upper body, stretching some of the kinks. "Do we have a plan?"

"We could have a round of wild monkey sex then break out of this joint afterwards." A spark of humor lit his face.

Eve couldn't fight the smile, or the choked laugh that escaped. "Always thinking with both heads, aren't you, Mac?"

His head tilted slightly to one side, an easy smile settling on his face. "Just kicking around ideas, trying to help."

A familiar tingling spiraled through Eve and her heartbeat sped up. How did he manage? One smile and she wanted to melt in his arms. She'd miss him when they finished the job. Eve's head pounded, but she forced herself to rise, the need to get free from his arms all the motivation required. She kept her gaze on Mac.

He kept his on her. He moved a bit slower, a reminder of the beating Mendoza's men had given him.

"Thanks, but I'll have to pass on the jungle monkey romp. I've got a—"

Loud voices and heavy footsteps were headed their way. Two guards, dragging a body, stopped at their cell while a third unlocked the door. Mac stood in front of Eve.

Seriously? Fury took over, and she elbowed him out of the way. "Dammit, Mac. Move. I don't need protection."

Mac blinked twice. His mouth opened, but a retort never came. Mendoza's men, without ceremony or words, tossed the man in and left. Mac raced to the cell door and shook the bars, his effort futile. Eve sank to her knees beside the body.

Mac joined her. "Is he dead?"

"I can't tell. He was in Mendoza's study earlier and still alive. Can't imagine why they'd throw a dead man in here."

"We're talking fucking Mendoza."

"True."

"Let's roll him over," Mac said.

The rare hint of fear in Mac triggered a strange uneasiness in her belly. *He thinks this man is Cade.* The idea had crossed her mind too. There was definitely something familiar about the man. She took a good look and put her hand on Mac's. "It's not Cade. Wrong clothes." She moved to roll the body. "Careful, now."

They turned the still form carefully. Eve jerked back. "My, God. Rex? What's he doing here?"

"What do you think he's doing here? The bastard's been in this thing with Mendoza and Carlyle all along."

Eve shook her head, stroked Rex's forehead. "You're wrong, Mac. He's had the bloody crap beat out of him. Why would Mendoza knock around his own man?"

"Brewer either fucked up, or Mendoza no longer needs his services. I'm surprised he didn't shoot him." Mac's voice was razor-sharp. "There's no honor or loyalty among men like this. I can't even begin to count how many times I watched the bastard kill his own men. Men like these turn on each other faster than sharks in a feeding frenzy."

Eve's heart was heavy with disappointment. Was Mac right about Rex? *Oh God, he is.* Not wanting to give him the satisfaction of seeing her concede, she sat back, and tried to dial back her emotions.

Rex stretched out a trembling hand and limply held her wrist. "I'm not working for Mendoza," he said weakly.

Eve leaned above him. "Rex, if you're not with Danny and Mendoza, why are you here?"

"You. I came for you." His grip grew tighter.

"Me? I don't understand."

"If I could find the flash drive, you wouldn't have to come back. I left you behind last time. It's my fault Mendoza hurt you. Couldn't let bad shit happen again."

"Don't buy into this load of crap, Eve." Mac put a warm hand on her shoulder.

"It's true, I swear." Desperation weighted Rex's words.

She studied Rex's face, studied Mac's. "He's telling the truth. You can't see it because you don't want to."

"I don't want to?"

"You're too damn biased about anything involving Rex." She gulped. "In Mendoza's study earlier neither he nor Danny had any idea why Rex was here. They thought I was out cold. They had no reason to put on an act."

Mac stood, ambled to a wall, and crossed his arms. "Okay. I'll give him the benefit of doubt. But if he makes one wrong move I'm tearing him apart, one piece at a time. You got that, Eve?"

She nodded, not willing to push. After all, he was trying—no matter how pitiful the attempt.

Mac looked at the man on the floor. "How about you, Brewer? You understand?"

"You're wasting your breath. Rex is passed out again." She let out a deep, almost whistling breath.

"Works for me."

Eve hated to ask, but she had to. "Could you help me drag him away from the door? I don't want him to be the first target Mendoza's men see when they come back. They've done enough damage already."

Grumbling in an unintelligibly low voice, Mac helped her shift Rex out of the way, then returned to the wall and resumed his cross-armed stance. "Happy?"

"Would you, just for a minute, put yourself in my shoes? What if I tried to convince you Cade had turned on you? Would you believe me, or would you defend him until you had absolute, positive proof he'd gone bad?"

Eve didn't expect an answer. Admitting he was wrong would be hard for a man like Mac. Of course, there'd be no happy dance in the park for Eve if she turned out to be wrong.

Eve was right. If anyone accused Cade of selling information, he'd never buy it. Mac would defend Cade until hell froze over. Brewer had taken a major beating. Mendoza preferred to deal with his men by putting a bullet between their eyes when they fucked up. If Brewer had crossed Mendoza, he'd be doing the three-eyed stare right now, not waiting in a cell to be tortured and beaten again.

Damn, Mac hated when he was wrong. Well, maybe not wrong. Misguided. He'd let jealousy about Brewer and Eve's relationship cloud his judgment. His need to protect her eclipsed common sense. If they got out of this mess—no, *when* they got out of this mess—he'd make things right. *Eve thinks we're parting company after this op is over. She's wrong. Fucking big-time wrong.*

"You're awfully quiet, Mac."

"Thinking." He secured his back against the wall.

"About?" Eve asked, kneeling beside by Rex, smoothing back his hair.

Eve fussed over her partner and a surge of resentment bubbled in his gut. Jealousy and bitterness shouldn't prevent him from be reasonable. At least he hoped that was the case.

"You may be right. Maybe Brewer's here in some stupid attempt to help."

"Is that your round-about way of apologizing?" Eve said, with a pinch of satisfaction.

"To you, yes. But I'm not apologizing to Brewer. Don't even go there. It'd be too painful to my man ego."

A smile lit her face and wrapped itself around his heart. She hadn't totally given up on him. He'd congratulate himself later. Right now, they needed to come up with a way to get out of San Carlos Lucas. "Let's figure our next move."

She stood. "After three failed escapes, I can vouch for the plans that won't work."

"Any ideas on what might work?"

"Be still my heart." She patted her heart with both hands. "Dillon McKenna is asking for a mere woman's opinion."

"You got one or not?"

"Yeah, I do. I started to tell you right before Mendoza's men so rudely interrupted. The way I see it, we have two choices. First option—we wait for Cade to come looking for us."

"Cade won't think anything is wrong until we haven't shown up after two hours."

"You're right. The rendezvous time is a little less than an hour from now. Personally, I don't like the idea of sitting here any longer than necessary. I have a feeling when Mendoza takes us from this cell again, the move will be our last."

"Unfortunately, I agree."

"I assumed you would."

"So what's behind door number two?"

Eve scooted her foot in a slow arc across the floor. "I lay here, fake some sort of seizure, and you scream for help, the guards will come running. You persuade them to open the cell door and step in. You'll have to put the fear of God in them. Convince them Mendoza will have their asses if anything happens before he gets his hands on me again."

Mac's face twitched a couple of times. *She had not just offered herself as bait? Had she?*

"Then, catching the morons off guard, I jump up and take them out." Eve continued explaining her plan, causing his facial tics to multiply.

Mac didn't speak, didn't move.

Eve frowned, propped a hand on her hip. "Don't stand there with your jaw down around your knees. Say something."

"I'll say something all right. Are you out of your fucking mind?"

"Jeez, Mac, I'm glad to see you're making such an effort to accept the fact I can actually do my job."

"Let me get this straight, Eve. You're going to take down what, two, maybe three, or four of Mendoza's armed men? Maybe a whole fucking army?" He stomped next to her. "If you try, they'll kill you before I can get near enough to help."

"I won't need your help, big boy. If I do, you can step in after I've drawn them close enough to use my knife. I can disable two of the guards in a matter of seconds." She tilted her head and cupped a hand over her ear. "News flash...the DEA really did train me for this."

He didn't bother to hide his own sarcasm. "And exactly where are you going to get this deadly weapon?"

She scooted in front of him, her back to the cell door, and held out her broken arm. Damned if she didn't pull a knife from her cast.

"How in the—?"

Eve tucked the knife back in. "At the safe house I hollowed out a spot and stuck the knife in while you were busy playing Suzy Homemaker. A perfect fit, don't you think?"

"It's been there all this time?" He backed to the wall again.

"All we've got to do is get the guards to come in and get close to me. They may seem mindless, but I doubt they'll let you anywhere near when they enter. So you'll have to back away. You're a threat they're well aware of. I'm not."

"I'm supposed to cower in a corner and watch, while God only knows what happens to you?" Mac liked the plan less and less.

"That's the idea. No matter what happens, you can't come anywhere near me until I've got the knife in my hand. Preferably, not until I've given at least one guard a big smiley face across his neck."

"Aw, shit, Eve. Tell me you're not serious?" He pushed off the wall.

"You got a better idea?" She grinned wildly. "Do you honestly think the rat shit guards are going to come in here if you're close by? Do you think they'd rush in to help if you're the bait withering away on the floor? "

Once again, Eve hit the bull's-eye.

"What about your injuries?"

"It's been weeks, and I'm much better. Even if I wasn't, don't you think I'd rather suck up a bit more pain than die?"

"*Almost* two weeks since Doc treated you."

"Minor details. It's a damn good plan and you know it." She elbowed his arm.

"There's nothing good about this whole deal, but you win. We go with your plan." He shook his head. "Fuck, Eve, Mendoza doesn't need to kill me. You and your dangerous plans will take care of that long before he gets the chance."

Chapter Twenty-Two

Eve jerked uncontrollably, arms and legs flailing.

Mac, on his knees, bent over her trying to help. He put more panic in his voice with each jerk of her body.

"Help! *Socorro*! Somebody help us in here!" One glance at Eve's face had Mac grimacing. She'd had the balls to wink at him. *Doesn't the fool woman know this isn't a game?* "Help! Please, somebody help," he screamed again.

After what seemed like hours, three guards came to the cell door. They stood, looking at the scene before them, then at each other, their confusion almost comical. Moe, Larry, and Curly in the flesh. Mac recognized Moe. It was Carlos Salazar, and he couldn't wait to see the prick die.

"Help her, for God's sake."

Eve, her back to the guards, twitched and seized a few more times, then threw a couple of moans.

He stood and paced toward the guards. They reciprocated by pointing their weapons at him. Mac held up his hands and stepped back. *Now comes the hard part. The part where I stand by, holding my dick in my hand, and let Eve risk her life. Fuck!*

Moe, a.k.a. Carlos, pointed his AK-47 at the still convulsing Eve. "What is wrong with her?"

"If I had any clue, don't you think I'd help her?" Mac knelt beside Eve again. “She needs a doctor to check her out. Something bad is going on.”

Carlos translated to Larry and Curly what was happening. Mac, fluent in Spanish, listened. Larry asked Carlos what they should do. He shrugged, a blank look on his face. Several ideas were loudly dispatched back and forth, anger and disagreement infusing the words.

If Eve had really been having a seizure of some sort, she’d be dead, or brain damaged by now. “You have to help her. Miguel will not be happy if you let Eve die while you three idiots play ask-a-thousand-and-one-questions. Do you want him to put a bullet between your eyes? Get your asses in here and help.”

The guards looked at each other and argued another round in lower, heated tones. Spanish curses flew. If Eve wasn’t involved, Mac would think it was comical. Carlos said, “We will now open the door and come inside. McKenna, you must step back from the woman and stand against the wall by your *amigo,* hands on your head.”

Mac had almost forgotten about Brewer. Leaving Eve exposed to these men would cost him. He wasn’t sure he could do it. Eve gripped his thigh. Still giving the Oscar worthy performance, she moaned again.

“Stick to the plan and get the fuck back,” she whispered through gritted teeth.

He smoothed his fingers across hers before he removed her hand and stood. *Time to play my role.*

He hung his head, sighing deeply. “I’ll do what you say. Just please help her.”

“Move back, McKenna. Miguel would be disappointed, but I’m sure he will understand if we must kill you to save Miss Taylor.”

Mac brought his hands above his head and backed against the cell’s wall. His foot hit a solid mass. Brewer. The man remained unconscious. Mac’s attention shot back to the guards, back to Eve. Carlos muttered something to Curly that Mac couldn’t hear, and Curly took off running as fast as his overweight bulk could carry him.

Carlos fumbled with a key ring, found the one he wanted, and unlocked the cell door. Keeping Larry in front of him, Carlos pushed forward to Eve's side. He kept his gun trained on Mac and told Larry to check on Eve. Larry knelt next to Eve and looked for a pulse.

Mac yelled, "She's not dead, you idiot. At least not yet."

Eve wasn't sure she could keep up the seizure act much longer. The muscles in her legs and arm were tiring. The guards probably expected her to start foaming at the mouth, or wet her pants next. On second thought, they weren't smart enough to know shit about seizures. Didn't matter. She wasn't about to give up or fail. Not in front of Mac.

There were two guards in the cell. One man sounded familiar, though she couldn't quite place him. The threat to Mac pissed her off, and she had to rein in the powerful urge to jump to her feet. Not yet. She'd blow everything if she didn't wait. *Timing is everything.*

A guard knelt next to her, reached a finger forward, and confirmed her pulse. He rolled her onto her back and tried to restrain her jerking body. He was close enough for her to take him out, but she wanted the second man within striking distance. That's when she'd pull the knife from her cast.

Eve focused.

She forced her body to spasm a little harder, moaned louder.

The guard standing treaded closer. Eve waited for him to move one inch closer.

"Help her. If she dies, Mendoza will kill you," Mac yelled.

She squinted and peeked at the guard standing. Now she remembered the voice, the man. Remembered the flurry of kicks he'd delivered to her belly, over and over, until she couldn't breathe. Remembered his endless, daunting laughter. His large, grimy, calloused hands pinching and twisting her breasts without mercy, until she passed out. An overpowering need to inflict pain on this former tormentor hit her, threatened to control her. She channeled the urge into energy. Carlos Salazar was about to die.

He was a big man, but no longer weak from blood loss, or the beatings she'd endured, she'd handle him. Her strike had to be accurate. Carlos was close enough now. Close enough Eve smelled the sour stink of sweat and tequila on him, heard his raspy and labored breaths. If she reached out, she'd touch him. *Or kill him.*

In a flash, she grabbed the knife from her cast, seized the kneeling guard by his collar, and pulled him close. The need to get her hands on Carlos drove her, kept her focused. She slashed across the first guard's throat. The blade slid smoothly across his skin, cutting through muscle and cartilage. Warm, sticky blood spread between her fingers. The man's body went limp. Eve pushed his weight off, eager to reach the man still on his feet. Ready to exact her revenge.

In one swift move, she arched her back and flew to her feet before Carlos realized what happened to the first guard. She took him down with a powerful roundhouse kick to his gut, knocking the breath from his lungs. He lay like a slug for a few heartbeats, then curled roly-poly style, and covered his head with his arms. Breathless and driven, Eve dealt one solid kick after another to his torso.

"Hey, tough guy? Not so damn funny now?"

Carlos uncurled and tried to get back up. "*Por favor*! Stop."

Eve held him flat with one knee to his chest, looked deep into his beady little eyes, and swiped the sharp knife across the intended target. He gurgled around the blood bubbling from his throat. The urge to keep slicing at him, to drive the knife deep into him over and over, shocked her.

Still kneeling on Carlos, Eve panted, her heartbeat racing uncontrollably. She stared at her battle-numbed and bloodied hands, hypnotized by her own fury. She rolled her shoulders forward and her vision blurred from the rage.

Strange, she couldn't say she suffered any remorse. Maybe a little satisfaction, but definitely, no remorse.

A hand touched her upper arm, and she jumped off Carlos' dead form and spun around, holding the bloody knife in front of her, poised and ready to strike again.

"Whoa, Eve." Mac jumped back, held up his hands.

"Dammit. Don't sneak up on me."

"Just wanted to make sure you're still with the program."

Eve let her arms drop to her sides and the blood rushed to her lowered hands. A tingling sensation soon followed. She forced her rapid, shallow breathing to slow. She used the dead man's shirt to wipe the blood off her hands and knife before tucking it back inside her cast. Amazing how much strength a good dose of adrenaline and rage could afford a person.

"I think the plan went well, don't you?" She hoped she looked, and sounded, a lot more composed than she felt.

Mac grabbed her, his hands digging into her arms and pulled her into a strong embrace. He tilted her chin up and stared deep into her eyes. Eve couldn't tell if he was upset with her or impressed.

"You took out Carlos." His hands dug in tighter, his gaze still searching hers.

"I did. Tickles the shit out of me. Killing a man shouldn't feel this good."

"I know how evil Carlos was and what he was capable of. I don't even like to think of what he put you through."

Eve flinched and Mac her go.

"He was a bastard. Second only to Mendoza." Her skin crawled remembering the things he'd done to her, how perverted he was.

Mac's hands came to her face and he smoothed away a few loose hairs. He touched her face everywhere. Forehead. Chin. Cheeks.

He gently cupped her neck. "You scared the living shit out of me, baby. Never in my life have I been so afraid, and amazed, at the same time."

That answered her question. He was impressed. *Now what?* Eve's gaze locked on his lips. Two cuts marred them, but they were pure perfection to her. She licked her dry lips, her tongue lingering on the swollen, bottom one.

Mac intended to kiss her. She saw it in his eyes. Felt it in his touch.

He leaned forward. His lips touched hers.

"What the fuck, Mac? I thought you were in trouble. Instead, I find you here making cozy with your lady?"

They jumped apart.

Gun ready, Cade stepped into the cell. He glared at them. He was not a happy camper. Mac and Eve moved from the shadows toward him. Cade took a step back, his forehead furrowed. His jaw fell open then closed again. A flicker of an *oops* moment darted across his face.

"Judging by your battered, ugly mug, I guess I don't need to tell you this operation has been compromised." Cade scowled. "Who beat the crap out of you?"

"I'll give you one guess."

"The bad guys?" Cade asked, admiration sparking his face as he caught sight of the dead guards. He nudged the bodies with his boot. "Looks like I'm a little late to help. Nice work, Mac."

Mac held up his hands. "I didn't take the bastards out. Eve did."

Cade grinned. "I really like this woman. She's kick-ass."

Eve couldn't stop the smile that tugged at her lips. "It was harder on Mac than me. He had to step back and let me take care of business."

"Ouch! I can only imagine how much that pained his ego."

Mac frowned and ignored Cade. The frown didn't quite reach his eyes, but a pinch of pride broke through his tough exterior. *Probably my imagination.*

Mac cleared his throat. "What's with all the chit-chat? We're still in a hostile environment. Time to pull out. I think Curly went to get reinforcements."

"If you're talking about the tall, bald mass of what one too many burritos can do to the body, he's been dealt with." Cade's brow lifted. "Permanently."

Mac nodded. "Yep, Curly was a big dude and cue-ball bald."

"Curly?" Eve said.

"Never mind."

She'd ask Mac about Curly later. For now, Eve would focus on completing her mission.

Looking at Rex, Cade said, "Where'd Brewer come from? Your boss is looking for him."

"He showed up, Mendoza found him, and threw his worthless ass in here with us," Mac explained. "My vote? Leave his sorry, no-good ass behind."

Eve stiffened. "We will not leave my partner here."

"Let him have a dose of his own medicine."

"You're the ass. I'll drag him by myself if I have to."

Cade squatted next to Rex, looking over his injuries. "I'm not seeing any major broken bones. How about I just throw him on my shoulder, and we head to the LZ?"

Eve didn't move. "Not me. I'm going to finish what I started."

"You didn't retrieve the package?" Cade's eyebrows darted together.

"We had the flash drive—*had* being the main focus." Eve continued, "Mendoza took it. He was waiting for us, tipped off we were coming. Danny Carlyle is dirty and still alive. He's been feeding Mendoza details on all our moves. He's got to have an accomplice on the inside, because even out of the loop, he stills knows our every move."

Cade said, "Hutch sent the word on Carlyle, and you're right about him having an accomplice. His girlfriend, Lori, Lydia, Lilly—whatever, is neck deep in this. Hutch and Sanders got the whole story from of her. If Mac bothered to answer his radio, you'd have known our mission has been compromised."

"Mendoza took my ear bud and mic, along with my weapons. We're lucky Eve had a knife hidden in her cast."

"I was prepared, not lucky." Eve wasn't about to let Mac make light of her part in saving their asses.

Mac had the decency to nod and acknowledge his mistake.

"Man, the woman keeps on impressing." Cade flashed Eve a wide dose of his pearly whites. The man was more than capable of breaking a few women's hearts.

"Aren't we in a hurry here?" Eve rolled her shoulders gently in a stretching motion. She took the AK-47 from the first dead guard. "You two get Rex out. I'll take care of retrieving the files from Mendoza's computer." She grabbed a couple full magazines from the guard's pocket, stuffed them into hers.

"Nice try." Mac blocked her. "Did the hit to your head knock you senseless? You're not going in alone."

He spun in Cade's direction. "Get Brewer through the tunnels and wait for us. Give Corelli a heads up retrieval of the package is delayed."

"I'll give you one hour, max. Then I'm coming in and bringing my arsenal along." Cade patted his duffle.

Mac snatched Carlos' mini uzi. "How about tossing me a few of the flash bangs and grenades you've got stuffed in your pockets. Bastards took mine."

Cade passed him a couple handfuls. "We'll be waiting. Good luck."

Cade lifted Rex into a fireman's carry as if he was feather-light and disappeared into the tunnels. Eve and Mac, loaded with weapons again, moved out. Once they were free of the cell area, Eve grabbed Mac's arm.

He swung around. "What?"

"I wanted to thank you for not asking me to stay behind."

"I figured I'd be wasting time, and baby, we're out of time. I'm tired of this place, so let's get this over with."

Chapter Twenty-Three

"Damn good thing Mendoza is such a cocky son of a bitch," Mac leaned in and whispered. They were poised at the base of the stairway leading up to the villa. "He won't be expecting us. He thinks we're locked in nice and tight, no longer a threat to him. Plus, his security sucks."

She nodded, tickling his cheek with fly-away pieces of her hair. "Works for me." She hiked the AK-47 higher on her shoulder. "This time, his cockiness is going to cost him big. I just hope he returns in time for me to take him out before we download the files and head out."

Mac said, "The line forms to the right."

"I get first dibs, pal. I owe him." Eve rubbed her healing shoulder and her fingers drifted to touch the cast covering her arm. Her eyes closed, and she sighed.

Warmth zigzagged down his body and settled in his groin. He shifted to relieve some of the pressure building in crotch of his camo pants.

Mac cleared his throat then cleared his mind of all thoughts involving sex with Eve. "So, this stairway leads to the study?" *That sounded lame.*

"It opens into the foyer. The study's off to the left—I think. I was a little under the weather when Carlos dragged me from the cells after using me for his personal punching bag."

Mac's face grew hot and his temper rose, igniting an all-consuming need to kill Mendoza with his bare hands. Mac had never wanted revenge so badly in his life. He tensed and his hands fisted.

Mac would love to be the one to take the bastard out, but at this point, it no longer mattered if he, or Eve, got the pleasure. All that mattered was getting the job done. If Mendoza suffered a little beforehand, who would complain?

"Mac? You're shaking."

"Just keyed up. I can't wait to finish this operation, and if we get a chance along the way to kill the bastard? Icing on the cake." He grunted. "I can't remember ever hating another human being the way I hate the sadistic son of a bitch."

"Mendoza's not human. No human being could enjoy torturing another person the way he does." Eve shuddered.

Mac held her hand and squeezed.

She didn't pull away from his grasp. "I guess working for Mendoza while you waited to ID the chemist, and get him out, was rough. Going undercover must suck."

"You have no idea." He tried to clear the images that assaulted his mind. "He never got his hands on another agent while I was there. I would've hated giving up the op before finding my extraction target, but I would never have stood by and let an operative die. I'd have blown my cover first."

"You'd have died right alongside the person you were trying to save."

"There would've been no other choice. I saw firsthand how he deals with his own men. Not a pretty sight. Mendoza would pull his gun and blow them away without blinking. Like flicking fleas off his body."

"Those dead men don't deserve your pity, Mac. They deserved to die. Die long, painful, tortuous deaths."

"I didn't pity them. I wish he'd killed few more." Mac tried to shake the images. "It's not over. Not until Mendoza's dead and his cartel is out of business."

"Then let's end this shit. Right here. Right now. Copy his files, and if luck is on our side, we may get another shot at Mendoza."

"I'm ready. More than ready."

They climbed the stairs and found the villa empty. An uncanny silence surrounded them. Eve entered a series of numbers on a keypad. The alarm's red light blinked green, and she opened the door to the study, relief marking her face.

Mac followed her inside and headed to the patio doors. The sharp blips from the alarm being reset sounded especially loud in the silent room. He pulled back the heavy drapes, checked outside, and dropped the material. As they swayed to a stop, he pointed at Eve, mouthing the word 'clear'.

"Would you give me a hand here? It'll save time if you help me dig the drives from my bra."

"My pleasure." He helped her pull her good arm from her T-shirt.

"Pull the drives from the seams." She put her good arm over her head. "And you can wipe the smile off your face. There'll be no touching the girls."

"Damn. You just ruined all my fun." Mac tugged a few times. "These babies are really tucked tight inside the material. Just...one...more...tug. Got it!"

The second one slipped out much more easily. Eve turned and held up the other arm. "Sorry, I can't lift this one any higher."

"No problem now that I know what I'm doing." Mac pulled the next two drives without effort and helped put Eve's shirt back in order. "Why do you need all four?"

"One of them is special. I'll show you some magic in a few minutes." Eve looked at the drives, put two aside, and sat at the desk. She turned on the laptop. "I hope Mendoza didn't change the password."

"Why would he if he didn't bother to change the alarm code?"

"True."

A short string of musical tones drifted from the computer. Eve tapped a few keys.

Seconds ticked by like hours. The tension etched on Eve's face flickered in the blue light from the computer. Her lips tipped into a grin, her attention still glued to the screen. "Yes. He hasn't changed the password. I'm in."

"Great."

Eve's fingers flew across the keyboard. "Still can't send the files. Gotta do another download."

"Finish and let's get out of here."

"Jeez, why didn't I think of that? Get the job done and move out. What a great idea." Dramatically, she smacked her hand on her forehead.

"That was an attempt to encourage you."

"I'm sure." She pulled one of the flash drives from her bra and popped it in, didn't bother to look up from her task.

"Any problems?"

"Nope. This won't take long. I already know my way around his files."

"I think we're on borrowed time as is."

"When Mendoza finds we're gone, he's going to guess we've swiped his files again."

"Wouldn't take an Einstein." Mac smiled at the image of one-upping Mendoza. "I'd hate to be the poor bastard who delivers the news of our escape. He's going to put a bullet between the man's eyes."

"Get ready for the magic show." Eve held up the other drive she'd set aside and kissed it loudly. "This time, when I've finished the download, I'm going to wipe his files, send them so deep into cyberspace he'll never find them. Sanders sent this wipe program and his note said to take all the files out. This is gonna be fun."

"You're gonna crash his hard drive?"

Eve's grin was evil. "I'm going to wipe the files. If I just crash the hard drive, there's still a slim chance he could retrieve them. If I wipe them, he'll be SOL. If he somehow manages to slip past us, he and his operations won't be able to function without the stored intel. He may remember some of the stuff stowed here, but no way can he remember everything."

"Why didn't you wipe the files after you downloaded them the first time?"

"We didn't want him to know we'd been here. IDEA didn't want any attempts from him to close up shop, transfer moneys to new offshore accounts, or move his operations to other locations. We didn't want him warning his associates we were coming for them. They would've scattered before we'd had the opportunity to bring them in."

"Exactly what Mendoza's been doing the last few days." Mac grimaced. "Well, there's no chance of hiding the fact we were here this time."

"Exactly." Eve looked up from her work. "Mac, I need you to promise me something."

He didn't like the sound of this. "What am I about to promise?"

Eve sucked in along breath, rolled her head from side to side. "Umm, I need you to promise that if anything happens to me, you'll get the flash drive to my SAC. No matter what, you've gotta get this stateside. Understand?"

"What the fuck are you talking about, Eve? You'll be handing the flash drive to Sanders in person."

"I'm serious. If I go down, even if I stub my little toe, you have to leave me behind and get out of here with the drive." A fine sheen of moisture covered her forehead.

"You seriously think I'd leave you behind just to get the goods on Mendoza's drug operations? I'm not Brewer."

"Please just do this one thing. No questions asked."

"Jesus, Eve. Tell me what's going on. Is there more to this job than retrieving data on a lowlife, murdering drug lord?"

She stared at her feet, her arms wrapped around her waist. "Sorry I can't elaborate. I wish I could."

"Eve, you gotta have some faith in me. At least enough to tell me what's going on." The truth hit him like a fist to the gut.

"Christ. You don't trust me, do you?"

"That's not the reason. The time we've spent together the last few days has been...well let me just say, I do trust you."

"But not enough to fill me in on what the fuck is going on?"

"It's my...oh crap. You have to trust me, too. Trust that I'll tell you when I can."

Eve was right. He needed to trust her. She'd tell him when the time was right. *This is a fucking compromise?* Right now he'd promise almost anything to put a smile back on her face. Anything except promise to leave her in Mendoza's clutches again.

"You win, baby, but remember one thing, you and I are in this together."

"Mac, I—"

Footsteps approached the study. Silently, Mac hid and Eve placed the laptop under the desk, the glow from the screen now hidden behind the toe kick panel. She picked up the AK-47 she'd laid across the desk chair and hid near the drapes, to the side of the outside doors.

For the first time, there in the dark, quiet room, Mac worked with, and alongside Eve...not protecting her.

She'd be an asset to any task force or mission. *My woman is good at her job. Fearless.* He added another detail to the growing list of things to tell Eve when they got out of this place.

He looked at Eve. She'd blended into the shadows. Vanished like a puff of smoke in the wind, her breathing not even loud enough to give her away. Heavy steps paused outside the door. He went on alert, his body shooting high-octane adrenaline to all parts. The doorknob jiggled, but the door didn't open and the footsteps continued on their journey. Mac let out the breath he held and let his shoulders go slack. His blood began to circulate at normal speed again and his trigger finger relaxed.

Eve slipped from her hiding place and sauntered back to the desk. She picked the laptop up and sat it back on the desk, her movements guarded. The glow from the screen lit her face once more. She radiated determination and confidence. Lips, barely moving, formed silent words while she skimmed the monitor's display. Her right hand floated to her injured shoulder and rubbed gently.

Mac lightly stroked her hair. "You want to finish our talk?"

Her hand dropped to her side and she straightened. "Not now. Let's get this finished. The download's complete." She removed the flash drive and put it in her pocket. "Give me a sec to download the wipe drive program."

Mac said, "He's going to be all levels of pissed."

"Yeah, isn't it great?" A grin tweaked her lips, exactly what Mac needed to see. He really did like the way the woman worked. Not to mention the way she looked. The way she smelled and tasted. The way her body fit beneath his. But he needed to focus on the business at hand.

"I'm doing a seven-level wipe of the computer, a wipe so deep nobody will ever be able to reconstruct data from this puppy. I helped build this program while I was still in tech support. It's bad-ass." She sounded happier than she had in a long time.

"Mendoza's going to find a business is hard to run without proper files."

Eve worked a few more minutes before shutting down the laptop. She closed the lid, wiped her hands together in an exaggerated gesture. "Done. Now all we gotta do is pray the arrogant ass hasn't backed his files up."

Mac said, "Not his style."

"I'm banking on it. Let's get out of here."

"Copy that."

Eve entered the code to unlock the door and Mac cracked it open. The foyer remained empty. They made their way to the stairway and hurried down, keeping their footsteps quick and silent. Halfway through the underground hallway, Mac spotted a group of three, maybe four men running full-throttle toward them. He fought the need to push Eve behind him.

He offered her a swaggering smile. "Okay, Eve. Let's kick some ass."

Eve darted to the right, Mac to the left. A shot pinged past her, ricocheting off the concrete wall, showering her with pulverized gravel that stung her skin like a son of a bitch. Aiming the AK-47, she pulled the trigger, waited for the recoil and blast. Nothing happened. Damn. The gun jammed. She tossed it and dodged the next spray of bullets.

She reached the shooter before he had a chance to fire another round. Eve took a deep breath, grunted, and swept her leg in a graceful arc, snagging him behind the knees. He twisted in midair and hit the ground facedown with a loud thud. His handgun skittered across the floor.

Using her weight, Eve dropped on both knees and landed solid on the man's turned neck. Vertebra snapped and crunched beneath her, and the garbled hiss of his last breath signaled she'd won this round. He went lax.

One down. Two to go.

Eve tried to steal a glance at Mac and the man he grappled with. A hit to her back knocked her off balance. The air rushed from her lungs. Her face met the floor, then her body, and jarred her injured shoulder. Pain screamed in two-part harmony and her vision tunneled. White spots danced before her.

"You bastard." She tried to get control of her breathing again, and refocus on the target at hand. "You are so about to die."

She rolled to her side first, onto her knees, and up. Once standing, Eve landed a forceful blow to the man's gonads. He doubled over and clutched himself. Using all the strength in her good arm, she gripped his greasy hair and jerked down while kneeing his face. A warm flow of blood from his nose soaked her knee. The man sobbed, but managed to get in a gut punch. He latched on to her waist. Eve shook off the hit and tried to break free. She curled around him and saw the M9 Beretta tucked in his waistband.

"Fuck this." She reached over his back, pulled the gun, planted the muzzle against the side of his head and squeezed the trigger. He wobbled like a Weeble for a couple seconds, then dropped like a bag of marbles.

Two down.

Acutely aware of the sound of fists hitting skin, she found Mac fighting another guard. Locked in battle near another stairwell, the man held Mac and delivered repeated blows to his right side. Eve raced toward them, ready to help. Instead, she got an up-close view of Mac head butting the man. The guard staggered back, wiping blood from his face. When he charged, Mac side stepped and grabbed the guard's throat. With a snap of his opposite hand, he broke the man's neck, and he toppled into a pile at Mac's feet.

He stepped over the carcass and took Eve into his arms.

His warmth soothed, but there wasn't time for comfort. Using all the willpower she could muster, she jerked away from him and took a step back.

"Don't, Eve. Don't turn away from me." He reached for her.

"I'm not. I just think we need to clear the compound and San Carlos Lucas while we still can." She eyed the mini Uzi Mac had taken from Carlos laying near the corpse of the man he'd just taken down. "Grab your weapon and let's go. Unless we come across Mendoza, we're finished here. There's no time—"

Shots rang out. Eve and Mac hit the ground and crawled to a sheltered area behind an arched beam. She ran her hand over herself. She hadn't been hit. Her focus turned to Mac.

Mac, are you okay?"

"Depends on your definition of okay."

"Oh, God." Eve heard his heavy breathing and panic rose up her throat. "Please, tell me you're not hit."

"Sorry to disappoint. Don't worry though, it's just a graze. I've suffered worse cuts shaving. We need to be more concerned about finding the shooter right now."

Shit. The beam wasn't big enough to protect them. Eve steadied her weapon in front of her, then around the beam. She peeked out and back again. She inched her way into a standing position and helped Mac pull himself up.

"Where are you hit?"

"My side."

"Damn, Mac. You're supposed to avoid those bullets when they come at you. Avoid them like a two dollar hooker with a bottle of cheap wine."

"And you know all about two dollar hookers?"

"Doesn't everyone?" Eve couldn't tell if he was grunting in pain or laughing.

"I'll try to do better next time."

"You do that."

"Miss Taylor, surely you're not leaving the compound without saying a proper goodbye."

She stilled. Mendoza's cold, menacing voice cut right through her. Her fingers caressed the Beretta. She had to think. Needed a new plan.

Mac moved closer and gripped her arm, his touch solid and reassuring. She turned her head and whispered, "Getting away from this place is turning into a real pain in the ass."

Mac said, "Got any ideas?"

Eve heard the tremor in Mac's voice, hoped she wouldn't have to make the decision to leave him behind to ensure the intel reached IDEA in one piece. "We did say we wanted the bastard. Now, I guess we get our chance at his ugly ass." She wanted Mendoza dead.

"I assume we're about to go in guns-ablazin'." He shifted, looked uncomfortable in spite of his joking. "Hopefully, the onslaught of wake-the-dead shots that've been fired will bring Cade running."

"That'd make three, instead of two, against Mendoza and how many?" Assuming Cade wasn't already dead, but she wouldn't share that suspicion with Mac.

"I'm sure Mendoza's got a shit load of back up with him." Mac sounded winded. "How many rounds you got?"

She popped the 9mm's magazine, took a quick look, and slapped the ammo back in. "Thirteen. You?"

He jerked his head toward the mini Uzi he'd dropped.

"You're on your own, baby." He paused and then added, "Unless of course you'd consider giving me the Beretta? I'll lay down some cover while you make your way out of this place with the flash drive. Who cares which one of us carries the package out?"

"Don't even go there, Mac. How about I lay—"

"Forget it. We stay together," Mac said firmly.

"Agreed. We stay together. For now." Eve would re-evaluate if Mac's injury began to slow them down, although she had a feeling she'd not be leaving him behind.

"Then fire when you're ready. I'll go for the Uzi."

Mac shifted away from her, the space behind her going from warm to cold. He settled into position, ready to hustle when she fired. Eve peered around the beam and drew a steady bead on Mendoza's heart.

"Put the gun down, doll face."

"Seriously?" Eve weighed her options.

"I said drop the gun, Eve. If you fire, I'll kill McKenna."

"Danny," she whispered. *Damn him.* Her fist tightened on the Beretta, and her mind waged an internal war before she reluctantly lowered her arm, but didn't drop the gun.

Mac filled the space to her side, his warmth instantly returning. He leaned forward and the side of his face touched hers. Heat radiated from him. His lips brushed against her ear.

"Got any other ideas, baby?"

Chapter Twenty-Four

"*Querida*, step into the open so I can see you."

Eve mulled over Mendoza's request then stepped into the hallway where the lighting was better.

Mac moved with her.

Determined to get control of the situation, she brought the Beretta back to shoulder level. Feet apart, she aimed at Mendoza's head. The room was quiet except for Mac's sputtered breathing.

Mendoza smiled at her. "You disappoint me, Miss Taylor. Look around. You surely do not think you can shoot your way out."

"That may be true, Miguel, but you'll be the first to die." She kept him in her sights, trusting Mac to guard her back.

"My men will mow you and McKenna down the second you pull the trigger. You may not care if you die, but I'm fairly certain McKenna won't appreciate your demise. Or you, his."

Danny added, "Listen to him, Eve. You just broke free from the cells for the second time. If you stay alive, maybe you can escape again. If you're dead, doll face, everything's over."

"You don't honestly believe Mendoza's just going to send us back to rot in the cells, do you? You can't be that naïve. He's going to kill us."

Danny shrugged. "Sad to say, you're right."

"You honestly don't care about Mendoza's deal with Afghani terrorists? You don't give a rat's ass he's selling a weapon capable of murdering millions of American men, women, and children?"

"What are you talking about, Eve? Mendoza's a fucking drug dealer."

He was either a damned good actor, or he honestly had no idea what Mendoza was up to. "Oh, Danny, you are so stupid."

"Miguel, what's she yakking about?"

"What does it matter? You need only concern yourself with taking the money I offer." Mendoza glared at Eve. "So you found my hidden files after all, *querida*?"

"Jeez, Miguel, what do you think?"

"It does not matter. I will also have this flash drive to destroy as I did the other one. Kindly hand it to Mr. Carlyle." Mendoza wiggled his gun in Danny's direction.

Danny stepped toward her, shock plastered on his face.

Mac blocked him.

"Move, McKenna," Danny said.

Was he pissed at Mendoza, Mac, or her? Hard to tell. No one liked to be taken for a fool.

"No fucking way, Carlyle." Mac stood his ground.

"Well then, that's a shame." Danny drove a fist into Mac's bullet wound.

Mac's curse echoed throughout the hallways. He doubled over and fell to the floor, gripping his stomach.

Eve flinched. *A graze, my ass.* Without lowering her gun, she angled slightly and yelled over her shoulder, "Damn you, Danny."

"Miss Taylor, your lover seems to be in dire need of medical attention. I can arrange for help if you would be kind enough to give up the flash drive without all the drama. And the gun."

Eve's hand tightened on the Beretta. "You have no intention of helping him, Miguel."

"That may be true, *querida*. What I can do is put him out of his misery. Perhaps you'd prefer to let him lie there and suffer. I will leave this decision to you."

"You're much too kind, a regular Boy Scout." Eve's struggled to keep her tone calm and even.

"Sarcasm in the midst of terror. I am impressed. Your courage and *determinacion*, ahh...determination, these are some of the things I find so attractive in you. But please, you must realize the time has come to hand my files to your old friend."

"Eve, do what he says." Danny whispered, "I swear, I didn't know about the terrorists. I'll figure a way to help you out of this mess."

Eve dared another glimpse at Mac. He'd twisted onto his side. Blood seeped between the fingers he pressed against his wound. He was pale and sweating profusely. She wanted to kill Danny for making his pain worse.

Eve could stall and hope Cade came looking for them soon. The agreed-on hour was almost up, and he'd surely heard the gunfire. "You win, Miguel. I'll give you what you want." She laid down the Beretta, dug a flash drive from her pocket, placed it in the fingers of her casted hand, and held it out. "Here you go, Danny."

Danny reached for the prize.

With all the strength of her good arm, she grabbed his wrist. Using her cast for leverage, she shoved her forearm under his chin, and yanked him against her chest. She snatched the knife from its hiding place and held it to Danny's throat.

Danny gurgled and fought to get loose. She dug the blade deep enough to quiet his thrashing.

"Drop your gun, Danny." When he ignored her request, she skimmed the blade across his neck. Blood drizzled from the long, shallow gash. "I said drop the gun. The next cut will be the final one."

"Dammit, Eve. What're you doing?" Danny squeaked.

"Giving you the opportunity to help us. You offered, didn't you?" Like she'd ever trust him. "Now, give up the gun and then we'll bend real slow like and get the Walther from your ankle holster. You're going to hand me the backup piece."

Danny released the gun he held and stood still. She kicked it in Mac's direction.

"Now the Walther."

Danny stilled.

"I worked with you a long time and know what you carry." She pressed the knife against his throat again. A faint line of blood sprouted from the new cut. "Let's have it."

"All right, all right. Give me a second."

"Don't try any funny stuff. I'd hate to see my hand slip. Of course you'd hate it more."

Danny squirmed against the knife Eve held securely to his throat.

Danny bent forward, Eve glued to his back and moving with him. He retrieved the Walther from his ankle holster and passed it to her.

"Now yours, Miguel. Easy."

Mendoza's laugh was loud and raw. "You think I care what happens to this man?" He pointed at Danny. "He is nothing to me. Less than nothing."

"Not funny, Miguel. Do what Eve says." Danny stiffened in her arms.

"No, I don't think I can do that, *mi amigo*. I am saddened to say, your usefulness has come to an end, *el fin*."

Mendoza fired at Danny.

She still held him in a tight grip as the bullet ripped through Danny's chest and sliced into the outside flesh of her upper left arm, burning on impact. The sharp scent of blood tickled her nose.

Danny was dead, and he wasn't faking this time. Eve glanced at her wound, noted the trickle of blood, and appreciated the sting was minimal. "Son of a bitch, Miguel, you killed your man?"

"Without a single moment of hesitation. Now you must decide how this amusing little game is going to end." He nodded to Mac. "Tell me, *querida*, have you ever watched a man die from a gut wound? It's very slow and very, very painful. In the end, McKenna will be begging you to let me put a bullet between his eyes. Begging you to end his suffering. This I can promise."

Mendoza slithered forward. "Give up your weapon."

"Stay right where you are. I will kill without reservation, also. This time it'll be your blood that spills." She held the gun steady on him.

He stilled. "As I have said, my men will kill you. They will also make sure McKenna suffers greatly before he dies."

"You did mention that. I do hate the idea of dying, but I can't help thinking how gratifying it'll be for me to look you in the eye and know I'm taking you with me."

Eve's grip on Danny grew weak as the blood and pieces of tissue blown from his chest made him slippery to hold. Danny was dead weight–literally. The morbid pun brought a smirk to her face.

Mac had told her all about dark humor. He'd get a kick out of seeing her smile at a time like this. Of course he'd also be damned pissed he wasn't on his feet saving her.

"You find humor in this? I do not see, or hear your McKenna laughing. Do you?"

"I do find this funny. I have some real bad news for you, Miguel."

Without remorse, she dropped Danny with a thud. His corpse hadn't done didley squat to protect her. Sure didn't stop Mendoza's bullet. She lifted her casted arm, held the flash drive, and jiggled it back and forth for good measure. "I wiped your files after I downloaded this little jewel."

He paused, stiff and perspiring. The man was never sweaty. He tilted his head and through squinted eyes, followed her waving hand. Back and forth, back and forth.

She released the flash drive and it landed in front of her right foot.

"Stop!" Mendoza took a hesitant step forward, still pointing his gun at her.

Eve, continuing to hold her Beretta on him, covered the

device with her boot heel.

"Uh-uh-uh." She shook her head. "No you don't. Before you take another step, I suggest you hear me out. I will crush the *last* remaining copy of your files. If you're going to force me to smash the flash drive with my big old size eights, you better damn well be sure your memory is long and precise."

Understanding marked his face, and then fear. He froze.

"I'd say by the look on your face you didn't back up the files. Dumb move, Miguel." She lowered her voice a notch, making sure she had his attention. "So here's the deal."

He said between clenched teeth, "I am listening."

"You're going to lower that fine looking pistol of yours. Then, we're going to take a little stroll back to your cells where I'm going to lock you and your men in. After you're all settled in nice and cozy-like, I'll toss you the flash drive, take Mac and get the hell out of Dodge. We'll all be happy campers." She tipped her head downward. "Well, everybody but old Danny here."

Mendoza's eyebrows scrunched together in sync with his lips.

Is he worried, or is that his pissed look?

Her smile widened. "Now don't you be fretting, Miguel. You won't be locked up for long. One of your brainless minions will eventually find you and let you out. Although I think they'd be wise to consider leaving you to rot."

"Do you expect me to trust you'll hand me the flash drive, Miss Taylor?"

"What other choice do you have?" She refused to look away when his expression filled with hatred.

Eve wished she had the confidence to back her tough words. Mendoza wouldn't take her deal. She needed to stall and hoped—no counted—on Cade to come to the rescue.

"Hey, Miguel, relax. Take a few. Think about my offer, weigh your options. We've got time." She hoped they had time. Hoped Mac had time.

"How do I know you wiped my hard drive? You did not destroy my files the last time you broke into my home."

"I had orders to leave your documents intact. Your deal with the terrorists changed everything. My boss not only gave me permission to wipe your files, he sent the program to do the job."

From the corner of her eye, Eve saw one of Mendoza's men creeping closer.

Mendoza raised his gun and shot his man. "*Idiota.*"

"Fuck, Miguel. If you keep killing all your men, there'll be no one left for me to shoot."

"No worries. I have many more men."

"You're the one who should worry, Miguel. I'm afraid without this flash drive it'll be nearly impossible for you to resume operations." She stretched her uninjured shoulder. "But we've got a little time to hammer out the details."

Mendoza stole a look at the boot heel guarding his files then over her shoulder at Mac. Smirking, he returned his attention to her. "I'm afraid I must disagree with you. I don't believe McKenna has very much time left."

Eve had run out of stall tactics.

Damn and double damn. *Where the hell is Cade?*

Chapter Twenty-Five

Mendoza firmed his aim, the muscles in his arm tensing. "You are bluffing, my *querida*."

"Think so?"

Eve stomped on the flash drive. She fired the Beretta at the same instant he fired.

His bullet missed.

Hers didn't.

Two separate splashes of crimson erupted on his chest. One to left side of his heart, one to the right. She'd only fired one shot. "How in the—?"

A barrage of gunfire exploded, and she hit the ground returning fire. The familiar thwack of bullets meeting flesh reverberated. Bodies fell like dominoes around her. Then, almost before it'd begun, the shooting stopped, leaving a haze of gun smoke swirling in the silent aftermath. Eve surveyed the carnage and counted five dead guards strewn chaotically about.

Mendoza lay sprawled on his back, unmoving, and like Danny's, the bright crimson circles on his shirt grew larger by the second. Finding no immediate threat, she stayed low, and back crawled toward Mac. He sat, gripping one of guns she'd taken from Danny. Mac was alive. She breathed a quiet, "Thank you, God."

"Glad to see me still breathing, baby?" He grinned smugly.

An unexpected storm of relief washed over her. She straightened upright on her knees and threw her arms around him. After leaning backward, she pulled away the hand he used to cover his bullet wound.

"Jeez. You okay?"

"Barely hurts."

Needing a better view, she tore his shirt open. If he'd moved half an inch to the left, he'd have dodged the bullet altogether. "The shot went clean through. I see the exit wound. You know, Mac, there's a lot of blood here for just a graze."

"'Tis but a flesh wound."

So now he thinks he's in a Monty Python movie?

"Flesh wound my ass. Seemed like an awful lot of moaning and twitching for a mere flesh wound." His face was still pale and covered in perspiration, but the bleeding had slowed. "This little graze of yours is going to need a lot more than a Band-Aid."

"I just exaggerated my injury—well, except when Carlyle punched it. That hurt like fucking hell." He flinched. "I wanted Mendoza to think I was on the verge of dying and no longer a threat."

Mac held Danny's gun in his hand. How many times had she stood at Danny's side and watched him fire it? Now, oddly enough, she couldn't even muster an ounce of sympathy for her dead team member. No remorse. No sympathy. Nothing.

"Eve?"

Her attention switched to Mac and she pointed at the gun he held. "You used Danny's gun to shoot Mendoza. I wondered where the second shot came from."

"Yeah, kicking Carlyle's gun in my direction was a great move."

She stood and helped Mac to his feet, needing to feel the connection.

He pulled her close and whispered in her ear. "I'll have a new scar for you to kiss."

"You're right." She winked at him. "I'll take care of that

later."

"Promises, promises." Mac rubbed his torso.

"Cross my heart." She drew a giant X across her heart. "We get the intel to IDEA first. They'll be more than happy to put the information to good use." *There should be time to stop the terrorist attack before anyone even knows it exists.*

"Hold on. I'm a little confused here. I saw you smash the downloaded flash drive."

"You saw me crush an empty flash drive. Back in Mendoza's study I pocketed all four drives Sanders sent, one full, two empty, and the one with the wipe program." She slapped her pocket. "You never know what might come in handy. The one with the downloaded files is still right here, safe and sound."

"I'll be damned."

They went around the room, gathered a few of the dead men's weapons they might need. Eve reached for Mendoza's gun. His hand still had a tight hold on the grip. She began to uncurl the fingers wrapped around it.

"*Puta cabrona*, you whore bitch. I should have killed you the first time I saw you." Mendoza struggled to raise the gun, to point it in her direction.

Eve landed a knee on his wrist and smiled. He squealed like an alley cat in heat, instantly releasing the gun. "And all this time I thought I was your *querida*. I am so crushed."

"*Chingate*. Fuck you."

Eve shook her head. "Not in this lifetime, asshole."

Mac joined Eve, and nudged Mendoza's prone body. "This piece of shit's still alive?"

"Barely, but yes, I'm afraid our friend is still breathing."

"Incredible."

"Parasites have a tendency to hang on and on and on. The only cure is to squish them. Like I did his flash drive."

Gasping for breath, Mendoza arched up. He grabbed his chest and fell back panting. "*Mierda! Ay Dios mio. Dios mio.*" His eyes closed and he whispered, "*Dios ayudame*. God help me."

"I don't think God is going to be helping a bastard like you, Miguel. Even God must have limits." Eve pulled away when he reached for her arm.

"Please, *querida*. Help me."

"I almost wish I could. Dying is way too easy an out for you."

Mendoza coughed weakly a few times, his breath hitching convulsively. He exhaled one long, last expiration. His eyelids fluttered to half-open and his head rolled lax to one side.

"He's finished," Eve said without emotion.

"I won't be shedding any tears."

"Me either. Well, maybe tears of joy." Sprinkles of sarcasm broke through her words.

An explosion, amplified by the tunnels, brought Eve to a standing position next to Mac, gun ready. A burst of screams followed and then all faded to quiet again. A cloud of smoke and dust floated toward them.

Mac coughed. "Cade's here."

"Hey, man." Cade stepped from the haze and stood near one of the dead bodies, taking in the scene. "Looks like I missed another party."

"Your invitation must be lost in the mail." Mac swiped the sweat trickling down his forehead.

"Sounds like you were having a party of your own." Eve rubbed her ears and fanned the cloud of smoky residue.

"M-67 fragmentation grenade. Designed to inflict maximum damage to nearby persons. My own modified version of Darwin's Theory of Natural Selection. I do the selecting."

"You sound like a fucking weapons infomercial, Cade." Mac laughed.

Cade smiled then rubbed the healing graze on his cheek against his shoulder. "Mendoza's men shouldn't have fucked with me."

Eve said, "I can only assume they figured this out a little too late."

"You assume correctly." Cade pointed to Mendoza's body. "Dead?"

"As a tree stump. Eve and I both got in a solid shot."

"You good to go?" Cade's gaze settled on Mac's bloody wound.

Mac lifted the hand covering his side. "I'm cool."

"Good to hear." Cade's stance loosened while he checked the pile of bodies. "Damn. You're a fucking killing machine."

"Eve took out most of these animals."

"I was talking to Eve. I know she's kick-ass." Cade smiled conspiratorially.

Mac turned to Eve. "That's a compliment, by the way."

She smiled and nodded her thanks.

Cade looked at his watch. "I'm sure you two would like to hang around awhile and admire your handiwork, but I think we'd best get while the gettin's good. I put down a shitload of guards with my trusty M-67 grenade, but I have no idea how long until another posse of slime assembles above ground and digs their way past the bodies and mess."

"I'm sure the minions are panicked, busy little shits, trying to find their great leader." Eve's heart filled with dread. She hated what she was about to do, but she was driven by the need. She bent over Mendoza, pulled his collar open, and rubbed her fingers along both sides of his neck several times. After thoroughly examining his throat, she checked for a pulse.

Cade shuffled next to Mac. "What the fuck?"

"Making sure there's no cadaver putty. I want to be sure he's dead," Eve answered. "He's definitely dead." *Now I can move on.*

"You know what she's talking about?" Cade asked Mac.

"I'll fill you in later." Mac gently braced Eve's shoulders and guided her from Mendoza's body.

"He's really dead, Mac."

"I know." Mac rubbed her back. "You okay?"

"Just glad he's gone. I'm kinda savoring the moment."

"Savor fast, baby," he told her. "We need to beat feet before the troops gathering upstairs descend upon us."

"I'm ready. We need to get that *flesh* wound of yours looked at."

Cade inspected Mendoza's carcass before joining Mac and Eve. "We'll grab Brewer on the way out."

Eve asked, "Rex okay?"

"He was still breathing when I left to help." He gave the room a final once over. "Help you didn't need."

Mac mumbled something under his breath about Rex. Eve couldn't understand a word he said, but had a pretty good idea. A nerve above her eye twitched. She chose to ignore him. Everyone had a right to their opinion. No matter how misguided.

Cade asked, "What's the status on the downloaded files?"

"Eve's got the new flash drive in her pocket. She wiped Mendoza's hard drive."

"No problem with the password?" Cade retrieved one of the dead guard's handguns and stuck it in his waistband.

Mac said, "Arrogant bastard didn't change Jack shit. He was so sure he'd shut us down."

"How the mighty fall." Cade tapped his watch. "Corelli's probably sitting on a hot LZ, itching to go wheels up." He added another gun to his growing arsenal.

Eve, watching Cade's actions with interest, raised an eyebrow at him.

"Hey, you can never have too much fire power." He winked at her. "I'll put in a call to Hutch when we clear the compound. He and Sanders can organize a sweep of this place. Clean up should be easy."

Mac said, "Once you've severed the head of the snake—"

"The body will die." Cade finished.

Chapter Twenty-Six

Washington D.C.
Eve Taylor's apartment

"Dammit, this son of a bitch is stubborn." Mac jiggled the key in the doorknob. He double-checked the apartment number. "You sure this is the right apartment?"

"Of course it's my apartment. Give me the key." Eve yanked the key from his fingers. "If you weren't acting like a horny teenager that's about to score—"

He silenced her by running a finger along her cheek. "I am about to score. And damned horny, to boot."

They'd spent the last five days in debriefings and apart. *A long fucking five days.*

Eve said, "I was surprised to find you waiting at my car when I finished with Sanders and the IDEA heads today."

"Good surprise or bad?"

"I'll let you know as soon as we get inside."

Mac finally got the key to tumble the lock and the door flew open. He scooped Eve in his arms and kicked the door closed with a bang.

"Your side, Mac."

"It's been five days. I don't feel a thing."

Mac laid his forehead against hers and her breath feathered across his face. He loved this woman more than life itself. More than he ever dreamed humanly possible. His groin went heavy with desire. "I'm not gonna make it to the bedroom." He covered her lips, taking all he could, giving all he had. Her soft, supple tongue danced with his.

"Me either." Eve murmured between kisses. "The couch?"

"Can't hold on that far." Mac stood Eve on the floor and began peeling off her clothes. "I can't wait till the fucking cast is gone." First to go, her T-shirt. Sweet Jesus, the woman was braless. Both breasts swung loose. He ran his hands across the pale, silky globes, stopping long enough to tease her nipples into hard peaks, and worked his way south.

In one fluid move, he unsnapped her pants and slid them off, somehow managing to take not only her shoes, but her socks along with them. The sight of her, standing before him in her panties, made him impossibly harder than he was a mere second before. Man, oh man. Lingerie models had nothing on his woman.

He eyed the table in her kitchen a few feet away. "Your kitchen table even looks miles away."

"Then let's go for it right here, right now." Eve pulled his shirt over his head. She ran her hand over his chest and spent a moment caressing the band aids covering the wounds on his side, front and back. Somehow Eve managed to turn even that small gesture into an erotic adventure.

Her hand drifted downward, found a new target. She unbuckled his belt, ripped it from the loops, and tossed it. The hunger and longing in her gaze sent Mac's libido into major overdrive. He wiped the small beads of sweat forming on his forehead. He panted like a love sick teen who just found his dad's stash of *Playboy* magazines. *Dammit.*

"Lose the pants, pal." She fingered the rough side pocket seam of his jeans. "And don't forget the shorts."

"What shorts?" He tossed her a sly half laugh, toed off his shoes, and rolled away his jeans. He moaned when she licked her velvety tongue over her perfect pink lips.

"Oh...my...God. Commando. Every woman's fantasy." Her voice was deep and breathless. With a lazy wave, she fanned her face, chewed on her bottom lip when his sex jutted forward, coming to rest against her belly. "You're killing me here. Hurry, Mac. Please."

Mac cherished every inch of her flawless bare skin. Her body was one of God's true engineering marvels, perfect in every way. Scars, bruises, cuts and all else, it didn't matter. Heaven-sent perfection. And she was his. All his. Forever his.

He ran his fingers beneath the smooth elastic of her panties and slipped them down her hips, past her knees to her feet. She stepped out of them, Mac lifted her, and she wrapped her legs, long and lean, around his waist. The moist warmth of her core against his sex sent his need rocketing into overdrive.

Eve's breath caught, and a second later she released a sigh of pure pleasure when he entered her. She arched, taking in more of him. Deeper and deeper. He knew—one-hundred percent knew—his heart was in as deep as his body.

"You feel so good." Mac breathed in the scent of her, spring-like with a hint of fresh lemons. He showered Eve's face, her shoulders, and everywhere else within reach, with hungry kisses. "I'll never get enough of this. Enough of you. Enough of us."

Eve tingled and an uncontrolled heat inched its way down her spine. Mac's very creative hands left a burning trail everywhere he touched. A deep, fiery burn emotionally charged and stoked by...what? Love?

And she knew. Eve finally accepted what she'd been trying to deny. It had happened without her consent. Love had taken control of her mind, and her body. Definitely her body. She'd almost had an orgasm on the spot. Then he drove into her again, and what little control she had left crashed and burned.

"Mac, it's too much. It's not enough. Oh, God, don't stop." Her eyes blurred as every inch of her being greedily absorbed him. Every minuscule nerve ending tingled from his touch. She ached for more, so much more. She wanted his heart. She wanted his soul. Demanded both.

Eve's legs hugged his body to hers, the need for him paralyzing. She would sink without him. Without this. She searched his eyes, his soul. He was an endless masterpiece of emotions. Wisdom, strength, and heated desire—desire for her. And love.

He was hers.

The heat between turned scorching, fusing them together. When she went over the edge, Mac followed her. The climax sent Eve's mind spinning. A million flashbacks from their past and their present, overlapped with pictures of what could be their future. A future Eve wanted. With Mac.

They collapsed, bodies drenched in sweat and breathing hard, onto the floor in a boneless pile of pure sexual satisfaction. Eve lay on top of him and Mac's solid, racing heartbeat mirrored hers. She lifted her head, looked at him, and smiled weakly.

"Am I smashing your wound?"

"What wound?"

He lifted a hand to her face, smoothed a wisp of flyaway hair behind her ear. "How about your arm and shoulder?"

"What arm and shoulder?"

He snorted. "Got me there. I guess we're a couple of tough ones."

"Yeah, we are."

He sat up, bringing Eve with him. Still naked, clothes strewn all around them, she snuggled into his lap. Damn, the man felt good, sweaty skin and all.

He palmed her chin and turned her face to meet his. "Eve, we need to talk."

"Talk?" She wiggled on his lap and a crooked smile crossed her lips. "I think our time could be better spent. I haven't gotten around to kissing your new scar yet. I promised, remember?"

"I remember, but can we be serious? What I have to say won't take long."

Blood pounded in her ears and she rubbed her temple. This

talk wouldn't end well. Talks never did.

Eve stood, gathered their clothes, and slipped into hers while tossing Mac his. *God, he's going to ask why I didn't trust him enough to tell him what was really in the Mendoza's files.*

"So talk. I'll listen." She closed her eyes and waited for the questions she couldn't answer.

"I love you."

"You love me?" She squeezed her eyes shut. "Well, that's not what I expected to hear."

"I love you. Is that so hard to understand?"

"I thought you were going to say something else."

"Nope. I love you." He made it sound so simple. His declaration was anything but simple.

"I love you too, Mac. I'm just not sure if—"

"Let me finish before you say anything else."

"Okay, go ahead." She gulped air, and keeping her emotions in check, forced a sunny smile on her face.

"I want us to be together, but I want to talk about your job with the DEA first. I've got this great idea. I want you to quit—"

Her hand covered his mouth. "Stop. Stop right now. I don't want to hear this." Eve's chest tingled, her heart filled with disappointment and dread.

Eve suspected this conversation would happen, but did it have to be so soon? Mac would demand she leave the job she loved. Again. Demand she give up what she'd worked so hard to achieve. He hadn't changed and she'd been a fool to think otherwise. *Trust him. Yeah, right.*

Eve's anger flared, and she ignored the warning in his eyes.

"You want, you want, you want." She tugged on her last shoe. "I'm tired of hearing what you want. We're never going to get past all the bullshit, are we?"

"Dammit, Eve, let me finish."

She jerked opened the door to the apartment. "We are finished. We figured this relationship crap out two years ago. We can't be together, can't seem to get our shit right. I should never have let myself fall for you and your empty words again. I had a pretty good idea I'd be hurt and guess what? I'm not only hurt, but I'm damned mad."

"Eve, please." Mac hopped toward her while he pulled one leg into his pants.

"No. I'm finished letting you rip my heart in two. I should've known you couldn't change." She said shakily, "You don't love me enough to change."

"And you think you've changed?" He ran a hand through his hair. "Shit, I didn't mean that. I don't know how to make you listen."

"To what? More lies? More promises?"

"Eve." Mac reached for her.

Tears filled her eyes, her bottom lip quivered. She turned away, didn't want him to see her like this.

"Please, Mac. Just go. Don't make me beg. I can't...I can't do this anymore."

"You're wrong about me, baby. I have changed."

Eve's shoulders shook and Mac caressed her upper arms. He pulled her rigid back against his chest. The rock-hard chest she'd worshipped and lavished with kisses only minutes ago. He gathered her in his arms, his solid and powerful muscles holding her tight. His deep breaths wafted through her hair, blowing and mixing the strands together. He buried his face in the back of her neck.

Eve fought her need to turn into his embrace, to seek comfort. Instead, she stiffened. "Please Mac, please let me go. If you love me, let me go."

He placed a long, soft kiss on the top of her head. She felt his reluctance. "You sure about this? Really sure?"

Eve nodded, afraid if she spoke, she'd beg him to stay. Her mind screamed with emotions she couldn't sort.

"Then I'll go, but I want you to know, to always remember, I love you. I will love you until the day I take my last breath. You own me, heart, and soul." He released her. "I never meant to hurt you."

The door closed softly and Eve instantly hated the emptiness in the room, the emptiness in her heart. She turned around, laid her cheek against the closed door and cried until there were no tears left.

Then cried some more.

ꟹ

Mac stared at the closed apartment door. He heard Eve crying inside and shuddered. A whole new kind of ache squeezed his heart, a need to comfort her, to quiet her sobs.

He rested his head against the door, suddenly defeated. He'd hurt her again, wasn't even sure how. He considered his options. Maybe he'd stand outside, pounding wood until she let him back in. Or walk away and give her some time to think. Leave her behind, alone and weeping with only her heart breaking sobs to keep her company.

Mac admitted, deep in his heart, there was no way on Earth Eve would let him in. At least not right now. She should've let him finish what he had to say. He stomped away, needing to kick something. He needed to kick someone's ass. Hell, if anyone's ass needed kicking, it was his.

A cat darted from behind some bushes, almost tripping him. His chance to kick something? Such irony. If he wasn't feeling so miserable he'd have laughed. But all he had time to think about right now was how quickly the playful twinkle in Eve's eyes had faded, the joy sucked out, replaced by disappointment and sadness. He'd done that. Not on purpose, but his fault just the same. His words came out all wrong, nothing he said had made sense.

"What the fuck? Was it possible to screw things up any worse?"

Chapter Twenty-Seven

Washington, DC
Three weeks later

Eve tossed her keys and purse on the table. Her cell phone jingled a cheery tune in complete contrast to the dejected way she felt. She dug into her jeans pocket for the slick little phone and flipped it open.

"Eve Taylor."

"How's my favorite partner?"

She smiled, feeling a bit more cheerful. "Rex. I'm fine. Just got back from the doctor. The cast is finally gone. I'm feeling great." *Unhappy, lonely and all around miserable, but hey, what's a little lie between friends?*

"Ready to come back to work?"

"I'm beyond ready."

Rex had no idea how badly she needed to get back on the job. Needed to do something to keep her mind off how much she missed Mac. How much her heart and body ached for Mac.

Eve had to stop thinking like that. She was still madder than hell. He was the bad guy here. She had to stay focused and remember that. A little covert action would go a long way to getting her mind off her Mac fixation.

"I hear you, Eve. I'm ready, too. Sanders put me on light duty until you return. We'll be going back on active status together. Meanwhile, I'm about to go bug-fuck crazy." Rex took a deep breath, a drawer slammed shut, followed by several choice curses.

A smile stretched her lips.

"Do you have any idea at all how tedious a DEA desk job is?"

Toeing off her shoes, she bit back her irritation. "I actually do have an idea."

Eve had put in plenty of hours behind a desk in Legal and Tech support doing research and whatever else had to be done to complete her assignments. If she hadn't had field training classes in the evenings to look forward to she may not have stayed in the program.

"Oh, yeah, I guess you do. I forgot you put in your time before getting into field work and turning into a kick-ass operative."

Eve smiled at another memory. Cade also called her kick-ass. Apparently Mac was the only one who didn't believe in her.

"So when will you be back?"

"The doctor cleared me to start Monday."

"Good. I figure I'm gonna need rescuing real soon."

"Any idea what our next assignment is going to be?"

Rex said soberly. "You know Sanders. He's a tight-lipped SOB. But, hey, I'm not going to complain if whatever op he puts us on gets me from behind this damn desk."

"Maybe we'll help with the cleanup in San Carlos Lucas." That'd keep her mind focused on more important things. Anything besides a certain Resolutions operative.

"Not much left to do. Mendoza's cartel is history. IDEA made a haul. Drugs, gazillions of dollars in laundered cash, and all kinds of stolen goods. The list of low-life criminals being extradited to the U.S. fills a prosecutor's wish list. It's like merry freakin' Christmas around here."

"Any updates on the terrorist deal Mendoza had put together?" The task force had finally been briefed on the planned attack.

"Still looking for the right terrorist cell, but in the meantime we've taken out a few. You have any idea how many Afghani terrorists groups there are?"

"I didn't until I saw the files. Sanders will narrow them down."

"Time's a ticking."

"At least Homeland Security is on board and sharing info on the group we're looking for."

"I guess in the end the mission was successful." Rex sounded upbeat.

"And the best part?" Eve added with enthusiasm. "Miguel Mendoza's dead."

"Six feet under."

"Justice served." Mendoza's stunned look when her bullet, and Mac's, hit their target was priceless. The bewilderment when he realized he was a dead man. How many times had he seen the same look on his victim's faces?

"What's the latest word on Lynda Turner?" Eve hadn't been updated on the woman's fate.

"That bitch is all about cooperation right now. Lynda is giving Sanders everything she's got—and then some—in return for taking the death penalty off the table. She thought Danny loved her. Who knows? Maybe he did."

"Strange what some people do in the name of love." If she'd stayed in Legal, Eve might still have Mac. Would it have been worth the price? Was he worth the price? Didn't matter anymore. Mac was gone.

"No excuse."

"You won't get an argument from me. See you Monday, Rex. I'll be the kick-ass agent minus an arm cast."

"Catch you then."

Eve dropped the cell phone on the table with her purse and keys. She un-holstered her new Glock and placed it on her hall closet's top shelf. Her back up piece would go on her night table at bedtime. A quick flip through her mail and she'd finished her tasks for the day. There was nothing left to clean in her apartment. After all, how many times could a girl re-arrange her underwear drawer? How many times could you take apart your guns and clean them? Especially when they were brand new?

She checked her watch. Damn, it wasn't even noon yet. She had nothing to do except think about Mac and how pissed it made her that he'd fooled her into thinking he'd changed. He hadn't even bothered to call and check on her. Hadn't begged for her forgiveness, or groveled on bended knees for her to take him back. If he truly loved her, where was he?

Eve refused to waste another brain cell worrying about what Mac had, or hadn't said. She refused to beat her mind senseless wondering where he was. Or what kind of extraction op he was busy executing. Or how dangerous his new mission might be. Eve wanted him safe...if only she could shield him from harm.

"Damn and double damn." Eve had an instant need to protect him. She remembered the moment of breath stealing, run-smack-into-the-wall fear she'd experienced when Mac had been shot. Her insides had turned to blocks of stone, impossible to chip away. She'd watched the blood flow from his body, an overwhelming helplessness clutching her heart. His moans of pain were imprinted in her memory, would be forever. Her first gut instinct, even then, had been to protect him from further harm, or die trying.

"Well, well, well, Mac. I think I finally get the whole I-want-to-protect-you, want-to-smother-you thing."

Eve was tired of thinking. Bone weary tired of letting her emotions get the best of her. She grabbed the TV's remote, plopped on the couch, and propped her feet on the arm. Time to indulge in some mindless channel surfing.

☙

"Dammit, McKenna," Mac growled to himself. "Grow a pair. Time to man up and get face to face with Eve. How hard could talking to her be?"

The answer to his question was clear. *Pretty fucking hard.*

Three weeks ago, he'd stood in the very same spot he stood in now, his guts twisted in a hundred and one knots, not sure if he should stay, or cut his losses and run. This time around he'd not be turning tail and running. Today, the only way he'd be leaving was with Eve at his side.

How could she turn him away?

His heartbeat raced like a thoroughbred on steroids. Mac ran a hand through his hair, rolled his lips together several times. Christ, he hadn't even lifted his hand to knock yet. At this rate, his knees would be the only thing knocking. So much for being a big, tough Delta Force soldier and Resolutions operative. Armed enemies and terrorists had never unnerved him this much.

Forcing his breathing to a normal rhythm, Mac knocked on Eve's door. No one answered. He knocked again, harder. Bare feet slapped the floor on the other side of the door. *Eve.* He was about to see her. Hold her. Love her. The footsteps fell silent and he pictured her looking through the peephole.

"Go away, Mac. I'm not speaking to you."

He focused on the hole. "Eve, open the door. You don't have to speak. I'll do the talking."

"After three weeks without a word from you, now you want to talk? You expect me to listen?"

"I'm not leaving before I have my say. I don't care how long I have to wait. My feet are planted right here."

"Suit yourself. I hope you don't mind a little rain."

For the first time since he'd left his house, he glanced upward. The sky did indeed look ready to spew buckets of rain.

Mac pounded on the door. The blows were probably heard four blocks away. It didn't matter how loud he knocked, Eve didn't answer. But the guy two doors over did. "She ain't home, asswipe. Go the fuck away before I call the cops."

Mac ignored him. "Come on, Eve. Open the damned door."

She still didn't answer. Mac leaned against the door, ready to wait for her to come to her senses. No matter how many angry neighbors yelled at him. No matter how much rain, how loud the thunder, or how intense the lightning the sky hit him with.

Two hours and one inch of rain later, Mac heard Eve's soft footsteps coming toward the door again. She slapped the wood. He straightened and stood where Eve could see through the peephole, the determination on his face.

"Leave, Mac. I don't have the energy to deal with you."

Mac took a step closer. She sounded tired, even through the thick door. "What's wrong? Are you sick? Hurt? What?" *God, don't let anything be wrong with her.*

"Mac, I'm fine. I'm just tired."

"Let me in so I can see for myself." He hesitated, and then said reluctantly, "I'll leave and never bother you again if you'll let me see you one more time." He was begging, and he didn't give a flying fuck.

"I'll let you in, but only because the neighbors are calling and complaining about a soaking wet moron hanging out in the drenching rain at my front door. You get five minutes before I throw your ass out. And no touching. Agreed?"

Five minutes. The same amount of time Mac let Brewer spend with Eve in Bogota. Five minutes had seemed generous then. Now all of sudden, five minutes seemed stingy.

"Do you agree to my terms, or not?"

He felt like a kid who had been caught with his hand in the cookie jar and gotten the mom lecture. "Agreed." *No way in hell.*

The door opened a few inches. Mac stuck his foot in, prepared to stand his ground if necessary. He wasn't about to miss the chance to plead his case. Mac was armed with a dozen yellow roses. He held them out to her.

"What are these for?"

"You."

Her eyes went wide. "Oh. They...they're lovely. Thank you."

"The florist said yellow roses symbolize new beginnings."

"Don't go there, Mac." Eve set the flowers on the foyer table and cleared her throat. "You said you wanted to talk. So talk."

Mac had to fight the urge to take Eve in his arms and cover her mouth in kisses. She was beautiful. The cast and bruises were gone. The only visible sign of her ordeal were the dark shadows beneath her eyes. She'd said she was tired and her eyes backed the statement up. Did she still have nightmares? Or God help him, had she been miserable without him the way he'd been without her? He took a short step.

She shook her head. "No touching, Mac. Say what you came to say, then leave. I expect you to honor your word."

Then you expect wrong, baby.

He'd brought her roses. No one had ever given her roses. *No, don't be sucked in by a few pretty flowers.* Eve blocked Mac from moving closer. That, and a shitload of luck, might keep her from jumping his bones, smothering him with kisses, and losing herself in him forever.

How could any one man look so good? His cocky, half smile was too much for any woman to resist. She took in every spectacular inch of him. A shallow minded woman could love Dillon McKenna for his body alone.

Eve fisted her hands and planted them on her hips. "Your time is running out."

She'd have a hard time getting him out of her home, not to mention out of her mind. And out of her heart.

"I have three things to say to you. I tried to tell you this the last time we were together, but somehow, in my special way of fucking things up, I...I...well, I fucked up. I'm going to explain my thoughts right this time. If you'll let me."

"Better start talking. You're wasting your five minutes."

He glanced at his feet. Mac? Nervous?

Had she ever seen him like this? *Wow. This is gonna be good.*

"First, I want to say I'm sorry—"

"Sorry for not calling? For being a prick? What?"

"Both. And more. I wanted to say, before I was interrupted, I'm sorry for being such an ass. I had no right giving you that ridiculous ultimatum two years ago. I should've never asked you to choose between me and a job you love. It's finally sunk into my thick head you are in no way, shape or form, anything like my mother. You're an excellent agent.

"My mother had no field training. Her death was nothing more than an act of fate. A matter of being in the wrong place at the wrong time. But, she died doing what she loved. The reality is she could've easily been killed crossing any street in the city. Dad couldn't have kept her home, couldn't have protected her. Neither could I. Dad was smart enough to know that. I wasn't. I'll never try to control your actions again."

In that moment, Eve wouldn't have been more surprised if Mac had sprouted a second head while standing upside-down in her foyer. She wasn't prepared for an apology from him, had no idea how to respond. "Thank you. I appreciate your candor." *A brilliant response. Who uses that word? Aargh.*

Mac stuck his hands in his pockets. "I was wrong, and because of that, we've spent two years apart that we should've been together."

Eve's belly felt like a hundred butterflies fluttered around inside, begging to be released. She studied the man before her and truly believed he meant what he said. He planned to keep his promise. She was afraid to speak. Afraid he'd take back everything he'd said if she whispered the wrong words.

"Second, and most important of all, I love you. I meant what I said when I left three weeks ago. I will love you until the day I breathe my last breath. I don't ever want to be without you again."

Still dumbfounded with his un-Mac-like attitude, Eve smiled and nodded like a bobble-head toy, wondering if an alien had taken possession of his mind. Or hers.

Mac cleared his throat a couple of times, swallowed hard. "Eve, this is where you profess your undying love for me."

"I do." The bobble-head still bobbled away. "I do love you, Mac. I always have."

"Good, we're in agreement."

"Just a minute, Mac. Since we're in the baring our souls mode, I have something I want to tell you. I understand your need to protect me. I had the same need to protect you when you were shot. My mind went crazy at the mere notion of you hurt or dying. I've spent the last three weeks worrying what kind of op you might be involved in at work. Worrying if you were safe."

"Eve, the difference is you wouldn't start making crazy demands that I quit my job. Now that I've come to terms with my mother's death, I know I was out of line."

"I'm glad you understand how I feel."

Mac, looking almost shy, pulled her against his chest, and held her tight. "I'm not finished with part two of my speech. How's my five minute deadline looking?"

"Fuck the five minutes. Keep talking. I'll just stay right here in your arms while you chat away." She snuggled in, her chest rumbling and purring like a kitten.

"I want to marry you. I can't imagine my life without you. I want the whole damn thing, marriage, a house, a big dog, and a bunch of kids underfoot. I may even consider buying a minivan."

She stepped back, looked up, and studied him. The man was serious as a heart attack. "We need to negotiate. How about if I agree to the marriage, house and dog, and you'll reconsider the size of the dog and the number of kids? By the way, I draw the line with the minivan."

Eve couldn't believe she agreed to marry Mac—and was happy about her decision. Ecstatic, in fact.

"Done. So what is that a yes, baby? Will you marry me? Make me the happiest, pig-headed alpha male in the world?"

Eve jumped into his arms, wrapped her legs around his waist. "Yes! Yes, yes, yes. I'll marry you."

Mac took a little black velvet box from his pocket and opened it. It contained a diamond solitaire engagement ring the size of Rhode Island.

Mac placed it on her finger, twirled her around a few times, and smothered her with kisses. He stopped abruptly. "I've got one more minor detail I'd like to run past you."

She couldn't read his face. Had no idea what the remaining detail could be. "Okay."

"I've spent the last three weeks tying up a few loose ends on a couple of my old cases and tossing an idea around with Hutch. After fine-tuning it, he's agreed to offer you a position with Resolutions. You only have to accept the offer and the job is yours."

Shit. Here it comes. Mac rips her heart out for the one-hundred and tenth time. Eve sagged, and she imagined her face drooped with disappointment. Drooped so low she'd trip over her chin if she took a step. She was tired of the up and down roller coaster of feelings Mac always managed to spark in her. Her temper hit the boiling mark.

"Doing what exactly?" She looked at him, trying to yank the ring off. "Working at a boring desk job? Your idea of a safe job for the little lady? No thanks, I'll pass—on the job offer and the marriage offer."

"No, Eve. You can stop right there and let me finish."

"You mean there's more? More of your empty promises?"

"No, they're not empty. Hutch is offering you a job as an operative, an extraction specialist. With an option to have, or not have, a partner."

The anger drained from her reluctantly. She wasn't quite sure if she was ready to give up her moment in the anger zone. But her muscles relaxed, she quit fingering the ring, and wrapped her arms around her waist. She stood face to face with Mac.

"Did you just say an operative?"

"Yep. You'd be an asset to the team. Cade and I have been bragging on you. Hutch agrees you'd be a perfect match for the Resolutions team."

"It's my choice to have a partner, or not?"

"That's right. I'm hoping you'll consider it. Hutch and I have agreed on the ideal person to compliment your skillset."

Her heart began to do the happy dance. "Just who would that partner be...if I were to choose to take one?"

"Me, of course."

She laughed. "You're slick."

"We make a damn fine team. I want to be your partner on the job *and* your partner in life." He planted a warm kiss on her lips, didn't try to separate her arms from their position around her middle. "But it's your call. If it's too much together time for you, I'm cool with it."

"If I take you on for my partner, are you going to pull all that alpha male crap and try to protect me every time we're on a job?" She pushed away from him, looked into his eyes, not wanting to miss his answer.

"Actually, I sort of planned on you protecting me. I've seen you in action, baby. I want you to be the one covering my ass."

Grinning, she offered her hand and they shook on the deal. They finished the exaggerated handshake. Mac didn't release her hand. Instead his long, firm fingers began to stroke it. She knew that touch, recognized the steamy look in his eyes. His hand began to walk its way up her arm, bringing her closer.

"Wait a second, Mac." She gripped his wrist, stopping his wandering hand. "You said you had three things to say to me. You only got to number two on your list."

"Ah, you're right."

Eve caught the gleam in his eyes and lust skittered from top of her head to the tips of her toes.

"I'm here to collect on the promise you made while we were still in San Carlos Lucas." Mac picked her up and carried her toward the bedroom.

Eve couldn't remember exactly what promise he meant, but from his hungry look, keeping it would be fun. "Promise?"

"The promise to kiss my new scar."

~ABOUT THE AUTHOR~

As a child, Teri's made up her own bedtime stories. When her children came along, Teri always tweaked the fairy tales she told her daughters, giving them a bit more punch and better endings when needed.

Now she spends her days turning her ideas into books. She lives in Marietta, GA with her husband.

Visit Teri online at: www.teririggs.com

Made in the USA
Charleston, SC
01 July 2014